FORTY MARTYRS

PHILIP F. DEAVER

PAPERBACK *bp* **ORIGINALS**

Published by Burrow Press
PO Box 533709
Orlando, FL 32853
burrowpress.com

© Philip F. Deaver, 2016. All rights reserved.
Book Design: Tina Craig
Cover Photo: Ashley Inguanta

ISBN: 978-1-941681-94-7
eISBN: 978-1-941681-95-4
LCCN: 2015949876

Distributed by Itasca Books
orders@itascabooks.com

ALSO BY PHILIP F. DEAVER

Silent Retreats
Scoring from Second: Writers on Baseball (editor)
How Men Pray

In memory of my father,
Philip F. Deaver, M.D.
1920-1964

PROLOGUE

THE FIRE

SCARS

"In the spirit of reconciliation, Wagner, repeat after me: 'I firmly resolve with the help of thy grace, to confess my sins, to do penance, and to amend my life. Amen.'"

Fr. James David Cavanaugh
White House, St. Louis, MO

PROLOGUE

VASCO AND THE VIRGIN

Vasco Whirly had been an English professor out at the college, but he didn't get tenure. So he got on the safety crew out at the Murdock Mine, and it wasn't so bad—his self-esteem was shot, and he didn't fit in, but he did make a lot of new friends. Actually he didn't. But he kept a lot of the old friends, Lowell Wagner in Psychology, Ann Rook in English, Gloria Steinem the local librarian, some others. All this took place in the dying prairie college town of Tuscola. This is more than you wanted to know.

Vasco never saw his friends much, and they never saw him, so it was hard to figure how they were friends. And his daughters, Michelle and Melanie Junior, were always off somewhere, and this left Vasco hanging around his old homestead doing things like staring down in the cistern or climbing around in the rafters of the garage. Sometimes he'd go all around the house opening drawers, and sometimes he'd take a shovel and dig in the narrow passage between his garage and the Rittenauers' garage next door. The house was old, built in 1882—he'd poked around for hours in the dim of the musty basement, finally even using a metal detector he'd rented. In fact, he did the whole yard with the metal detector, working day after day, half the community driving by on Niles Avenue and seeing him do it. He metal-detected Melanie Senior's tulip bed out by the garage, under the grape arbor, along both edges of the drive, in the parkway, under the bushes that surrounded the front porch. He came to the conclusion he was looking for something, the way he was always rummaging around.

Though this was his childhood home, though he'd inherited the place at his mother's death, he could never seem to think of it as his own. And he was always broke—broke, broke, broke. His ex-wife, she said it was a midlife thing, all this stirring around and being broke. She couldn't understand why you'd ever work at the Murdock Mine unless it made you rich. One night on the phone she told him in no uncertain terms that he was pitiful and that he should get a life.

"Well, I just think that's totally rude," Melanie Junior, his daughter, offered supportively when he told her about it the next morning at breakfast. "What's she—like, the Queen of Sheba?" She was talking too loud. She had dyed black hair, cut short, with bleached blonde roots, wore all black, and was sitting there eating Raisin Total, headphones on, Jesus Lizard ramming into her brain.

Vasco called Lowell Wagner, got some free advice. It wasn't a bad thing to do. Lowell might have been a psychologist, but also they were friends, they went way back to the days when Lowell first arrived in this crazy town and they were young teachers just starting. And Lowell offered: Relax, it's a stressful time. Don't get too absorbed in your work—keep the balance. Stay with literary scholarship, your true love—keep reading. And finally, keep in shape—a man your age, you got to keep in shape. To back it up, Lowell challenged him to racquetball.

Late March, and they went to the courts at the college. Vasco's lungs, he imagined, were turning to black crystal, which will impair your racquetball game if you're not careful. Plus, he was down and gloomy, couldn't concentrate. Lost the first game 21-8. In the second, narrowly dodged a skunk, 21-3. Contrary to the intent, the encounter was only serving to illustrate his deterioration.

Halfway through the third game, he began to get angry and play a little wild, hitting the wall in his follow-through, diving, slamming around in disgust when he lost a point. His face felt hot. Then all of a sudden, a colossal pain shot right to left across the center of his chest and down he went. He couldn't breathe, he was gasping, losing consciousness, clutching his chest and neck. Even in this horrible moment, Vasco later remembered thinking, "Okay. Maybe this is just as well."

Luckily, there was an emergency medical technician class going on in the gym. Word got out that a guy'd had a heart attack in the racquetball courts, and up they came, twelve of them, two minutes flat. They had their red metal cases, and they were all over Vasco, and even though by then he didn't really think he was going to die, he looked up at the one who was about to give him mouth-to-mouth and he muttered, "Get the hell away from me—can't you see I *want* this?"

Lowell rode with Vasco to the hospital in the ambulance. Michelle and Melanie Junior finally arrived. After four hours of tests, a doctor told Vasco that it had been a warning sign. They released him, and he rode home crammed in the non-backseat of Melanie's Honda CRX, depressed, with bandages and cotton balls from various invasions hooked all over him. He ate pizza and resumed his rummaging around the house. Didn't read. Didn't exercise. Didn't have balance. Waited for the next chest pains. It was the beginning of the end, anybody could see that.

•

Then on the thirteenth of April, while standing in the driveway, leaning on his metal detector, staring through the spray of the lawn sprinkler, contemplating the split linden tree in the sideyard and, in the bright green shade of its new leaves, the early sprouts of his mother's peonies, Vasco spied, just above the peonies and slightly to the left, the Virgin Mary. It was a crystal clear and very real apparition, the Madonna herself.

His daughters were off somewhere or Vasco surely would have called them to check it out. Fine. They had to go to the Dairy

Queen, endlessly drive by all their friends' houses. They had to go eat hamburgers, get gallstones at an early age, play like youth would go on forever. They had to cruise the park, laugh and run around, leave their dad out, that's too bad. He was home having a visitation from the Virgin Mary.

Vasco and his ex-wife hadn't done too hot a job of raising the girls, religiously speaking. And, after Melanie Senior moved to Mattoon to live the wild life (this would have been about eighteen months before—actually, she left due to his manifest failures as well as her interest in enhancing her personal freedom), he'd woefully neglected the religious thing with the girls. He hadn't squired them off to mass at Forty Martyrs Catholic Church on his alternate Sundays or on holy days. No communion, no confession, no confirmation. No throats blessed, no ashes on the forehead—they hadn't been conditioned to the assumptions of the church, to its language, and to the people of the Bible. A visitation from the Virgin Mary wouldn't have meant as much to them as it did to him. So it was right and just, in a manner of thinking, that Melanie and Michelle were out somewhere chasing boys and the Mother of the Lord was visiting their father in the sideyard above his deceased mother's peonies.

The moment he saw her, Vasco knew this was what he'd been looking for for the past few months. Not buried treasure, not his lost youth and hairline. Not his health or old friends who were gone. Not his rapidly deteriorating character, eroded by episodes of situational judgment. Not family, not a woman to love.

No, what Vasco had been looking for was a change-your-life miracle of some kind. There was, when he looked back later, something foregone about this strange occurrence, something he had been carrying around inside that he had known way ahead of the fact in some unarticulated, unrealized way. It was part of his dreamscape, an affirmation from on high. There she was, backlit by the brilliance of the prairie sun, wearing a sky blue flowing gown of some kind with white something or other beneath, exactly as he remembered the statue on the altar in Forty Martyrs. She had a glorious smile that seemed to engulf him and everything within thirty feet of him. It engulfed his mother's spirea, under the dining room window. It engulfed the split linden, making it seem less forlorn. It graced the whole yard, causing it to glow in new greens and blues. He was having a miracle, Vasco Whirly was—a miracle for sure.

She spoke to him personally. Said that he was kind of going off, like with the deal on the racquetball courts, the metal detector stuff, et cetera, and that she could help him concentrate again, help him get his career back on track and be a better person—if only he would get down on his knees once in a while and pray the rosary, and stop buying lottery tickets. She said she knew he didn't have much money and that that was a source of pain, but that there was poverty in worrying so much about it, and he was *always* worried about it, and she said she just couldn't understand why an intelligent, literate man like himself would drop five to fifteen dollars a week worth of futility and delusion on lottery tickets. She asked him if he had any idea about the odds. She went on to assure him that she could see into the future and that, well into the next century, nobody by the name of Vasco Macon Whirly would be winning the Illinois lottery or any other lottery in the solar system.

Also she told him he had character problems. She said she'd help him work on it. She said he was self-involved. She understood one has to be a little bit, but she said in his case it was too much. Communicate, she said. Don't get inside yourself so far. And reach out to your friends, she told him. They are lonely, too. In fact, she said, whatever your feelings are, safe to say they are the feelings of at least fifty percent of the population—the males anyway. Give. Think of others. Faith, hope, love, the whole bit. She was on his side, she said, and he was no more hopeless than Republicans, the NRA, or the prison system. Finally, she said she would come to visit him, in this very spot, on the thirteenth of the month. Which month? She was gone before he could ask.

•

All through April Vasco said nothing about this to anyone. And as the event receded in time, replaced by deadening routines, he began to lose the sense of the immediacy and reality of it. Finally, one afternoon sitting in his chair in the den, he couldn't get himself to imagine it had really happened. A man of long-deferred gratification, of vivid wishes and dreams, he had probably merely conjured the Blessed Mother in dream. She hadn't really visited. It was a little odd that he had ever thought she had. Okay. He got up from his chair, strolled the three blocks down to Huck's, the convenience store on Route 36, and bought a six-pack of Stroh's, a package of Slim Jims, and four Lotto tickets. He skipped work.

One day in early May, Michelle, his sweet sane tenth grader, told him, "You're getting weirder all the time, Daddy." She held up the half-eaten package of Slim Jims she'd found next to the couch. She looked him dead in the face with her mother's heartbreaking eyes. "Really," she said.

Vasco realized he didn't have words for what was going on inside himself. He couldn't get free advice from Lowell again. He couldn't call Father Kelleher, the priest over at Forty Martyrs. The girls wouldn't understand. Melanie Senior, ha, forget it. He decided he would keep his mouth shut and suck it up. He would move forward in time, like he always had. He would be a stoic. In silence, he would fall on this matter and smother it with his life. For a while he was serious and stuck with it. Then he drove down to Huck's for some more beer.

•

But still. First thing in the morning on May 13th, a Saturday, Vasco was in the yard, on that side of the house where the split linden and peonies were. He tried to convince himself he was out there just doing what needed to be done. He set up the lawn sprinkler so it would dampen down the grass, he edged along the driveway, he analyzed the side of the house to see if it needed paint. All the time, of course, he was keeping an eye out. She didn't make him wait. Mid-morning, around ten, the Virgin Mary came into view in the halo of spray from the sprinkler—in the sun and dappling of morning shadow in the sideyard, there she was.

She was approximately fifteen feet off the ground, about five feet five inches tall. Her hands were out as though she were bestowing a blessing on the multitudes. Vasco stood motionless. When he tried to say something, no words would come. She, too, was silent. For half-an-hour the vision held. Thoughts of peace came to his mind. His own personal peace, peace in general. A thought came to him that world peace was important. It occurred to him that we were lucky there hadn't been a nuclear horror, since everybody had a bomb. He had lived whole months or even years thinking only of his British Literature syllabus, coal, affording pizza, and coping with the varying personalities in his homely little family. The Blessed Virgin embraced a bigger jurisdiction. She stared at him, a calming but not solemn smile on her face. He marked this spot in his mind so he wouldn't slip backwards again. This was not only real, but for this moment it was the *only* real thing. He was there, she was there, that was it. Okay.

•

When the image above the peonies had faded, Vasco realized there was a car parked in the driveway, somebody sitting in the driver's seat looking at him. He went up the driveway to see who it was. It was Gloria Steinem.

Not the real Gloria Steinem. Gloria Steinem the librarian. Her name wasn't really Gloria Steinem, but he could never think what it was. She looked like Gloria Steinem. He'd graduated from high school with this woman thirty years before.

"Vasco Whirly, what are you doing?"

He smiled at her. It rhymed with "Gloria," but it wasn't that, what was it?

She looked at him. "Standing there like that, what were you doing? I'm serious."

"Good morning," Vasco offered out of a hesitant fog, struggling for the name.

"You didn't move for ten minutes." As she looked at him, she was examining his behavior, noting various weirdnesses—he could feel it. "I thought it was a statue of you, standing there," she said. "Because of how still you stood. It was odd, I thought. It creeped me out there for a minute. Not one movement, more than ten minutes. Twenty maybe."

"I was just standing there." He smiled at her again. "It's my yard."

"Yeah, well," she said. The car was backing out of the driveway. "Get help, okay?" She was smiling. She was probably kidding.

"What did you want?" he called after her.

Half out in the street and changing gears, she said, "I wanted to let you know *Hiroshima* is overdue."

"For what?"

"I mean way overdue. A month."

"You mean the book?"

"Get some rest," she said. "I'll speak with your younger daughter, the one remaining Whirly we can depend on." And off she drove, down the pretty brick street toward downtown and the library.

•

In the early afternoon, Vasco phoned his ex-wife down in Mattoon.

"Melanie Templeton."

He hated her answering the phone with her maiden name. "Hi, it's Vasco."

Quiet for a moment. Then: "What's up?" She coughed, cleared her throat. "Did you pay Citibank?"

"Listen, I need to talk to you. Something's been happening to me lately. I should tell you face to face. You got a second?"

"Be swift."

"Okay, but sit down. And let me warn you, this is a—large and odd, even by our standards." He stared out the window at the lawn in the sideyard. "I've been experiencing an odd thing, an odd kind of real odd thing."

"Of course you have. Talk." He could hear her pulling up a chair.

"No, I mean a *real* odd thing."

"Okay, *okay*. Tell me."

He cleared his throat. Here goes. "Such as visitations from the Virgin Mary, basically."

At this time, Vasco needed a very quick, reinforcing response from his ex-wife, but that had never been her thing. She stirred around a little on the other end. She was in her studio, probably cleaning up from painting earlier. Melanie Senior was an artist and photographer now.

"So," he said, "What do you say to that?"

"What do you think I should say?" She was quiet for what seemed like a long time. "You're serious, am I right?"

"Yup."

"Have you called Lowell?"

"You mean because I'm crazy?"

"Well. Medication maybe."

"I don't think he'd understand, do you? He's on the agnostic side of Methodist, he's on the Jung side of Freud, he's a psychologist so he can't do prescriptions. And he's my friend—I'd lose every remaining smidgeon of credibility."

She gave him her best sarcastic grunt. "Uh-huh. Yeah. Well…"

"I figured maybe you could give me some advice on how to proceed. She'll be back June 13th."

"Oh boy."

"You hate me. Why am I calling someone who hates me? Listen, Mel. Let's say, in the abstract, that it were true what I just told you.

What would you do?"

"Maybe, I dunno, have the girls open a lemonade stand and see if we could parlay the whole thing into payments on Citibank and the water. You know, I got a call yesterday, and they're going to cut you off the water any second. Bill Epps, at the water company."

That reminded Vasco that the sprinkler was still going in the sideyard. He stretched the phone cord toward the window. In the moment he looked at it, the high, vaulting spray of glittering water from the hose wilted to a dribble. "Yeah, Bill Epps did call, didn't he. I remember now."

"Yeah, he's a friend, but if you don't pay he can't just—" She trailed off. Then she started up again: "It's just one more sign that the system's breaking down," she said. "I've told you this before, babe—you better watch it." She was talking about the kids. Melanie would take the kids if it could be proven in a court of law that Vasco was haywire.

"Hey, Mel, the system already broke," Vasco said, laughing. "I'm notifying you of an upswing, are you listening to me? From now on, it's a different dimension. It's the Virgin Mary, for Christ's sake."

She hung up on him.

•

Later in the week, Vasco called Lowell and asked to meet him at the Hungry Bear for lunch. The Hungry Bear was the lunch and snack bar for most of the college people on Lowell's side of campus. It was ancient, its terrible decor a tradition guarded with care. They arrived around eleven, and the place was mostly empty. Lowell met Vasco with a smile, shook his hand. They sat in one of booths back in the shadows by the cash register. In a front corner of the room stood a real, stuffed Grizzly bear, six feet six inches tall, ancient and moth-eaten, staring through its glassy eyes at the Olds dealership across the street.

"You look pretty good without an EMT sitting on you," Lowell said. He laughed as they settled in. They ordered BLTs and ice water for lunch. Vasco could tell Lowell was wondering what this was all about. Within two minutes, he asked: "So, what's the deal?" He fingered his graying beard.

Vasco smiled at him. "Okay yeah well, to get right to it, there's something going on with me. That I wanted to tell you about. I seem to be being visited on a monthly basis by a vision. In my yard." Vasco watched Lowell's eyes. They seemed to flicker, but he proceeded. "It's a vision. The thirteenth of each month, for the last two months." He cleared his throat. "I haven't said anything to anybody about it. Except Melanie, and of course she thinks this is the big midlife crack-up she's been expecting from me since I was twenty-two."

Lowell looked down. "A vision of what?" he asked doubtfully.

"Well, don't laugh."

"I won't."

"It's the Virgin Mary."

This made Lowell spew water onto the table. It leapt out of him, not his fault. Something about the timing. He regretted laughing, Vasco could tell.

"She's quite pretty," Vasco said after Lowell got himself settled down. "And gentle. I know you know I'm in a tough time right now, but she says that's precisely why she's visiting me."

Lowell stared at him, eyes watering, unable to speak.

After a while, Vasco said, "I'm virtually certain there's no scientific explanation for this."

Lowell, in the middle of a sip, almost sprayed the table again getting it swallowed. "Yeah, probably not," he said, coughing.

Vasco couldn't keep looking at him, stared away. Nobody talked for a few minutes. They ate their sandwiches.

"Look," Lowell said finally. "People are talking. They see you wandering around in your yard. I'm worried about you. You're going to walk out of here today, and I'm going to hear something bad happened. I think we need to do something. Maybe we need to get you checked in some place."

"Pooh," Vasco offered.

"It happens to a lot of people. Look at you. You're under incredible stress. I hate to see this. It wouldn't have happened if that fucking English department had gone ahead with the promotion."

"Okay, there's a little stress, but things are better. They really are."

"It's money, isn't it? I heard Annie Rook paid your water bill."

"So? I'm not talking about Ann Rook. I'm talking about the Virgin Mary."

"Oh for God's sake, Vasco, *please!*"

"Lowell. There's nothing you have to do. I just—I just want somebody who kind of likes me to know about it and watch what happens. I don't know what's going to happen, but somebody else—a friend—needs to know about it. Something's definitely going to happen."

They were finished eating. Lowell put money on their table for the lunch. "You've got my phone number. Any time, day or night."

"Okay." Vasco looked at him as he started to depart. "But you're here right now. I *did* call you. You're here."

Lowell was making his way to the front door, past the staring bear.

"Can't we deal with it now?" Vasco asked, but Lowell was out the door.

When he got home, Vasco called Lowell.

"Hello."

"Lowell, it's Vasco. I…"

"I really wish you hadn't told me this one," Lowell said.

They said nothing more. Unaccountably, when Vasco hung up the phone, he felt better.

•

Previous to all this, Vasco had worried that the mine would be all there was to his life. Now he found that he could lighten up. This didn't mean that a former English professor was well accepted by the miners. They laughed at him. He didn't care. He could get on top of things. He had existential breathing room. Somebody, not just anybody, had his back. It was an *internal* process, however. Anytime he brought it into the light of day, it didn't work so well. For instance, he told Dean Ferguson, the superintendent of the Murdock Mine, that he was feeling better about his job. He volunteered the information one day, as Dean and two other managers were walking by the slag pile.

"Listen to me, Whirly, and listen good," Dean told him. "You still don't fit out here. Don't start thinking you do." Vasco turned and walked toward his car. On his way to the parking lot he got thwocked on the helmet with a piece of coal.

"This is totally embarrassing," Melanie Junior said to him one day not long after that, while Vasco was setting out warm plates of Spaghetti-Os for dinner. "Mom told me everything, Dad."

In the heat of the moment that Saturday morning, in his call with Mel Senior, he thought he'd asked her to keep a lid on this. What the hell. No telling what she was saying and to whom. Michelle was at the breakfast table, too, stirring the hot red food. She placed her hand gently and consolingly on his arm. "Daddy," she said. "Everything's going to be okay."

"Thanks, doll." The beginnings of being parented by your children. How long had they pitied him? "What about *Hiroshima?*" he asked, hoping for a diversion.

"Oh, that's all over." Michelle smiled. "It cost us three dollars and eighteen cents."

"Vietnam cost in the millions," Mel Junior observed.

"How do libraries survive?" Vasco sighed. "Did you ever wonder that?"

"Dad, Dad, Dad," Michelle said, exasperated. "You're such a worrier."

•

Lowell called the next morning to try to stop Vasco from reading the *Tuscola Review.* It was a weekly. In the "Column One" section, left column of the front page, there was an editorial. It had the heading,

"Huh??" Vasco dreaded reading it, but did. It referred to "a certain hapless gentleman in the community, frequently seen wandering aimlessly in his yard on Scott Street."

"Well, guess what," the editor wrote. "Now apparently the gentleman has observed the Virgin Mary above his driveway." The piece went on to suggest that Vasco should secure from her, on her next visit, a prediction of the outcome of the Arcola-Tuscola football game, three months hence. At that very moment, the article was being read all over the community. Vasco shuddered in his chair.

•

The next morning, as he was arriving home from a night at the mine, he discovered Melanie Senior pulling away from the house in a U-Haul. Melanie Junior and Michelle were in the cab with her. His heart aching, he followed them down Niles Avenue to the highway. On the highway, he pulled up beside them, then veered in front of them, forcing them into the white gravel of the Poplar Motel parking lot.

He got out of his car and stomped to the truck's driver's side window. "What's going on?"

"We'll talk later, 'kay?" Melanie Senior said to him, not quite looking him in the eye. Her tone indicated she didn't want a scene in front of the kids.

"Melanie, I need the girls right now."

"We think you're coming apart, sweetie. We know you need them, but they're the kids and you're the dad. Don't get it turned around."

"Daddy, we'll come visit," Michelle said. She was sitting in the middle. Melanie Junior was chewing gum, staring straight ahead on the other side. Her headphones were on.

Their mother sat agitated in the driver's seat, chewing gum, her eyes flashing. "We may have a week or two of peace before this crap runs in the Mattoon paper and humiliates us off the face of the earth."

The rental truck revved.

"Mel," Vasco said, appealing to Melanie Junior. "Don't leave me." Headphones blaring, she couldn't hear him.

"Gotta motate, hon, sorry," his ex-wife said. She smiled that hard, tough smile of hers.

"We'll come visit, Dad," Michelle sang out to him again as the truck lurched away.

•

Okay, fine. They wanted to leave him alone, go be in Mattoon with Doubting Thomasina right at the most inspiring moment, great. He drove home. He went upstairs. He looked in the girls' rooms. Their clothes, their toys, their beds, their chests of drawers, their gerbil, their goldfish. Gone, all of it. Lint and pieces of paper and parts of old games littered the ruglines where furniture used to be. An old wrinkled math test was on the floor in Melanie Junior's room. In Michelle's room, a stuffed bunny was sitting straight up in the corner like she left it there as a signal. Fine. Vasco went down the long hall to his room and sat on the bed. The house was quiet. It was a two-story house, big, the house of his childhood. This is way more than you wanted to know: He decided to lock himself in the room. No more rummaging around. No more coal mine. No more people. He'd come out June thirteenth. It was only twenty days away.

He called Gloria Steinem and had her call her friend Harold Luce, the town handyman, to change all the locks in the place. Locked in his room high and deep inside his locked house, he should be okay. He moved in a little refrigerator that was going to be Melanie's at college. There was enough food. He had a phone. The master bath was right there. He locked the bedroom door and pushed the dresser in front of it. He had a rosary and a few books. He got down on his knees and ran the beads through his coal-blackened fingers. He slept. Late that night, he showered, slept more. He set up some pictures on the dresser, pictures of the girls. A day or so passed, then a few more. Nobody missed him. Fine.

More time passed. On a few occasions, he heard a knock on the front door. After a while, visitors gave up and ran away. Once he heard someone in his yard below his window. He peeked out. It was Father Kelleher, the parish priest. No moon, it was very dark out, and Vasco couldn't be certain what he was seeing. For sure it was Kelleher. And he appeared to be working his way along the edge of the driveway with a metal detector. Vasco raised the window and was almost ready to speak to his visitor.

Kelleher looked up, startled. "Er. Hi. It's you. I was looking around." He tried to hide the metal detector behind his back.

"Well, feel free," Vasco said.

"Look. You've got to retract this business. It's going to ruin us all. Very bad. Very."

Vasco closed the window.

"Not for just me," Kelleher shouted. "All of us!"

After a while Vasco couldn't hear him down there anymore.

The house telephone was hooked to an old answering machine. Mostly there were whole days between phone calls, especially right after Vasco locked himself up. But eventually the messages began to flow in.

Melanie Senior called, said she was going to call the police if he didn't snap out of it. "Vasco? Vasco pick up the phone this instant. Vasco." She just realized he'd had the locks changed on the house, and she couldn't get in. If he was dead, she said, she didn't want him rotting on the carpet.

Gloria Steinem called: "Vasco Whirly?" She waited a moment. Then he could hear her laughing. "I'll tell you what, you're a lot more interesting these days than when you were in high school." Pause. Gone.

One day Lowell Wagner called: "Hey, buddy. You okay in there? I'm next door at the Rittenauer's. You need to send out some kind of message or wave at the window so we know you're alive and you didn't off yourself or something. Your ex-wife wants them to break down the door and rush the place because you're whacko. Orson's out here, if you want to just wave and let him know you're okay."

Vasco went to the window and waved at Orson Morrell, the police chief. Henry Green, the editor of the paper (and author of the Column One article), was standing next to him pointing a camera with a long lens toward the window. Vasco shot him the bird, pulled the curtain. As he was pulling it, he noted something. There seemed to be a lot of cars parked along Scott Street.

One afternoon the low and rumbly voice of Abe Holden, his friend on the safety crew at the mine, came on the recorder: "Hey Vasco. You in there? Listen, is it true you've gone crazy? Hey, the boys at Murdock, they hope you're okay—seriously. They like you, they said. People are talking all over the place. You gotta get out here and defend your honor, boy." Then he whispered: "Hey, oh yeah and Dean says you're not fired yet. He'd of come here and told you himself, but he broke his nose yesterday. Walked into the wrong end of a shovel." Click.

Vasco heard a lot of activity outside. But he didn't look. He lay on his bed, staring at the ceiling. Why would the boys at the Murdock start liking him all of a sudden? That night a rock crashed through his window while he was sleeping. He stared at it, on the floor in a stray beam from a streetlight. His heart was whamming. Wrapped around the rock was a Letter to the Editor, torn from the latest issue of the college newspaper. Oh how he dreaded reading it:

Virgin Mary, Quite Contrary...

I've been following this Vasco Whirly business. If anyone wonders why we on the college promotion and tenure committee failed to provide tenure to this individual, maybe it is clear now. One of the dangers of coming to a provincial region to teach in college is that we can sometimes become ensnared in the unseemly small-mindedness around us. It is now becoming clear that Mr. Whirly is a case in point.

As we in academia so well know, the most profound grief of all in this country, in this generation, is bound to be the grief accompanying the arrival of the greatest realization in history: that there is no living God, and there never was. We are alone out here, and we will have to make our own way. In the backwater regions, such as this one, where religion's roots have traditionally been fundamental and deep, that grief is bound to have its most profound impact. For some, it could even cause insanity.

> Benjamin Carlyle, Ph.D.
> Chairman, Dept. of English

It was nearly a day before the answer machine clicked on again. Ann Rook: "I hope you're enjoying your water," she said in the quiet voice she was known for. "Sorry to bother you. I wanted to call and tell you some stuff nobody else is probably telling you. The community development committee just signed a deal to build a big store. The big cheese in from Chicago heard about you and the 'sightings,' as this stuff is being called. He said, 'We believe this is just the environment for a Wal-Mart.' High school kids have a t-shirt that says 'BVM, welcome to Tuscola.' And did you hear about Ben Carlyle's letter in the college paper? That's been the funniest of all. It turned all the churches in your favor! This past Sunday Father Kelleher proudly said from the pulpit that he spoke with you recently, in your yard, that the two of you are pretty good friends. He'll be over to see you again soon, I'm sure. He's on crutches right now with a sprained ankle. Well. I've been thinking of you. Okay. Somebody's at my door. Later." Click.

On another day, a call from his daughter Michelle, plaintive and forlorn: "Daddy, what's going on?" Pause. "We love you." Click.

On the first of June, the recorder picked up a call from WCIA in Champaign, the TV station. They wanted to interview him on the phone. In a big, frosty broadcaster's voice, the woman from WCIA said she wanted to discuss the "sightings" issue, plus Ben Carlyle's letter to the editor in the local college newspaper.

On the tenth of June, the phone rang and it was Lowell. "Hey, pick up the phone. I'm next door at Rittenauer's again, and the lady from WCIA is right here." Vasco took a breath, tried to collect himself, and picked up.

"Hello."

"Ah. He speaks," Lowell said. It was the first Vasco had spoken to anyone in many days.

"Lowell. Thanks for hanging in there."

"Hey. It's been unusual. We'll talk later. Here's the TV lady."

"Hello?" she said, big broadcaster's voice.

"Yes."

She said her name, but he didn't hear it. The Rittenauers' cordless phone was getting too far from its base. "Okay. Okay, now, Mr. Whirly?"

"Yes." Sometimes Vasco could hear a little voice squawking into the woman's earphone. It was like he was talking to an intelligent electronic impulse instead of a human.

"Okay, tell me in your own words exactly what she said." The woman was intense, her voice big but flat.

"Who?"

"You know who. We're live."

"Well, if it's in my own words it won't be exactly what she said."

She was away from the phone a moment, then back. "You know what I mean, right?"

Vasco didn't respond.

"Okay. First, tell me what you thought when she was talking to you."

"Well, it would have been just my luck, she appears to me and then speaks Hebrew or something."

Vasco heard someone squawking in the earphone.

He went on: "It happened so quietly. In the movies, you know, they've got the closeups and the background music."

"Go on."

"And well, there was some personal stuff I'm not going to tell you, and she popped off a few good ones about baby boomers."

"No."

"She said she was irritated by the yuppie rush-hour joggers, that crowd, that runs in their little shorts and designer shoes in pure carbon monoxide rather than run unseen on side streets. And she was equally irritated by these people who must go to the biggest, best-dressed church, and all those people who think they're saved. She said all of them better get that smug look off their face. There's a hell. She promised me there is a hell."

"Did she say that?"

"I'm paraphrasing but you get the idea. She popped off a couple about money, too. Money as religion, greed, that sort of thing."

"She sounds very down on American society."

"Yeah, but—I mean—she was cute about it."

The woman was away from the phone a second, then came back. Her earphone was really crackling.

"Yes. Well, Mr. Whirly just a little background. This happened at your house? The house I'm looking at right now?"

"I don't know what you're looking at right now, but yeah, in the yard, yeah."

"What's your profession?"

"I'm a college professor. English. But I lost that job."

"Where do you work?"

"I'm in Safety at the Murdock Mine, in Murdock—actually, sort of under Murdock. It's a coal mine. Coal."

"Coal. I see." He vowed not to try to be funny during the rest of the interview. "Mr. Whirly, what are you going to say to the many people who refer to you as a real whackjob?"

"You think they will?"

"Yes. Many people think that already, members of the public and community, et cetera. You've had yourself locked up since May nineteenth." She paused a moment. "They'll say, playing devil's advocate here, people will say, Mr. Whirly, that you're in some kind of state of mind. The local paper referred to you as, I'm quoting here, 'hapless.' And there's a complicated divorce and a tacky little redneck struggle over the children. Collapse on the racquetball courts. You were dumped from your job at the university. Mid-life. The whole drill, *you* know."

He sighed. "Well, I…"

"There are allegations that you're funded by the Religious Right, did you know that? But I don't think so, now that I speak with you. Now that I look at this picture of you in the paper flashing an obscene finger sign. I've talked with people around here that know you. I think you might be some kind of peculiar misfit. You've been round-hole-square-pegging it for a long time in this community."

"Well, I…"

She said, "I can hear something in your voice, hostile and unstable. Or I think maybe you're pulling my leg here, the public's leg as it were. With this whole business."

"You don't think the Virgin Mary would appear to somebody?"

"Not in Illinois, no."

Vasco hung up.

It was a full hour later before the phone rang again, and Vasco was just about to jerk the cord out of the wall. But it was Melanie Junior: "Dad, guess what happened. You know the lady from TV you were talking with? Well, the WCIA news truck just hit a pole over by the courthouse. The driver split his lip, and they've taken the interview lady to the hospital with a broken leg. I mean, she *totally* broke her leg!"

•

June 13th began on June 12th. Lowell and Ann Rook kept phoning, leaving new developments on the recorder. Traffic in the area was reported to be increasing. The local motels were full. The Catholic Diocese of Springfield put out the word, and the Franciscan Monastery at Illiopolis and the Benedictines from Aurora had met together and come up with a concelebrated sunrise mass that would be held outdoors in the Tuscola park amphitheater. The merchants planned sidewalk sales.

Scott Street was blocked off from Court Street to Ohio, and Niles Avenue from Daggy to Ficklin. Big gray plastic portable toilets were set up in a row on Scott down by Judge Helm's house.

Vasco was looking out the window, watching the flapping of the canvas awning over the t-shirt stand down by the Rivertons'.

What a strange life, he thought.

•

On the morning of the 13th, he moved the chest of drawers blocking his bedroom door, went down the front stairs, and walked out onto the front porch of his house. There was scattered applause. He calculated it for about nine o'clock. Gloria Steinem had had Orson Morrell rope off the whole area in the sideyard between the Rittenauers' and Vasco's own place, using crime scene tape. A modest crowd was there, and quiet. Some people in the crowd had signs. One said:

VASCO FOR POPE!!

Another said:

SUPPORT THE THS BAND TRIP, FOURTH OF JULY PARADE, CHICAGO

One said:

HAIL MARY, FULL OF GRACE

He was struck by the color and the quiet of the little crowd. He saw everybody, Melanie Senior and the girls, Lowell, Gloria Steinem—Ann Rook, in the distance, standing alone, in the shade of Ruth Fuller's horse-chestnut tree. He even saw Ben Carlyle there, too—mysteriously, his arm was in a sling. Vasco went around to the side yard and turned on the sprinklers.

It never occurred to him that after all this, she might let him down and not show. He stood in the driveway watching the area where she had appeared before. In time there was a stir in the trees and the sun seemed to spin like a pinwheel. She was visible only to him. He felt his soul open to her like a rose. On this visit, she spoke only of him and his character, and he listened the whole time. Maybe *this* is what you wanted to know: at the end of it, she blessed us all, though Vasco Macon Whirly was the only one who knew it for sure.

THE FIRE

LOWELL AND THE ROLLING THUNDER

L ong before the fire, back when things were going fairly right, Lowell Wagner found himself out in the Douglas County countryside on a car ride with Wally and Carol Brown. They were coming back from an AA meeting in West Ridge during a phase when they'd all quit drinking and this short car-pooling journey put them together, as friends and fellow recoverings. Ironic perhaps—perhaps somewhat inappropriate, too, in that Lowell, at that time, was Carol Brown's shrink. It was a small town.

Lowell had counseled Carol for years, predating her marriage to Wally. Though Lowell knew Wally a little (they both were professors at the college, Lowell in Psychology, Wally in History), he didn't know him well. From a distance, he seemed bright, intense, often funny but a little sullen sometimes. Not that Carol said much about him—she didn't. Just that it was a small town.

So that's where things stood on the day of the West Ridge drive. And while Wally seemed quiet and odd en route, he was completely out of whack driving back. He had expressed the opinion that cross-country was shorter and quicker than the highway and, being the captain, he insisted. Lowell, not wanting a boring male-ego argument about the best route, and having no classes or appointments that afternoon, acquiesced. Accordingly, they headed home from West Ridge on the diagonal, northeast to southwest. It was early June, and they sank into the humid countryside, fields of soybeans, knee-high

Illinois corn, bluest sky, brightest sun. Lowell was comfortable, riding shotgun, sitting sideways so he could see Wally and also Carol, who was sitting in the middle of the backseat. Wally, eyes dead ahead, leaned forward over the wheel and pressed a mile west, then a mile south, then another mile west, doggedly pausing to decide at every unmarked crossroad.

Carol was originally from New York City and, even for an AA meeting held in the modest West Ridge Methodist Church basement, was dressed up. In fairness, the West Ridge AA meeting was known to be more upscale than what you got at the Green Street Y in Champaign or the Boy Scout Cabin facility in Tuscola or the Catholic Church hall in Cerro Gordo. Drying-out doctors county-wide opted for the West Ridge meeting, as did many attorneys and thus the other entitled professionals, including the most landed of the farmers. In fact, the West Ridge gathering had the feel of the Kaskaskia Country Club, which was where this same caste had nurtured their alcoholism before one by one they bottomed and went on the wagon. Carol wasn't overdressed, though she wouldn't have cared if she had been because she did like to look good.

And she seemed to enjoy the company of two men on the leisurely drive. She chattered and waved her arms, positing gossipy theories and stretching each actual case to make the story better. Meantime, as he listened, Lowell began to notice that, despite the air conditioner pumping frigid, beads of sweat were welling on Wally's forehead and lip. One drip streamed from his sideburn down his cheek and, after a flash from a sunbeam, slipped into the creases of his neck. Then for a moment Lowell was drawn into a Carol story, and when he checked back again, their silent driver had gone blotchy and dank. Whatever was coming over Wally was coming fast. Carol acted as though she didn't notice, and maybe in fact she didn't, or maybe, Lowell rationalized, this was normal enough for Wally and nothing to be concerned about. But about the time he considered that, Wally slowed the car and steered it to the slanting edge of the country road, on what would have to pass for a shoulder but was more of a ditch, and rolled to a stop.

Carol leaned forward over the seatback. "Are you okay?" She touched Wally on the shoulder and leaned forward so she could see his face. "Yikes, you look awful."

Wally looked over at Lowell. "It might be good if you took over."

"Okay," Lowell said. Quick, he slid out to go around. They were so much on the slant that his door fell open, and he stepped out into gravel and weeds. To close the door he had to lift it until it latched. And then, as happens sometimes in this world when things are going right, Lowell made a casual but fortuitous decision. Instead of taking the easier route out of the ditch around the front of the car, he was, after wrestling with the door, sort of leaning to the rear and so went around that way instead. He was, in fact, exactly behind the car when suddenly the most astounding thing happened. It took off. The tires spewed gravel and clods of tar, sandblasting him, and the Browns' aging Chevrolet peeled out and tore away down the road. Lowell stood staring, mouth open. In the first flash, he wondered if they'd conspired to leave him out there. He knew that wasn't it, but it was hard to imagine anything else. He heard the Chevy's eight-cylinder engine wind out and then go *above* wound out, to a sort of high-octane scream, the car swerving left and right between the ditches. Rumbling toward them from the opposite direction was a loaded gravel truck, clouds of dust behind it. The Chevy swerved, corrected, swerved again, tires raging against the sun-softened blacktop. The truck went deep into the east-bound ditch and Lowell involuntarily raised his hands to his head as the Chevy whipped by it, narrowly missing, the truck driver blasting the horn, the Browns' motor loud against the quiet of the countryside even though the car was now a chrome dot sailing into the distance. The rumbling, angry gravel truck whammed past Lowell, the bearded driver offering him his middle finger, as Lowell stood dumbfounded in the middle of the road.

Now the Browns' car was out of sight and the countryside was quiet again. Light wind and the call of the redwing blackbird. An airplane high above and far away, car tires on a distant road somewhere else. Prairie wind. There was nothing else to think: the Browns were dead. Had to be. The car had ducked a bumper, went end over end, rolled a few times ejecting the pilot and his dressed-up wife, skidded on its top into a field. Boom crash bang. Had to be. Lowell stared up the road.

Presently a car appeared. Presently it was clear it was the Browns' car, coming back for him. Presently it pulled up, Carol driving.

"Sorry," she said.

•

While Wally sat in the back seat and Lowell drove, Carol rode shotgun and apologized a lot. Between apologies she told Lowell every detail she could remember about the wild ride.

What happened?

As Lowell slid out of the car and wrestled with the door, Wally lost consciousness. It was a bench-style seat, and as Wally slumped over, his right leg and foot pressed the gas pedal. The car was still in gear.

Luckily, Carol was already leaning over the seat. Though the acceleration threatened to throw her back, she managed to grab the wheel. Then she was half standing in the back, leaning way over and craning to see out the windshield, with one hand trying to steer, the other attempting to rouse her husband back to duty. His thighs were pressing up against the lower arc of the steering wheel, and freeing the wheel by pushing down on his legs resulted in pressing his foot harder on the gas. It crossed her mind to turn off the ignition, but something told her that would lock the steering wheel. The swerving threw her around and that caused more swerving—she knew she would flip it. The motor roared and the tires squealed, and she could see the gravel truck coming, and she yelled at Wally, "Wake up, you stupid fuck—you'll kill us both!" and was driving with one hand and pounding on him and tugging at his shoulder with the other, but the red stripe on the speedometer stretched past eighty miles an hour and Wally didn't move. She knew they were both as good as dead. She saw the intersection coming. She bent her legs like a jockey standing in the stirrups and they shot onto the rise where the two roads crossed. The tires left the ground—she could almost feel the air beneath them—before it slammed down a little sideways on the other side, and in the lurch from that she hit the gear shift, wonderful old gear shift on the column, and found neutral. Then, even though the motor was revved, the car slowed and glided and slowed some more and finally stopped just as Wally sat up in his seat.

On their way back to town, Lowell drove, and Wally rode embarrassed and silent in the backseat. Lowell stole glances at him in the rearview mirror. What was up with this guy? The sun went behind afternoon clouds, and Lowell dropped himself off at the college. He had no idea what to say. He gave them a perfunctory goodbye, then got in his own car and watched as Carol slid back into the driver's seat and drove away.

•

Lowell was married to Veronica. Had always been. Would always be. He'd lived crazy in his youth. After he was married, twenty-two years ago, things got better. Recently, he had ten active clients, enough to make a steady flow. Apart from teaching class, department committee work, and all that. His clients would sit a few at a time in his waiting room, then come in and talk to him for an hour. Astounding, the things he heard in those sessions. The range of human behavior, the irony, the confusion, the primitive simplistic maneuvers and convolutions, the courage, beauty, loss, inconsistency, grief. The lies. For some, things never went right and, for many, though he would never say it, there was no hope.

Veronica, for some reason, was hope for Lowell. Always had been. Years before they were married they'd attended a Dylan concert in Chicago. Rolling Thunder Revue. Lowell had been to many concerts, but this one caught him in a different way. Even though they were close to the stage, he had binoculars—not dopey little opera things but real field glasses. Through the haze of weed, the blast of music, and the dizzying wonder of bouncing girls, Lowell stared at the famous Mr. Bob Dylan, icon. The binoculars were powerful. He could see the eyes. He could see the guy was as crazy as he was rich—and somehow also he was innocent, dangling right at the end of his boy-wonder phase, a little Howard Hughes starting to show at the gills, as he mutilated old favorites—"Blowin' in the Wind," "Just Like a Woman," "Tangled Up in Blue," "Don't Think Twice."

Maybe all poets and/or rock stars were like this, Lowell was thinking. Maybe that was their thing, pushing themselves further and further until they were pretty much out of earth orbit. Or maybe that old motorcycle accident had done something profound and permanent. Then, inside the round optical field of the binoculars, as Lowell watched Dylan begin the traditional folk song "The Water Is Wide"—did this happen?—suddenly Joan Baez stepped into the circle of light and joined Dylan at the microphone. She had grown into full adulthood—beautiful and somehow open, her hair shorter now, a grace and calmness, Nixon gone, the war over. The audience raised a big cheer. She smiled and then through the speakers her voice joined Dylan's—hers lithe and steady, braided into his rasp and growl. Something loose and desperate in him, something anchored and solid about her. He was doing his thing. She was trying to get him to remember their rehearsal. Through the binoculars, Lowell watched them stare at each other as they sang.

In bed the night of the Browns' Car Debacle, Veronica and Lowell, on clean sheets in their small, sweet-smelling home on the northwest side of town, lay close. Their daughter, who was in college but lived at home, was in her room down the hall.

"So, how was the meeting?" Veronica said into his ear.

"What meeting?"

"I thought you went to AA."

"It was good."

"Good," she said. She kissed him on the neck. They stayed quiet again for a while. "So," she said, "what's up, besides not you."

Yes, he was preoccupied. Until then, he'd said nothing about the drive home from West Ridge. In the hours since, in his mind, the story had evolved into a new insight into his client, Carol Brown—her super-human insistence on survival—some fierce thing in her that stood up to her own death and said, "Not this time, pal," and about how a day that had seemed ordinary, even peaceful, had so suddenly become dangerous. There, in bed, Lowell still smelled the oily metallic burn of near death.

Staring up at the ceiling, he told his wife about it. She was speechless.

"But anyway..." he said, hand relaxed on her leg, "turned out fine."

Then up on one elbow, she stared at him. "Well." She was tense. He could feel the heat. "Worst case, I'd have gotten a phone call this afternoon, and tomorrow your daughter and I'd be arranging the funeral." She sighed big, thrashed her pillow to get it right. "Lowell, Lowell, Lowell." She flung herself back to the other side of the bed and was fidgety for a while. Soon she said, "Do you remember the Trumbull Street house in New Haven? And we slept the whole summer on a fold-out couch?" She always did this. When she was bedeviled in some way about him, she would tear into the past for something stable to shore up their common foundation. It was her intuitive way of re-establishing their balance.

"Yes." Yes, Lowell remembered.

She stayed on her side, her back to him.

Softly, she said, "And those Yale guys breaking in to the apartment to steal Cheerios?"

"Yes," Lowell said. He'd confronted them in his underwear, stomping down the hall with a baseball bat.

"Do you remember where the mailbox was, at the condo?" The two of them had lived in many places, and in their folk history and oral tradition the places had shorthand names. "The condo" was a place where they lived for a year up in Freeport. "The apartment" was where they first lived, near the railroad tracks in Wheaton. "The white place" was an apartment they lived in just before he was drafted, second floor of a big white antebellum beauty, Geneva, on the Fox River.

"There was a mailbox on the front porch," Lowell said. "It was a wrap-around, remember?"

"Right," she said, deep in covers, staring away, her back to him. "I forgot that porch." Quiet again for a few minutes. "Lowell," she said then, turning back to him.

"Hmm?"

"I have a lot of questions about the Browns. Carol Brown—I like her, but I don't know if I trust her."

"Trust her how? It's not like you work with her."

Now Veronica was looking right at him. "You do."

Ah. There it was.

"You've been seeing her for long enough, don't you think? Doesn't she need a female counselor to spill her pretty little guts to?"

Lowell saw Carol Brown once or twice a week in therapy, group and one-on-one. He'd been seeing her for a long time, through her divorce, through her single years, and now into her time with Wally. In fact, Carol did not discuss much of this journey in therapy sessions. For her, therapy was a game, cat and mouse, hide and seek. She had mastered appearing to work at self-revelation, but it rarely happened. Sometimes, but not always, Lowell would push her, but forget it—there would be no throwing open the kimono from Carol Brown.

"Besides," Veronica said to him now, "you shouldn't be going to the same AA meeting as these people, Lowell. You *know* that. It's trouble. It's a dual relationship."

Lying there, Lowell pictured Carol talking to him at the office, upright and straight-backed in Lowell's most straight-backed client chair—how she performed, looking right at him, then averting her eyes, coyly talking away from him into an empty space in the room.

It was a form of flirtation, for sure, but flirtation was a form of behavior. There was information in it. Lowell liked Carol, despite her cagey indirections. He looked forward to their sessions. She was a runner; she was an accomplished pianist; she was a good mother— most of her talk in therapy was about her high hopes for her wonderful kids, kids from the previous marriage. All available signs were she was a devoted spouse in her own dicey way. In therapy, her story was a little pat, but Lowell was thinking that his chance participation in this recent event could help launch a new frankness maybe.

Veronica had nothing to worry about with Carol. He wanted to be a good counselor more than he wanted to court this small attraction. If there was a truer truth beyond that, Lowell didn't want the thought coming into his head now.

•

Before the fire, he used to take the occasional glance through a peephole he installed in a painting in the waiting room of his office suite. He'd bought the painting for this very purpose at a student art auction. He fitted it to a hole he drilled through the wall. The peephole was similar to the ones in hotel room doors, only subtler. The tiny fish-eye lens allowed him to see the whole waiting room. His colleagues over in Child Development, in the new Education building, had conference rooms outfitted with one-way mirrors; this was Lowell's jackleg version of that.

Lowell's office was a set of four rooms with a small foyer. He needed this space, because his private practice, by permission of the administration, was meshed with his teaching day and his psychology-related obligations to the school. In other words, he could use the third floor space for his small private practice, on the condition that the college community would have first access and free consideration.

The office suite was in the big administration building at the college, as were most of the faculty offices. The building, one hundred and twenty years old, sometimes called "Old Main," was the centerpiece of the campus. It was brick on the outside, oak on the inside, and if the floors were a little wavy and tended to creak, still it was a stately old thing, high ceilings, big heavy doors, a pretty red and blue domed skylight five stories above the matrix marble floor of the main lobby.

Long ago, Lowell's office had been the college president's suite. It had a secret back exit. Behind his desk was what looked like the door to a small closet. Behind the door was a metal spiral staircase that plunged from Lowell's office, with no other access, down three floors into the basement where there was a small, odd-looking door leading to the outside, padlocked and unused for the last fifty years. The staircase and the peephole made a professional life of stirring around in people's fears and obsessions kind of interesting.

Sometimes Lowell would watch James Kelleher, the local Catholic priest, pastor of Forty Martyrs parish, older, long-time resident of the town, wearing an open collared sport shirt, prayer book in his lap, glasses down to the end of his nose, waiting for his hour with one of the associates. Weekly, Lowell would take a glance through the hole at a Vietnam head-case named Howie Packer, who was hearing voices in his head, before having him for his hour. Once in a while Rachel Crowley would be out there, divorced, remarried, divorced again. Rachel was raising her little girl, reading, going to Weight Watchers, "doing" therapy, taking yoga, faithfully working her little job in the Dean's office, and hell-bentedly engaging in a part-time live-in arrangement with a chiropractor from Arcola. In the waiting room, Rachel and Wally would ignore each other, even though she lived directly across Van Allen Street from the Browns and had for years. It was such a small town.

Carol would be out there twice a week, though, by design, never when Wally was. Lowell would watch her, too. She'd sit right across from the little peephole, eyes down, legs crossed, one foot kicking with nervous energy. Michael O'Meara, Lowell's new associate, might walk by her, say hi, and they'd talk and Lowell would watch them.

It was interesting to watch Carol animate in her certain special way, because, after all, for her this wasn't *Candid Camera*. She knew about the peephole.

In the weeks after the Browns' Car Debacle, Lowell managed to get Wally back into exercise. A phase evolved in which on many afternoons Wally would mosey down the hall to Lowell's office and wait for him to get free so they could run or go to the gym. Through his little peephole, Lowell liked to spot Wally and study him a bit. There he was, Professor Brown, History, his compulsory copy of the *New York Times* in his lap. If he wasn't reading it, he'd be staring out the window, closed posture away from the rest of the room. Overtly he'd bend, acting like he was real interested in someone down by the pond or passing on the sidewalk. He had a broad, gnarled way about him, a tight fist of a man, private in his soul. This could be mistaken for the *standard* posture of a professor in late mid-career, but it was way more than that.

In that dark season, Wally'd had another spell. He'd passed out in the bathroom at home, landing on his face on the edge of the claw-foot bathtub. Concussion, broken nose. Carol did tell Lowell about this—Wally didn't, because Wally had become Lowell's running and racquetball pal, not a client. When Lowell asked him about these events, as a friend, Wally called them "episodes"—the car debacle, the bathroom disaster. He was plenty annoyed that Carol had told Lowell about the bathroom thing, like the condition of his face the week after didn't require explanation. Staring at him through the little hole, Lowell watched and worried about Wally Brown.

When they began their workouts, Lowell had coaxed Wally to schedule a physical, and that led to a prescription for Prozac and the doctor's strong admonition for Wally to improve his diet and get serious about exercise. Lowell had hoped to play a part in getting Wally going, then to ease out. They started varying the routine. They'd lift weights sometimes instead of running. In addition to racquetball, they'd do power yoga. Lowell told him to run alone more often.

He told him to run sometimes with his own wife—Carol had been running for years. The main thing was, Lowell didn't want Wally's exercise routine to depend on anyone other than Wally. Sometimes it did seem like Wally had gotten more independent about it. Lowell might see him at the gym lifting weights alone. Once he spotted him running out in the countryside, no one else in sight. Lowell would rejoice for a few days, but then he'd look through the hole and there Wally'd be, in his usual chair by the window, waiting.

By the fall after the summer after the late spring of the Browns' Car Debacle, there wasn't a single sign that Wally's exercise was working, and one day Lowell happened upon a scene in the registrar's office, first floor of Old Main. Dropping something off there, he saw Wally in the middle of a nasty argument with Ed Ewan, the rickety, white-haired registrar, over some lame class load issue, way too little a deal for such a big deal. Lowell stuck an arm between them, and as he did he saw that look on Wally's face, like when Wally was about to pass out on the day of the debacle. Staring into Wally's distracted, bloodshot eyes, Lowell said, "How's it going, bro?"

It took a few seconds for a response to rise up through the clouds. "Great," Wally finally said. "It's going great," he said, and his red hand let go of Ed's starched white shirt. He backed toward the door, looking around the office—then, head down, he retreated into the hall and was gone. Make a note, Lowell thought: Call the doc, switch the meds.

"Your pal's gone off his nut," a ruffled Ed Ewan said. Then it was Lowell looking around the registrar's office. The whole staff was staring at him.

•

Veronica and Lowell had a daughter named Monique who had always been called Misty. She was twenty and a student at the college. For a few bad years, Lowell and his daughter had been sideways. Lowell's fault, midlife and booze. But then things started going right, and before long he and Misty were doing better. Sometimes on a weekend afternoon, they'd run together in the neighborhood. She was fast and he wasn't, but she slowed down for him. After things got better between them, Misty seemed to enjoy mothering him, in a kidding sort of way. "Dad, you gotta drop some weight." "Dad, please don't wear black Levis anymore when my friends are around." "Dad, do you ever watch Wayne Dyer on TV? You should, you could learn something." Happily, she'd become a psychology major, which seemed to signal some faith in him. "Dad, don't you think you might be slightly ADD yourself?" Admittedly, his edition of the diagnostic manual was older than hers, and he hadn't looked at it recently, but Lowell was of the bias that ADD was a fad diagnosis created to expand the market for some drug that was used to treat it. Still, it did his heart good that his daughter was majoring in his field and testing her diagnostic mettle on him.

She was a real runner, and she wore a heart monitor. The apparatus had two parts—a heart sensor that was part of a strap around the runner's chest, and a watch worn on the wrist that was in communication with the heart sensor. Real runners could use this instrument to maintain their heart rate at a certain level for maximum aerobic benefit. Old guy runners, like Lowell, could monitor their heart rate while running and avoid overexertion and an unattractive death on a neighborhood street.

"Dad," Misty began to say to him from time to time as they ran, "a man your age should be wearing a heart monitor out here." She probably said it because of how loud he was panting as he tried to keep up.

Amazingly, one day she bought him one.

He only used it once. That day, running by himself, he was well into his fourth mile, tired and hot, and suddenly realized all he had to do was look down at his wrist and he could see what his heart rate was. So he glanced down and, through sweat running into his eyes, he saw a pulse rate of 197. That didn't seem too good. So he put away the heart sensor strap and used only the watch function, for timing his runs.

Then one day that following spring he and his daughter were jogging on the streets near the house. He knew she was slowing down for him, but still he felt like he was doing well, strides long, breathing good, the rhythm right. Then his running watch started beeping. It had never beeped before. He didn't know how to stop it. He put his hand over it to suppress the sound, hoping Misty didn't hear it. After a while it would stop, then later while they were in the middle of some conversation it would beep again.

"Damn."

"Watch your language, Daddy," Misty said with a daughterly laugh. "It's just your heart monitor."

They ran on for a while. The beeping would relent. Half a mile later, for no reason known to science, it would beep again.

"Just shut it off, Pops."

"I'm not wearing the monitor."

"What?" she said. They kept trotting along, beep beep beep. "Real nice. I bought it for you and you don't wear it. Geez. A hundred bucks."

"Well, I'm not wearing the damn thing, and it's beeping anyway."

Misty traded places with him, let him run at the curb while she ran on the side toward traffic. No more beeping. Down the street they went for a while, smooth as silk.

Finally she spoke again. "It was *my* heart monitor, setting off your watch, case you didn't notice."

"You mean your heart beat?"

"Hard to explain."

"You mean my watch?"

"Trust me."

"But shouldn't there be some kind of privacy code or something, so our monitors don't get crossed up?"

"Shshshshshshsh. Settle down, Pops." She was joking with him.

"Couldn't you find out all my secrets? Would my heartbeat show up on your cell phone?"

"Yeah, right. Paranoid!"

He loved her. It didn't bother her at all to joke around and run too fast at the same time. Down the street they went, steady as can be.

"This is pretty good," he said. "I sort of like wearing a watch that's in touch with *your* heart."

"Awww," she said. By then they were in mile five, and it was all he could do to keep up with her. It didn't seem one bit right. He'd watched her being born. And on they ran for a while. As they came into the last of it, they were both quiet and concentrating—lift the legs, steady the pace. And right about that time Veronica pulled up next to them in their Corolla.

She spoke quietly but fast. "Hop in, you guys—it's bad news. Old Main's on fire."

•

Lowell was getting a second doctorate at the time. He had a Ph.D. in Clinical, but after he stopped drinking he found new energy and now he wanted an Anthropology doctorate, too. He'd been at it a long time. His desktop computer, with dissertation on the hard drive, backup disks on the bookshelf, laptop with backup copy on its hard drive, backup tape system with desktop and laptop hard drives backed up, and zip drive backup system to make sure, were all in his office. As Veronica drove them toward the college he saw smoke from blocks away, rolling in a spark-filled black ball up into the sky and filling every downwind nook and cranny of the neighborhood. Old Main was five stories tall including basement and attic, and nearly a block long. As they got closer to the fire, Lowell was doing inventory on the things that would be gone. Twelve years of client files, his father's Buck hunting knife, pictures, the Anthro dissertation lock-stock-barrel. A lifetime of books. Parallel losses for his associates. The great place itself, the comfortable familiarity of its spaces, the windows looking out over the lawn and the fountain, the peephole, the secret spiral stairs behind his desk.

"Jesus," Misty mumbled as they rounded the last corner. The south end of the building was engulfed top to bottom. Arcola, Tuscola, West Ridge, and the local chemical plant's fire trucks were either already there or just arriving. Fire hoses stretched across the streets and across the grass, but police hadn't yet stopped traffic.

"They'll never put this one out," Misty said. From the back seat, she leaned forward and put her hand on Lowell's shoulder. "Dad, the whole thing's gonna burn." His heart monitor watch started beeping.

From all directions, the fire was being blasted by water. A paper brigade had been set up at the main door. Students, faculty, and staff passed records and files from the various administrative offices hand to hand a safe distance out onto the building's big expanse of lawn. On the upper floors, people dropped things from their office windows. They were saving all they could. Police were blowing whistles and waving their arms. Everyone ran, all directions. Lowell could hear the fire crackling, big pieces of Old Main falling.

Veronica pulled up on the drive at the north end of the building, amid a scattering of fire trucks. Lowell looked up to his third-floor office. It seemed fine, at the far end of the building from the fire. Actually, if one thought about it, there was a little time left. He got out of the car. Veronica said something to him, but he got the door closed just in time.

He walked toward the building, glancing at the small defunct door that was at the foot of his private spiral staircase. A fireman stood guard at the north entrance. To get to him, Lowell had to walk under yellow tape just being strung by the police department and climb a set of steps to a concrete porch where the north door was. The fireman, a member of the Brotherhood of Tuscola Volunteer Fire Fighters, held a large ax on his shoulder.

"Hey," Lowell said to him, "this is good duty. It's pretty hot on the other end."

"You got that right," the fireman said. His dirty yellow fireman's jacket had the name "Burroughs" on it. "Listen, you gotta get back behind the tape, sir." He pointed.

"What?"

"You gotta get back behind the yellow tape down there. See it?" He pointed at the perimeter the police had set up. "We're clearing the building of people."

"No, no, I've gotta go in the building." Lowell smiled at him.

"You've gotta what?"

"There's not a lot of time. I've got to get some stuff. I'll hurry."

Burroughs was young, the age of a lot of the older college students. "Sir, I'm telling you, get away from the building." The fireman's gloved hand was pointing the way.

Right then Lowell punched him—hard, just below the ear, a quick right jab—and then shoved him over the porch's pipe railing, ax and all. It was about a six-foot drop squarely onto his helmet, the fall broken by shrubs. Lowell's hand hurt because the punch caught a little bit of the helmet, but he was in the building.

He bounded up the first flight. The smoke in the air was poison—the one short breath he took told him he better not take another. On the second floor, he looked down the long hall toward the fire, a rolling ball of red-orange rage in a havoc of black smoke. There seemed to be a lot of noise and no noise all at once. At the top of the next flight, he was across the hall from his office door. No keys, of course, and needing air, he didn't take time to try the door. He went right into it with his shoulder. Old Main's doors were old, tall, and heavy, and this one held with the first hit. He stepped back and went at it again, this time like there was no tomorrow. When the door popped he ran inside and quickly pushed it shut.

The air was acrid, but he could breathe okay. He stepped up to his file cabinet. In the past he'd never have attempted to move this monster, but in the past, of course, he'd never considered punching a fireman. He grabbed it and would not accept that it was heavy and wouldn't move. He shoved it with his shoulder, all the way to the window. He tipped it so that the upper part rested on the windowsill, then lifted the goddamned thing from the bottom, a five-drawer steel cabinet chock full, and blew it right through the closed window. It fell three stories, landed in the bushes with a crunch. Through the destroyed window, he saw his daughter going crazy out by the yellow tape. He waved. "Hi, Baby," he said to himself. He saw Veronica, too, wearing a bright yellow blouse. She was staring toward him, her arms folded across her, motionless in a group of people under the line of maples that bordered the north drive. He jerked the cords out and tossed the computer, making sure it didn't land on the cabinet. Then he tossed down the cords. He heaved his father's sheathed hunting knife in the direction of his daughter, who scampered under the yellow tape to fetch it. He grabbed his laptop, the hard copy of the anthropology dissertation, the zip drive, his blue and orange Fighting Illini coffee cup, then from his desk drawer his wedding ring that he'd had cut off after he gained weight, his grandfather's magnifying glass, a great picture of Veronica from the desk, a picture of his parents from off the wall above his bookcase. He put it all in a copy-paper box. Smoke was coming up through the floor. He looked around for what else. The books. The painting with the peephole. The desk chair he'd bought himself when he turned fifty. He grabbed a loose pile of CDs that was part of the clutter on a bookshelf. He could hear people yelling outside. Smoke was whipping past the windows. What else could he carry? What wasn't he remembering? The fire was coming. Sirens. The place was a blur. Goodbye. Goodbye to all of it.

He decided he didn't want to come face-to-face with the fireman when he exited the building. Burroughs would probably still be mad. Box under his arm, he took a breath and with a free hand opened the door to the great old secret spiral staircase—at last, a use for it. Looking in, the first thing he noticed was that the air in the stairwell was still good. The second thing he noticed was Wally Brown, cowering in the shadows a few steps down in the dark.

"Hey, bro," Wally muttered, looking up at him.

"Hey, how's it going?" Lowell said.

The ordinariness of the question made Wally laugh. "Not too bad," he said. Tears streamed down his sooty face.

•

Lowell and Wally spent the night of the fire in the little Douglas County jail, Lowell because he hit the fireman and Wally because he burst out of the building with the assailant himself—blasted through the locked but decrepit side door at the bottom of the spiral stairs with his ample lowered shoulder. Lowell followed him out carrying the box of stuff from his office. Deputies "subdued" them, so the newspaper read a few days later, and hauled them off. Around seven that evening, Misty came by the jail with Lowell's checkbook, some jeans (blue), and a sweatshirt. Lowell was still wearing his running shorts. He was escorted out by a female deputy.

"My goodness," his daughter said, using her mock-motherly tone, looking at his handcuffs. "Are those real?"

They both laughed for a minute, until the nice deputy jerked his chain. "You got your clothes. Let's go."

Before he went back, he slipped the closed loop of his arms over his daughter's head and down around her shoulders and hugged her. "How's your mom?" he said.

"That's not allowed," the nice deputy advised them.

"Mom's a little stressed out," Misty said as he was being towed back to the lock-up. "She wasn't about to come over here with me, I'll tell you that." She gave him a "chin up" smile just before the big door bammed closed.

The following morning, a Sunday, the judge phoned the jail from home before church, talked to the sheriff, who passed the message along. The judge said he could understand what Lowell did and why. Still, he said, there was the matter of a public servant who was injured trying to do his job. He assessed Lowell a fine of four hundred dollars, to be paid directly to the Brotherhood of Tuscola Volunteer

Firefighters' Fund. The judge had Fireman Burroughs go over to the jail, him and his wife, so Lowell could apologize. It was a small town, and people did what the judge said. Lowell came out of the lock-up with his wallet, belt, running clothes in a paper sack, and female deputy escort. He handed the check directly to Burroughs, who was standing there, exhausted, gauze taped over his eyebrow, now looking smaller in his ironed Levis, farmer's tan, wet hair slicked back, his young wife next to him glaring at the lunatic who'd hit her husband.

Lowell looked them both in the eye. "Sorry," he said.

·

Nobody was sure why Wally was arrested. He'd been with Lowell in the building, so they took him in, figuring they'd sort it out later. Fraternities, the whole football team, a lot of the faculty who had offices there, had run into the burning building, helped save critical records, grabbed the heirlooms and books they couldn't live without. None of them was hauled to jail but Lowell and Wally. That next morning the judge let Wally go, no questions asked.

That morning, the community was shell shocked, of course. It was the biggest fire ever, bigger than when the Douglas Hotel burned and left the downtown looking like it was missing its front teeth. A single-file line of cars streamed down Main Street to stare at the ruin still burning in its own crater.

That night Lowell and Veronica went to bed early. He hadn't slept much in jail the night before. Though he was stressed and distracted, the music coming from Misty's room was comforting. He could feel the safety of his home and people. Within their locked bedroom, he and Veronica made love. Afterwards, after a civilized interval in the dark, Veronica yawned her affected yawn, which was how she would begin a discussion she really needed with an attempt at casualness. "Did you think about us when you ran in there?" She was standing at the bedside, a shadow sliding back into her nightgown.

"I guess I didn't, no." He knew he didn't. There'd been no reflection. "I was sure I could get in and out fine if I didn't stand there and talk about it." In the dark, the room threatened to capsize like those nights he came to bed drunk, but this time that wasn't it. "Do we have to talk now?" he heard himself say.

"Did you think about your daughter?"

There'd been a picture of Misty as a baby in his desk drawer. Had he grabbed it? "I saw you both, out the window. You were on my side. Misty was jumping up and down."

"In horror."

"She was cheering. Stop it. And you—you were with me all the way."

"Horror, my love. Bushels of it. I watched them arrest you! Oh my God!"

They were quiet for a while. She went to the bathroom. "It was a new low, babe," she said, splashing her face with water. That made him thirstier, and he got up and he filled his bedside glass, though something stronger would have been nice. He forgave himself the lapse. You aren't human if you don't think that after a fire. Then they were back in bed. She said, "Did you listen to the messages? People called all day. Buddy Blue phoned at the crack of dawn. He was laughing. He goes, 'Good luck saving a computer by dropping it three floors into the dirt'."

Lowell laughed. "Such a cynic." Buddy's real name was Wilbur Gray, Sociology Department, a marathoner. He was too quick to run with, but he and Lowell played a lot of racquetball.

"Vasco Whirly phoned saying he was 'proud to know you'—those were the words." After leaving the college and the mine, Vasco had become sort of a local shaman. Every town needs one.

"Vasco said that he and a couple of your other jock pals got your filing cabinet and stowed it where the college is storing things for the time being, and not to worry."

"Some of these people actually like me."

"Mike O'Meara called, too. He apparently helped Vasco. He said he got in the office before you, rescued a few of your things. So that's good. He said he left the office door unlocked."

"Hmm. That explains some things," Lowell said. Such as how Wally got in.

"We *all* love you, crazy man. Think how we'd have felt if today we were matching burnt bone to dental records."

"Okay." Despite Veronica's attempts at distraction, Lowell was upset. He was thinking about Wally Brown in the old stairwell, Carol in the driver's seat out on the countryside on that day. Carol's pretty legs in her nice dress, foot-tapping, eyes averted, observed through the hole in the waiting room wall. He was thinking about all that was confused and teetering, all that he didn't know, and all that was lost.

"And by the way," Veronica whispered to him. "Misty's worried about you. Now that you're off the sauce, she wants you to live."

Lowell stayed quiet.

"So wear the heart monitor, will you?"

"Grrrrrrr."

She laughed and was apparently waiting for more of a response, but none came. "You're off somewhere, aren't you?" Lowell knew his distraction made Veronica's world uncertain. She stirred and started talking. "Do you remember that time in Yugoslavia when we got so hungry in the middle of the night that we stopped and heated a can of stew in the ditch?"

"Dinty Moore."

"We were insane."

"Absolutely," he said.

She sighed and snuggled for a few minutes. "Lowell. Do you remember in Charlottesville in the townhouse when I caught you panning the high rise across the street with the binoculars?"

They were the Rolling Thunder binoculars. Damn. Gone in the fire. A small camera, too, with half a roll of pictures in it. Lowell sighed.

"Did you want to see a naked woman?"

Charlottesville. Okay. What *was* he doing that night, he now began to wonder. "A naked woman would have been nice, I guess. I think what I was doing, I was looking at slices of lives. Like Hitchcock's *Rear Window*. Or something. I don't know."

"You felt guilty about it. You tried to hide the binoculars when I walked in."

Yes, he supposed he did. "Honey, I was curious about how people acted. I was like a dog that eats grass. I had an experiential vitamin deficiency."

"Now you do all this leering for a living."

Quiet a while in the dark. "That's clever, but inexact."

"I guess if there's anything good to come out of this, it's that your sneaky little peek-a-boo painting at the office is torched."

Sometimes Lowell swore to himself that she had mental telepathy. He wouldn't tell her right away that he'd saved it.

"What are you thinking about?" she asked him. "You've got to talk this through, honey."

"I'm thinking about Wally." Actually, he was thinking about Carol. "I'm thinking about AA. Vasco and Mike lugging my filing cabinet."

"Wally looked real peculiar when the two of you scrambled out of there." Now Veronica sighed. "For friends, you have this whole brotherhood of wounded weirdoes."

Prozac. Lowell hadn't called Wally's doctor.

"So what else are you thinking about?"

He stood up abruptly, went into the bathroom for some more water. He looked at his very thirsty, rumpled, transparently whacked-out self in the bathroom mirror. "You know," he said, "later on that night Wally was fine—quite lucid and funny."

"You mean, in the slammer?"

"Well, yes, we *were* in jail." They laughed. He climbed back in bed, sitting up. "He was on the upper bunk in our cell. He was quoting Chuang Tzu, as translated by Merton, about finding happiness by not pursuing it. And some Stoic from one hundred years AD about how we must wish for things to happen as they do happen instead of how we want them to."

"Pretty good," she said. "He was confessing, right?"

"Wally was one overeducated prisoner, I'll tell you that."

"Where was Carol? Are the kids with her?"

"I don't have a clue about Carol," Lowell said much too quickly, though he truly didn't. Veronica had him all self-conscious about Carol now. The room turned again. In the old days, Lowell kept a bottle behind the furnace in the basement.

"Do you remember when Shadrak—back in Muncie, at the Sycamore house—when he chased that rabbit and ran into that wire fence at full tilt and knocked himself out?" Veronica was chuckling. "What a goof. I miss him."

Their common past. Ballast. Shadrak, their malamute, stolen in Charlottesville. It reminded Lowell of a picture of him and Shadrak next to their old blue VW, on the office bookshelf. Had he saved it? "Honey, do you know where that box is, that I carried out yesterday?"

"It's in the trunk of the Toyota, all safe," she said. She stretched and then was quiet a while. Maybe a yawn. "Mike said he grabbed a camera you had in the office, a few other things. He said give him a call."

"Hmm. There's hope for a few things then," Lowell mumbled. "Hope is good." Things *had been* going right there for a while—so it seemed, looking back. But he was back in the struggle now, for sure, one-day-at-a-timing it.

Veronica cleared her throat a few times. Something was on her mind, and it was going to get said, of that Lowell was certain. "Also," she said, her voice a little bigger than it had been, "I think the jury is in on the Browns. Since they've actively figured in your two most recent near-death experiences that I know of." She kissed him. "Don't you think? Carol needs a new shrink, somebody who'll kick her around a little." He felt Veronica looking at him, her eyelashes brushing his skin as she blinked. Finally, she said, "Lowell. You know Wally burned down the fucking building, right?"

Okay. He needed a drink. How bad would it get? Veronica, in their dark bedroom, her dark French beauty and voice that he loved, her smile that he knew was there even in the absence of light—her hands that he remembered from when she was seventeen, twenty-one, thirty, forty, fifty, her arm across him, her legs braided into his, dear God the years—she pulled him down into the covers. "There's tons of hope, babe." She got him face to face with her. He could hear the thump of rock 'n' roll coming down the hall from Misty's room, or was that his heart beating. Then the sheets flew away, and Veronica rolled on top of him. He looked up into the dark where he knew her eyes were. She was staring down at him. She bent toward him, lips close to his ear. "I love the Stoics, don't you?" It made them laugh. "Remember the blue VW?" she said. "That perfect color of blue?" She leaned way back. "God," she whispered toward the ceiling. "Remember the Alps, honey?" she said in a hot whisper. He took deep breaths. He had ahold of her. Her hands pushed down on his chest, she lifted and came down again, and then very much in earnest she started to move.

COAL GROVE

Nick was glad it was raining. Walking Dave, his dog, long
before a June dawn, passing under streetlights that showed
a medium downpour (not the annoyance of drizzle nor the
thrill of rain in windy sheets), Nick got a glimpse of his own shadow,
and it reminded him of Buck, his son—how the shadow walked, how
the head was carried, the shoulders when they were properly back, the
odd attitude it conveyed, a strange combination of optimism and not-
having-a-single-clue. Rain falling, Nick tried to hum a happy tune
but he couldn't remember one. Buck, twenty-three, was home in bed.
It was just the two of them these recent years. And Dave.

Nick wore a bucket hat, the wet canvas brim soaked and dripping.
Dave, the chocolate brown Springer Spaniel trotting along ahead
of him on the leash, didn't give a shit if the rain was coming down.
Water was his thing. He rounded his ears, and his eyes got blinky,
and maybe his head was lower, but overall he was the same old Dave
wet as he was dry, watching the bushes for adventure and lining up
to piss his whole dog-autobiography on everything that was upright
and would stand for it. Rain didn't addle him like it did some dogs,
so why should it addle Nick? Occasionally Dave glanced back for
the approval of the dog-slave on the other end of the tether. It was
a forty-five minute walk Nick had devised, across the campus and
along the canal that fed into the Hocking, and then back into the
neighborhood and down the streets among the big old Midwestern

houses. They walked fairly fast this morning, and Nick mostly ignored the dog and thought about Carol. He'd be seeing her today.

In the old days, back at the college where he taught before this one, Nick would always drink beer and sit around and loudly wonder about women. "I mean, what the hell do they *want*?" he'd say, his voice and beer mug raised, and with bemused delight Lowell Wagner would lift his mug, too.

"They probably want the *truth*!" Lowell would offer, the perfect straight line. Lowell was Carol's shrink. That other place, it was a very small town.

"Oh God, not *the truth*!" Nick would call out, and they'd both laugh at the boys-will-be-boysness of it. Lowell never knew about Nick and Carol, although this had always made Nick wonder what Carol did talk about in their therapy sessions.

In those days, everybody was always saying this or that about what people wanted, like it was really discoverable or like it even mattered. Mostly, men acquiesced to just about anything if the sex was good and there was a modicum of wiggle room. Women were more mature about it, it seemed, and more particular. During Nick and Carol's secret rendezvous, Carol would lie back and receive every bit of the conveniently little Nick could offer in cramped space and stolen time. Nick loved the illusion that this secrecy and stolenness was what women wanted, and Carol let him have that illusion for many months before, suddenly, out of nowhere, she married Wally Brown.

"Jesus!" Nick would bark, and Lowell would raise his hands in the air, the universal gesture of men's feigned puzzlement about women. "No, I mean it. Women are like dealing with a frigging cat."

Nick hadn't made friends like Lowell in the new place. The bar they always drank at was at the township line, out in the country, because back then the town itself was dry. Nick's eyes would take in the waving oaks through the neon Busch sign in the bar's small front window. They were the trees of Rice's Woods, a dense oak forest with random roads leading in—one of Nick and Carol's favorite parking spots. The fact that Lowell hadn't known all that was going on was yet another in the chain of betrayals Nick regretted, and also doggedly maintained, in his scattered little life. To make it all worse, toward the end of his time there, Lowell quit drinking. No more loud commiserations out at Squeak's.

Nick and Dave came up the front walk at last, and Nick worked the lock and slid back into the house. Still dark, but NPR had clicked on which meant it was six o'clock. In the kitchen, he toweled off Dave who submitted to this rubdown like Al Capone at French Lick.

He showered fast, put on jeans and a jacket, pulled his cell phone off the charger, and looked in on Buck, who was still hunkered, bunkered, and asleep. "Davie's walked and fed. See you in a couple of days."

"Uh-huh" came the grunt from under covers. "Where you goin'?" Two blankets covered the boy in so many heaps it was hard to discern a body in the bed.

"Down to the river to meet with some turkeys from Louisville, I told you before."

"Okay." The sleeping behemoth rolled over. "Have fun," he grunted. A third blanket was artfully draped over the window so Buck could sleep well into broad daylight. "Did you walk the dog?"

"It's handled. Sleep good."

•

Even Athens, Ohio had a beltway, Highways 50 and 33, and after hitting McDonald's for supplies, Nick got on a stretch of it and went down two exits to the interchange with Hocking Road. He had a bag load of bacon, egg, and cheese biscuits and three large cups of coffee, and at the Hocking exit he slowed way down and tried to spot Mac Pellier, his old homeless Vietnam buddy. He squinted down through the fog and saw something moving. Had to be Mac. So Nick rolled down the ramp with the flashers on because stopping on an exit ramp in the dark and the rain, even at the lightest beginnings of

Athens' miniature rush hour, was a good way to get smacked, and this promised later to be a fairly busy exit ramp or Mac Pellier wouldn't be out there leaning on his crutch with his "will work for food" sign. Nick honked and flashed, and Mac waved. Checking his rear view, all clear, Nick took one sandwich out of the McDonald's bag and set it in the passenger seat. Out of the drink holder on the floor he got one of the cups of coffee. He pulled close to the left curb at the bottom of the ramp. Mac was already up off his golf stool (Nick gave him the stool in the winter) and wielding his crutch expertly to the car.

"Hey, man, it's fucking wet out here," Nick said through the window.

"Ah, not too bad."

"Ha. Not too bad."

"It's nothin', to tell the truth. To what ya get sometimes."

"Whatever you say." Nick handed him the food bag. He checked the rearview again. "Nobody's coming—just set it down and come back so you don't spill this." He lifted the big cup of coffee.

So Mac did that, he put the sandwich bag down on a tuft of soaked scrub grass next to the golf stool, then gimped back to Nick's car. Nick looked into the dark, the shadows of the overpass, the undergrowth planted by the state on the slope up to the highway. Rough mean cable fence. Hard wet galvanized metal guardrail. God what a life.

He handed over the big cup. "I'm going to keep the rest of the coffee then, if that suits you."

"Whatever floats your boat," Mac said in his growly voice. Now he was holding his cup, leaning on the crutch and using both hands to get the flap up on the plastic lid. His hands were shaking. He looked in the car. "You all packed for something?"

Nick shifted into drive. "Yeah. Going down to the river to meet some people. Just overnight. Where'd you sleep?" Nick knew he probably didn't want to know.

"Didn't yet. Going into the shelter this afternoon. Got a toothache." Mac looked up the exit ramp toward the highway.

Now from this angle Nick saw that half the ruddy old face was swollen. "Oh damn, I hate a goddamned toothache. You okay?"

"My dad pulled his own tooth once," Mac said, and he was laughing. "I couldn't do that in a million jillion." He sipped at his very hot coffee.

Nick slipped the car into park and checked the mirror again. He popped the trunk and climbed out into the rain, careful not to knock Mac down with the door. In his bag, in his shaving kit, he thumbed out a few aspirin, and he also spotted one of those tiny plastic airplane bottles of Johnny Walker—God knows how long that had been in there. He thought about it for a nanosecond and grabbed it, too.

Standing out there with Mac, he pulled down his bucket hat. "Why don't you go into the shelter earlier?" Before Mac could answer, he said, "You got a pocket?" He dropped the aspirin and scotch into Mac's ugly bent hand and Mac jammed the stuff into his big raggedy blue-green army overcoat. Then Nick handed Mac a ten-dollar bill and that went into the coat, too. "Won't the shelter take you before the goddamned afternoon?"

"I ain't at the shelter." Mac drank coffee, stared at Nick. This was the logic Nick loved. Under Mac's raincoat was a sweatshirt with a hood, and the hood was soaked, draped over his skull.

"Well, it's raining, man. You need to be at the fucking shelter. That's what they're for. That's why they call 'em that. C'mon, I'll carry you over there right now." Nick's current girlfriend, a woman named Emma, worked at the shelter, and he really didn't want to encounter her as he slipped out of town on this particular mission. But she didn't get in until eight o'clock, so the coast was clear for a couple of hours.

"Afternoon's fine."

"C'mon, Sergeant, get in the car."

"Afternoon's fine. Just call me Mac."

Mac and Nick had a friendship that was this and this only, based, for Mac's part, on their commonality, which was that they'd both served in Vietnam, and actually had both gone deep into Cambodia back in the day. This particular thing they had in common really made them brothers, because it wasn't just every Vietnam veteran who was there in the time we were chasing Charlie over that border. Mac seemed to like Nick because of this and didn't know the whole Nick-in-Vietnam thing was a huge fucking lie.

Nick looked into Mac's eyes and vowed that someday he'd straighten this story out. Mac leaned hard on the crutch, looked up the exit ramp over Nick's shoulder. Nick stepped off the curb and into his car. "They got a dentist at the shelter?" He dried his face with his coat sleeve, found a McDonald's napkin and tried again.

"They got pliers there and somebody that can get ahold of it. That's alls ya need." Mac laughed, and Nick remembered Mac was already missing a front tooth. "You got any sugar?"

Nick looked in the bucket seat next to him, nothing. "Hey, maybe it's in the bag with the food." He indicated down on the ground behind Mac, the plastic bag. "If it isn't there, we're out of luck, sorry." The rain was really coming down now. "If you get something in the stomach, your tooth will feel better."

"Okay, Mom."

"Last call on the ride to the shelter."

Mac worked his one-legged way back to the golf stool, and when the light turned, Nick shot across Hocking Road and back onto the beltway heading south on Route 50 toward the Ohio River. The first sign of light was beginning to show in the dark blue, water-filled sky.

•

He was glad it was raining, even if Sergeant Mac had to hobo wet today. He was glad for the cottony wafts of fog that ran across the road in the low places, and for Carol's voice once she called and began chattering to him as she made her way to the same place from her own direction. She told him about her recent piano recital, held in great old Music One, a special recital room in the venerable music building he remembered so well. He remembered the wintery sound of her piano. He remembered the warmth from the radiators that heated each glassed-in practice room, so that the outside windows would first steam, then stream with condensation, the cold held at bay outside, the red flush of Carol's cheeks as she played, and the music and the timelessness of the rooms themselves holding the warmth in. That was back when they'd first been together, when she'd been between marriages. He turned up the volume on the phone so he could hear over the road noise and wipers, and once his wet jacket was off and stretched over the back of the passenger seat, and the car heater was cranking and the coffee was cool enough to drink, he was pretty happy.

"Ben came," she said. Ben Carlyle, cranky chair of the English Department but a lover of good music. "He sat with Wally and the kids." Her voice was desolate when she said his name, always had been. Lord knew what *their* history was. She'd been married to Wally four years come August. Shortly after the wedding, Nick and his son had moved to Nick's new job in Ohio.

"Did Wally enjoy the recital?" Nick asked her. It was a probing question, and there was information in the tone of her reply.

"Hell if I know."

The driving was automatic. Old highways of the north have their own cracked-up rusty awful charm. There's a Reduce Speed sign, then 45, then 35, and the road worms into the heart of some dead business district, chipped glass beads on a worn strand of string. Normally the car dips through the town, grudgingly conforming to its speed requirements, then shoots out the other side with some considerable relief. Good. At least that's not where we're going. Good. *That's* not where we always lived, a tiny place on Fourth Street across from the church and Grandma's waiting for dinner. Good. Onward, miles to go. He drank the coffee and slowed down the wipers.

"Yeah, I guess Wally enjoyed it," she said. "Is it foggy where you are?"

"I think so. I think that's fog."

"Very funny. You have some coffee?"

"How's Wally doing?"

"Who knows? Not me."

Nick leaned back in his bucket seat and remembered Wally Brown, his big, dark brown eyes, his focus and intensity, his eccentric bent way of fast-walking across campus, books under his arm, steaming toward his classroom where he'd give 'em hell.

"Still getting stellar evaluations from the students though. He's great with the kids."

Nick sought to change the subject. "What did you play in the recital, honey?"

"The usual stuff. Wow, it's foggy here, too."

"Where are you?" Nick loved cell phones. When people used to talk on the phone, "Where are you?" wasn't a likely question. You had to know where a person was to be talking on the phone with her. The phone was hooked to a place.

"In some hills or something. I don't know where I am, actually. How's Dave?" Dave was a pup when Carol last saw him, before Nick moved away.

Her voice brought back the old days. No matter how good your memory is, when you talk to someone you once knew, and still kind of do, the edges of what's specifically that person always come back and surprise.

"He's been a pretty good dog. He and Buck will have a good time while I'm gone."

"Buck's a good boy, too," she said. "Not in a dog way, of course."

"Yeah. Buck is a good guy."

The connection crackling, Carol said, "I want to tell you something before we get cut off."

"Good news or bad news?" The connection was fading fast.

"No, really. I want to be real honest with you. Can you hear me?"

Then there was a beep in his ear. "I'm getting another call. Back in a second." Nick fumbled with the phone. "Hello?"

"It's still me," Carol said. "I want to tell you something."

He clicked away, trying the switch again. He got a glimpse of the phone screen and saw that the second caller was Buck. He looked back at the road. This is how people have wrecks.

"Hello?" he said.

"Hey, Dad," Buck said. "Your girlfriend called, wants you to give her a buzz. She's at work."

"What does she want?"

"Didn't say."

"Okay, I'll call her. Everything else all right?"

"Yeah. Rain. I hate it."

"Me too. I'll call you when I get to the river."

"I'm gonna make spaghetti. Bye. This afternoon I mean. Bye."

Nick clicked back to Carol. "Back. It was Buck, speak of the devil. I have to call somebody. I'll be back to you, maybe an hour or so. I'm about two hours from the river."

"Wait, I have to tell you something."

Nick didn't want to hear whatever she was going to say.

"First off: I'm going to have to leave early."

Nick could hear the road running along under her tires, wherever she was.

"And I didn't throw away the letters. Don't be mad."

"I knew you'd say that." He took a deep breath. They were good letters. Maybe he was glad she still had them. "I've got to make some calls. I'll get back to you later. I have a confession to make, too. Bye."

He cut her off as she was saying "okay" and fumbled through his contacts list—all this and driving at the same time. Now he was feeling sour. Carol was the other person he'd lied to about Vietnam. He remembered when it came out of him, six years before. And, for him, it had plagued the relationship ever since. It was always a really bad lie, which was why he didn't tell it anymore, but there was a time when he thought he could handle it or when he thought he needed it or when he thought whatever he thought when, on a moment's notice, in some cul-de-sac of conversation, he slipped into it. Over the years, this particular lie, hanging out there between him and Carol, wore him out, and he felt plenty of self-disgust when it surfaced from time to time and he came to the road's fork where either he had to rid the world of it and be humiliated or sustain it with a couple of relevant remarks and quickly engineer a change of subject. He'd told the lie only a couple of times and always hated himself afterwards, but from it he learned, over long years, the natural force of truth, which had a tug like an undertow and his arms were growing tired of resisting. He and Carol had rendezvoused a number of times over the years. This time he was going to fix the lie even if it cost him the woman. And then, while he was bleeding, maybe he'd come home and purge it with Mac Pellier, too.

He called Emma. "You rang?" he said.

"Yes, Buck gave you the message?"

"He just said to call."

"Okay, well, two things."

"Why didn't you call me yourself?"

"I had something I wanted to talk to him about, too. Some work. That's good, right?"

"Yes. But calling him is brutal at seven-thirty in the morning."

"I noticed that," she laughed. "But you know, he's going to have to get up in the morning for any job."

"True that. So it was a test?"

"Stop it. Not a test. Anyway, two things. A job we have here for Buck. And this: we sent somebody out to pick up the Sarge and he said he saw you this morning."

"Yes."

"He showed me a small bottle of scotch that he said you gave him."

Nick sighed audibly if not theatrically. "God, that guy'll say anything." And he winced inside himself. "What has happened to the mental health system in this country?"

"Anyway, he got it somewhere."

He laughed. "I'm telling ya, you just can't trust the homeless anymore."

Always earnest, Emma didn't hear the joke. "Not you, okay. That's what I thought. He didn't drink it—we're real proud of him."

Nick sighed again. "I gave him the scotch."

"Oh," she said. She was quiet for a moment. "That's not a very good thing, in his specific case."

"I know. I did it on a whim. The guy's face was out to here with that toothache."

"That doesn't matter, Nick—don't make excuses."

"Well I also gave him coffee and two bacon, egg, and cheese biscuits, and I didn't see you guys out there in the rain making sure he had breakfast in the roadside weeds standing on his one-and-only remaining goddamned leg. A war patriot. Gave a limb to that fucking mess over there. Begging food on the Hocking exit."

"He didn't eat the food. He got tormented by this bottle of scotch and phoned us from a pay phone on Hocking. He was all worried he'd go on a bender and be tossed from the program. He said he doesn't trust you anymore."

"That sounds more like you than Mac Pellier, but okay, I stand reprimanded and deservedly so. It was goofy and terrible giving him the scotch. I'm glad he's in the shelter. Help him with the tooth, for God's sake. And save the whisky for me when I get back. What else is happening?"

"You don't get it."

"I do. I get it. Next topic. What else is happening? Be nice for a minute."

"No, you are making light of it, Nick, like you do. Who are these Louisville people you're meeting?"

"Business people, I told you—from a previous life, you know. Old friends, really, and we probably ought to be going to a ball game, but anyway—back tomorrow evening." Change the fucking subject. "How's your apartment doing?"

Quiet on the other end.

"Did they get it pumped out?" Too much recent rain and her ground floor apartment was flooded. Nice royal blue rug under an inch of stinky storm sewer backup.

"You know I can't talk about personal stuff on the office phone. Give us a call when you get back from visiting with your friends from Louisville." And she was gone from the line.

"They're not my friends," he said, too late. "And what's so personal about wet carpet?"

Emma was the most beautiful woman Nick had ever been out with. He loved her commitment to the homeless shelter, which was where he met her. She was active in the same parish where Nick ran the annual fund drive for the Guatemala relief program. She was prominent in local politics and had run for mayor a few years back. She marched annually against strip mining in the foothills and sat on the resources advisory board for the Appalachian Center that was a sort of United Way for the poverty regions nearby. Except for some very occasional fun, Emma was relentlessly focused on "the issues," as Nick's friends in business in Louisville would have put it, if he had any. She was a serious woman, and that, Nick noticed again, as if for the first time, was a major part of the turn-on.

The highway stretched ahead, and he rode it through the next half hour hoping he'd begin to feel better. When he was short on sleep, things would nag at him. Lies. He was in a swamp of them. Lies make you weak. What else? The letters. He'd not destroyed Carol's either, though a couple of times he'd said he had in an effort to get her to follow his lead. She didn't. Oh well. So in Tuscola, Illinois, and in Athens, Ohio, hidden somewhere in piles and bundles were equal halves of a six-year love affair in letters (compared to the time and effort of the letters, Carol and Nick's actual time together was miniscule), and while Nick was sure he could handle it on his end, he was not sure Carol, innocent and pure of heart in so many ways, and married with a couple of young but savvy kids around the house, could muster the required duplicity to properly stash her end of the mess and protect them both. It was a chance they both kept taking, because their love was like a vortex—pulling them together, pulling them down, pulling them down together.

He kept his cache of her letters in a U-Haul moving box taped shut with silver duct tape, a roll of it. There was a slot like a mailbox or piggy bank in the top, and after reading her letters he'd slide them each through the slot into the darkness where they piled up, read once and banked. He lived only with Buck, who was his older son, who was into his own thing and never gave the activities of Dad much thought. Certainly he would never go into one of seventeen million sealed boxes in the garage with a packing knife, which was the sort of effort such an intrusion would require, and once someone cut into the box, there was no way Nick wouldn't be able to tell. So how was Carol handling security? Her letters had to go. Nick vowed that he'd revisit the issue this time and get that solved, too. The Vietnam lie and the letters. Both. Now was the time.

He knew how it would go.

"They are beautiful letters, Nicky. I'll hide them better but I don't want to throw them away."

"Why?"

"They're love letters, that's why. They're to me, and they're love letters. From you. I can't burn them. Yours are gone. So in a way they're all that's left. I'll hide them so nobody can ever find them."

There would be tears. He would see from this how much quiet stress and real pain Carol was holding in as she lived these two lives, one wife-and-mother life visible to all, and one sharp little shard of doomed and secret pain and glory, their affair hopefully hidden well.

•

Nick was glad the sun was shining, finally, when he got where he was going. In Coal Grove, the Ohio River helped define the town's shape, sliding swollen and brownly behind the Super Walmart and the car parts/wrecker service (a hundred rusty hulks with hoods gaping and trunks too) and four warehouses that opened to docks of barges the teenagers loaded as summer jobs. There were hills, and Nick parked on the shoulder of one, a side road above the main highway, so he could see a good distance down to the Super Walmart parking lot, the place where he and Carol would meet, as arranged, as they'd done one other time in this town. From this point, parked in shade on the grassy slope, he could watch her pull in. The day before, she'd driven from Tuscola to Cincinnati, where she was supposedly seeing her mom, who was supposedly staying with her sister, Carol's aunt, who was sort of sick but they might go out from time to time, perhaps even a day trip, down to see the dogwoods, or something, hard to reach you know, will call when possible, etc. Convoluted and twisty trail. With luck, no one tries to follow.

What would she look like this time? Big trucks rattled by on the highway. A car wash was busy across the road and down a ways, and Nick watched some fishermen with their dockworker sons pamper their pickups and one housewife with kids in car seats wiping down her SUV. Her untucked t-shirt said "Exotic Landscaping." She was young and pretty. Nick still had good eyes. He was playing Van Morrison, "Into the Mystic" on repeat, and he had a headache though he didn't notice until he shut the engine off and stepped out. For a while he stood by the car in fresh mowed grass. The side road he was parked along led up to a private school on the hill, and this whole area was groomed and planted as a way of promising passersby that the invisible school above and out of sight would take good care of kids.

Closing his eyes against the headache, Nick leaned on the car and ate an apple, listening to the music, a different song. The cell phone rang again, and he reached in and got it. Buck.

"Hey," Nick said. "Is everything fine?"

"Yip."

"Had lunch?"

"Nope."

"Whattup?"

"Emma called again, and I said why don't you just call him—you got his cell number—and she said she tried and nobody answered."

"Ah." Nick finished his apple and lofted the core into a wooded area next to the road. He reached for a second one out of a bag in the backseat. He checked the register and sure enough, he'd missed a call.

"And I wanted to ask you something anyway."

"Shoot."

"When do you think you'll be back and can I take the car for a few days?"

Nick said, "Day after tomorrow, and yes. Where you going?"

"Columbus, and I know you don't want me taking the bike up there."

"Right you are, buddy boy. How long will you be gone?"

"A few days. Two or three. That okay?"

Of course it was. Buck needed a life, too. "That'll be fine," Nick said. "I haven't ridden the motorcycle for a while." Together they owned a Honda Shadow. It was black and fast. Mostly Buck used it, mostly locally.

"Yeah, you haven't ridden it because I don't go anywhere where I need the car." They both laughed ruefully. "In fact, I don't go anywhere at all." Nick could hear his son opening and closing cupboards as he talked. "How's the poor SOB car running and is the transmission work we did holding up? I know the muffler's in the toilet, but… well I'm glad you're road testing it and we should paint it while the rust…"

Suddenly Nick picked up a vibe. "I'm going to ask you a direct question, Buck, and I need an answer. Have you been into the pharmaceuticals this morning?" He could hear it in his voice, an altered, yammering, scattered stutter running through his son's regular talk like brain static.

"Nah, I'm just tired," the lad said too slowly.

Nick's heart sank. He had the urge to drive straight back home. The center wasn't holding. "I don't feel good about this. If I can tell over the phone, it's a problem."

"Well, anyway, your girlfriend called so you should call her right back."

"Clean up the act before I get home, or you'll be peeing in a bottle instead of taking the car to Columbus. It's out of the question, this shit starting up again."

"That's cool," Buck said. "Have a nice time down there, and old Davy and me'll hold the fort. Is the bacon in the refrigerator still good?"

"Yes." Pretty bad when you can't leave town even for a few hours without things caving in.

"That's good because I'm fierce about hunger at this time."

Nick was ready to go home. Oh how he hated this. Big pressure in his chest. His son. He didn't say anything.

After a few moments, Buck spoke. "Okay. Well, you hang in there, Daddy-o. And I'll catch ya on the flip-flop, or whatever you used to say on the CB."

The boy was stoned. Jesus.

•

Nick stirred and paced for a while, a couple of times around the car, over to the fence row in the deep shade of a stand of poplars to stare at the trickle of a stream. He remembered Buck as a little boy, all energy and go go go. He went by Nicholas, Jr. then. Now Nick remembered once when Buck was about five, he and his brother playing in a school playground on a Saturday. From a distance, Nick watched as several neighborhood kids surrounded the boys and teased them, particularly going after Nick's younger son, Matthew. Buck thought they were going to hurt Matt. He picked up a fallen tree limb that seemed twice his size and charged into the group of six or seven taunters, sending them running in all directions, and then led Matt back to Nick, who was standing by his car. Nick had remained amazed at that ever since. He desperately wanted for divorce not to be the ruination of that wonderful, brave little kid.

On the cell, he dialed up his ex-wife. It was mid-morning in Kansas.

"Hello." Same voice as ever.

"Hi, it's Nick." They hadn't talked in a year.

"Hi. How are you?" Automatic stroke, didn't really want to know. Same tone as ever.

"Okay." Nick took a deep breath and dove in. "I just wanted to tell you I think Buck's back into stuff. I'm on the road. He's been fine for a good long time, best I can tell. But today I've been gone for just a few hours, and I just talked to him—it doesn't sound good on the phone."

"I'm sorry to hear that."

"Yeah."

"Hmm. Are you sure?"

"I'm thinking of bagging the trip and heading back."

"Right." She cleared her throat.

"How's Matt?" Although he hadn't talked to her in a long time, he talked to Matt weekly, and Matt always *said* he was fine. But it was checking-up time.

"He's fine."

"Grades good and all that?"

"Oh yeah, all that. He's being scouted, he probably told you, and of course if the baseball's going well, you know and so on. And we're traveling all over hell's half-acre to games. He's a jock, when it's all said and done." She cleared her throat again. "At least now we're seeing light at the end of the tuition thing."

"Uh-huh. That'll be a relief."

"Shall I call Buck and sort things out?"

"I'm not asking you to, but if you want—sure. He's seemed fine, and I've been watching."

"To the extent you can."

"Yeah. I've been watching close," Nick muttered.

"Maybe the scars from last time are wearing off."

"Probably so."

"Why don't you make some stuff up. Tell him police again. Tell him jail this time. Tell him people are suspecting and this time it'll be bad. Make shit up. You're great at it."

Nick stared into the trees.

"Use it to do good, for once." She laughed the dark laugh.

Nick stared deeper into the trees. He was remembering a few things about why things didn't work out. Every time he called, for the last many years, he imagined that maybe the anger would have relented. After each call it was clear to him it never would. Grudges aren't what women want, but they carry them well and far.

"Okay, Nick," she said, maybe some reconciliation in her tone. She'd landed the punch of the day and felt better. "I'm glad you told me. Not much I can do from here. I don't think I'll call him. He needs somebody to trust him."

Nick was quiet.

"So where are you?"

"I'm down by the Ohio River, meeting some friends from Louisville, a little R&R. It's spring break for us."

"A little R&R, huh."

"Yeah."

Quiet on her end now.

"But I don't have to be here. If crap's gonna fly, I can head back just as quick. I'm thinking seriously of it."

"No, no. Do the R&R, Nicholas. You probably need it, with your rough life."

He stood there for a few moments, quiet, staring into the trees, holding the phone to his head like a gun. Finally he said, "Okay. I just wanted to tell you. Bye."

Nick clicked her off, good fucking riddance.

•

Carol had worn a ribbon in her brown and frosted hair last time, in Indianapolis fourteen months before. That was their fourth go-around since he'd moved away, and Coal Grove, then, the fifth, was not intended to be Coal Grove at all but instead they would, he hoped (planning not being his strong suit), drive deep into the mountains in Eastern Kentucky and find a proper B&B. He looked up toward the private school, bit into the last of his second apple, and gave more thought to going home. Maybe he would feel better if he did. In a way he was really looking forward to Carol's arrival, in another way he was churned up and wanted to start the car and drive home immediately and nothing less would suffice.

Right then her car shot by. There *was* a ribbon, white. He watched the rented Mercury Sable, creamy white, as the turn signal came on and she spun into the big horrible parking lot. She would circle once looking for him, then find a shady spot with a decent view from which to watch for him to arrive. But he was here, watching her arrive.

He hopped in, turned around, found a slot in the traffic on the main road, and cruised fast down the hill just catching a yellow light and turning in with his rusty-red Oldsmobile Cutlass—he and Carol had done the deed in it one night back when they lived in the same town. He drove cars to their knees. This one was from the early nineties and he was proud for her to see he still had it and thus hadn't changed a bit.

She saw him turn in, and instead of parking they drove up side-to-side, facing opposite, and hopped out fast. They kissed in broad daylight because in Coal Grove they could. Besides Indy and Coal Grove, they'd met in Washington, D.C., Kansas City, and Tampa— always only for precious hours stolen in a hotel room paid for by whichever of them was on the road for whatever convincing reason could be divined.

They put all Nick's things in Carol's trunk and left the red clunker parked in shade next to a collection point for shopping carts. Nick hopped in the rental, and Carol smiled and chatted behind the wheel—Nick half listened and looked at her fresh face and laughing eyes. Her diamond flashed in the sun as she turned left into grim and gritty downtown Coal Grove, with its cracked concrete streets and littered asphalt lots. The old brick buildings of the business district hid behind aluminum-and-glass rehab solutions done in the 70s, now dull and fading. They'd have been quaint at this age had they just been left alone.

"How is everybody?" Nick asked.

"You mean Lowell? He's great. I see him around the college all the time. Looks exactly the same."

Nick was thinking about the old days and didn't hear Carol's reply. She had a tendency to branch, and he had a tendency to drift while she branched, and they'd been together less than ten minutes and all their tendencies were kicking in.

Nick looked up from his reverie surprised to see where they were going. "What are we doing?" he asked, interrupting the tail end of a story about Wally and the kids and some bad pizza.

"What are we supposed to be doing?" She smiled.

"I figured we could get lunch and decide where to go. Further south, though."

"Nick, I *brought* lunch. You know that."

"The mountains are pretty."

"You never listen to me."

"Dogwoods." Nick smiled at her. She was right. What had she said this time that he missed?

She was turning in to the grimmest Holiday Inn in all Ohio, dusky green streaked with brown. In effect, it was a museum of Holiday Inns—a time capsule really—dingily preserving some corporate iteration from 1960, the days when they were proud of their aluminum window sills and air conditioning. The management could snatch victory from the jaws of mortification by shining it up and making the fact that time had passed them by into a marketing device. But Nick figured if they could spot potential like that they wouldn't be running the Coal Grove Holiday Inn.

"I thought we'd go down into Kentucky and find a B&B in the

foothills. We said that's what we were going to do, isn't it? And I know you don't think I listen but I don't remember you saying we were going to the Coal Grove Holiday Inn." He gestured toward the poor thing. "Or I'm almost sure I wouldn't have driven down here."

"Well, now, that's a point," she said.

"Seriously. Not here, please."

"Ah," she said, parking under the portico of the motel office.

"Ah what."

"Ah fuck it." The word was unlike her, and they both laughed.

"C'mon. We promised ourselves something nice for once."

She looked at him.

He watched her move in her bucket seat, turning toward him. "You deserve better than Coal Grove," he said.

"Listen, Nick, this will be perfect," she said. "Perfect for us." She smiled, touched his hand. "Quick. Go in and get us a room. I want to make love now." She leaned over and kissed him. She pulled back just enough so she could talk and said, "I told you on the phone, I have even less time than usual." Her hand was on his chest, then his face. "Let's make the best of it and not drive around Kentucky looking for the ideal mythical nonexistent perfect honeymoon spot like we did in Tampa and ended up in a Holiday Inn anyway."

"Ramada."

She kissed him again. "Go in there, madman."

And in he went. He ambled straight to the abandoned front desk in a pantomime of not being anxious, leaned over it to see if anyone had ducked down to avoid business. From a back room out of a cloud of cigarette smoke came a portly man with a flushed face and a Holiday Inn plastic nameplate. Clint, Shift Manager. The arrangement was made for one night, and Nick begged to check in early. Clint was up for it for a mere twenty dollars more, bringing the total to seventy nine dollars, which is what the establishment should have paid Nick and Carol to stay there, but anyway. Clint handed Nick two big brass keys. Old school all the way.

•

Nick was happy that Carol had brought lunch. It was her custom to do so if she was driving to the rendezvous point and thus had room for everything. She had an ice chest in the back, sandwiches lovingly packed that morning as she left Cincinnati, grapes, strawberries, Perrier, oranges, Dijon mustard, four Harp ales, and a funny card in an envelope marked only by the dazzlingly erotic imprint of her lips in the shape of a kiss. Nick had brought champagne and two flutes and the same set of five cinnamon candles he'd brought the last two times they'd met. But their time-honored traditions felt bleak to Nick right then.

The room was on the second floor, and they carried in the bags, ice chest, and various sacks, all of it, before they locked the door and closed the heavy drapes. During the hustle of moving in, in the locked bathroom of their room, Nick had the opportunity to check his phone. Emma had called—there would be two messages from her when he got a chance to hear them, and now Emma and whatever it was that was on her mind became yet another gnawing thing, joining his stoner of a son, his brick wall of an ex-wife, his big lie, and the ticking bomb of their letters.

They made love before anything else. Carol whipped down the bedspread of the window-side bed, a smile on her face, and rose gorgeously in the room's dim greenness from that fine, delicate last move of undressing that Nick loved so much, when the last ankle was at last freed from the beige panties and how those panties sailed across the room light as gossamer itself. Then the two of them were in each other's arms on crisp sheets, rolling, him on top, her on top, him, her, and laughing between kisses, and holding each other tight so that, for Nick, nearly a half hour passed without preoccupation or worry, and during that time, brief as it was, he genuinely took joy in Carol Brown, in the ease of her, in the fun she wanted to have, in her happiness as she reached for it, in all her words that he heard and all those many, many words that for some reason he didn't hear. She was pretty. She hated the word but it was so exact. He wouldn't say it, but he could think nothing else. They were stealing this moment and this love from the world around them, stealing it from a world that stole joy and freedom from them on a regular basis and this was revenge. No, it wasn't revenge, it was escape. No, not that, it was comeuppance, it was the coming around of what-goes-around-comes-around. It was a rite of adulthood, to be defiant if they fucking well pleased. They waited months and sometimes years between times of seeing each other. Steal love. Steal it. Time had made them both familiar *and* new to each other. Lovers in the familiar stretch of bodies and the fabulous way skin knows other skin, and strangers in the details, the thickness creeping in, the gray in Nick's hair now dominating the brown, smile wrinkles deepening for them both, and more, much more, subtle stuff that was hard to spot or name. And at the end of it, Carol was on her back, and tears, mascara-tinted, streamed from the corners of her eyes down into the fine hair that framed her face. Nick dabbed at her eyes with the edge of the top sheet, and kissed her again, her tears making the kiss humid and, he noticed, sweeter yet for all the sadness. She was only being emotional—happy, not sad, she would have said if pressed—but he didn't press and soon she pulled the ribbon out of her hair and rolled away from him. "I don't know what's going to happen to us," she muttered.

"Nothing is," he said after a while, and he really believed it, for better and for worse. He thought about that, and other things, and drifted. He saw the shaking hands of Mac Pellier—what was he thinking giving that man booze? He thought of Emma's strong, level, committed, right-or-wrong-and-nothing-in-between gaze. Buck resurfaced for him. He stared at the ceiling, and sank back into his rickety, chaotic, barely-glued-together reality though he tried not to show it.

Carol was saying that Tuscola was going wet. The new student center had a bar. Somehow she'd gotten that far from the existential question, and her long white arm reached from under the sheets to open the cooler and bring out the grapes, and the large bunch was passed back and forth. They weren't saying anything. He got up and opened beers, lay back down, and the grapes and beer held their attention a while. She went to the bathroom, stayed fully five minutes, came out in her robe with a hairbrush, a familiar hairbrush she always had with her when they met, and brushed her hair in the motel mirror in the dim light. Then she lit candles like it was late at night, although it was barely noon. Pretty in that flickering light, she sat at the foot of the bed facing him.

"You asked what I played."

"Yeah."

"I played our Mozart—the stuff we like. Some Ravel I keep trying, a few other things. I want to play for you again some time."

"Ah." Nick was still drifting. Buck had been in rehab twice in the last few years, jail once. Drugs had been whopping trouble for him and for everybody. How could they even let him near the shelter? Emma knew all this. What was she thinking? Was she trying to do something great for Nick by turning a blind eye to his son's record, trusting him and giving him a job? And why does Buck turn up high this day? *This* day.

"I don't know why I keep doing recitals," she said.

Nick stared at the dark ceiling, but he did hear her.

"To keep my head in the game, I guess."

"Yes."

"So my kids know their mom is accomplished at something."

Her two children, ages nine and seven, Stephen and Rebecca, from her previous marriage. Focus, Nick. Listen. "What's up with the kids these days?"

"What do you mean?"

"Just asking."

"Our neighbors have them while Wally's at the college, or Margaret does, and then he's got them. They love the Fosters, and they're right next door. It works."

"Ah."

"They're taken care of, if that's what you mean. While I'm…"

Nick remembered the days. He missed them in fact. It was all in a tangle now.

"I know they'd be taken care of, Carol. I was just trying for an update."

"They're growing up. They remember their father well, and he comes by, and Wally seems to get along with him."

Tangles everywhere. Nick thought of Dave, earlier this morning, getting toweled off. He'd come out of the towel, his face beaming, his eyes looking straight into Nick's. He'd be sad while Nick was gone, but he'd sleep plenty, cocking his ears toward the street from time to time, full of dog hope.

Carol was up to get the sandwiches. She'd said something, and Nick didn't hear it. "Hey. Saint Elsewhere." She wiggled his foot.

"What?"

"Are you praying or something?"

His hands were folded on his stomach just so.

"I was saying that I hate to tell you but I'm going to have to go home." She was looking at him. "In a couple of hours. Drive back. I really forced this. I wanted to see you. I needed to. I can be home by ten o'clock if I leave by four."

"Okay," Nick said.

"You don't mind?"

"Buck called a couple of hours ago stoned." Overstated, the usual.

"Oh no, Nick."

"A miracle he managed in the mere four or five hours I've been gone." Nick picked up his beer and finished it. "So I should go, too."

Nick's ex-wife's pointed digs were gnawing at him now. It must have seemed to Carol from his body language that he was thinking of leaving immediately. She said, "We can stay here for another couple of hours, though, right?"

"Okay," he said, and looked around, trying to get ahold of himself, wondering how long he could keep from bolting.

"We have to take our customary picture, too."

Nick sighed. By all means, let's add more pictures to the cache of letters and pending disaster.

"Another exciting Coal Grove panorama with the two lovers in the foreground," Carol said.

"Yeah, we can go up on the road where I was waiting for you. Green in a sort of generic way. It's on the way out."

"Has Buck been clean and dry until now? I mean since…"

"Hell if I know. I think so."

"Is he dating?"

"Not right now," Nick said. "Who knows. They don't 'date' anyway, you know. But no."

"Have *you* been seeing anyone?"

"No." This was a sudden and surprising question, and Nick answered too quickly. He hated it. Carol had to know he'd be seeing someone in Athens, and to think otherwise surely would have run against all she knew about him. He rationalized that she'd expect him to say "no" to such a question, the two of them only partially covered in the daytime curtained dark of a motel.

She'd set a sort of picnic on the round table next to the bed. "Well. You'd said you had a confession to make, so I thought that might be it. Plus the unanswered call from someone named Emma on your cell phone." She opened the second set of beers, drank from one, gave him the other. She quickly went on, looking down. "You know, I played the Mozart sonatas at the recital." She was letting him off the hook. "I played them for you, and I thought about you while I was doing it. I played the Ravel piece, I played *Les Adieux*, I played my Chopin butt off." She laughed.

"I wish I could have been there."

"People liked it."

"The woman—Emma, on the phone—she's calling about Buck. She works at the shelter where I volunteer. And she knows his case, from the old days."

"Ah."

Carol kissed him and they rolled into each other again, among the crumpled sheets. Maybe they both were less heated this time, calmer and slower, probably more preoccupied, or best case, maybe watching closer, running the tape, hoping to remember each secret move and feeling during the next long time apart. Maybe by the time they'd snuffed the candles and were in the shower together they were already beginning to go home, both of them, starting to feel rushed, people waiting, both of them understanding and not meaning to be mean but mentally rotating and being pulled back, both of them, not just him because he got what he came for, or her because this was half of what women want—both of them, in mind of home because this is how people are. If they had gravitated together, here was the other force, centrifugal, equal and opposite.

In the rental car heading back to the river, in the parking lot of the Super Walmart, they said a few things and kissed again. Her hair was wet and combed back. Maybe she'd put the ribbon back later. A man with new fishing tackle consented to take their picture right there in the parking lot, red hulk of a car and brown river behind them.

She hugged Nick. "Buck will be okay," she said. This was quite easy for her to say, but the jury was still out.

"Drive careful," he told her. And goodbye.

Moments later, Nick, sour and unhappy, was driving fast, panicked to be home, pounding up the same highway he'd just pounded down. It wasn't raining anymore and for that at least he was glad. He dug frantically for the phone in his bag in the seat next to him, accessed the messages, both from Emma. The one she'd left first said she was sorry for ragging on him about the Sarge. The Sarge was relieved of the troublesome tooth and doing fine and only just before she called had told Emma he liked Nick and wasn't mad about the scotch. Emma still was, however.

Then the second message: "Now look Nick, I talked with your very upset son. I had him come over to talk more about the job and suddenly I was having to settle him down. I have taken a very close look at him, and he's not on drugs. I tell you, you are going to have to get on top of this thing and show some trust or you'll lose him, you'll lose your son! It would help if you could communicate even the slightest bit with those of us who love and need you. You even sicced his mother on him! Please! I'm not calling from the office phone because I knew this would get personal and loud. See you in a couple of days or whenever, and when you get a minute from your Louisville business pals, or whoever, be in touch with this good boy and apologize to him!"

Nick pulled over on the shoulder, ears red and ringing. It was about three in the afternoon. He'd call Buck soon. He doubted he was wrong about this, but at least if Buck didn't seem high to Emma then he wasn't too far gone. After a few minutes of sitting there, the dominant emotion was relief. He loved how Emma took him to task, how she really cared about Buck. He sat there a few more minutes, trying to go blank. He pictured Dave the dog, earlier, in the mental fog of morning and rain. Now he'd be home on the couch, sleeping, not one care in the world, his probably-still-damp leash hanging from the ladder-back chair in the foyer. Nick found himself sorry Carol was gone. The lies and letters were still steeping. Confrontation was not his strong suit. Lies make you weak. He turned in the seat, looked back toward Coal Grove through his dusty back window. Maybe he could catch her, still in town getting gas or something. Retrieve the day. He turned back and stared up the highway toward home. He clicked the cell phone off, that awful tormenting thing, speaking of leashes. He took a deep breath, prepared to pull back onto the road. For all the mournful facts in the matter of Carol—that they lived far apart and were separate in the trajectory of their lives, that he'd told her some giant lies that she carried with her as true, that pressures from home tore at them both during their few hours together, that each time was darkened by the cold fact of risk and the ominous swirl of circumstance—still, Carol Brown was a grand friend and gorgeous woman whom it was his privilege to be with, and her love was generous and fun, and she played him with the mastery with which she played Chopin—including the coda where she'd touched the keys lightly—then let him leave fast and without coming clean. Because that was how this music went.

PROJECTS

One particular dark day in the dark days before prison, remembered dark but really probably they were sunny he supposed, Carol gone and the kids, Stephen and Becky, playing at friends' up on the north side, Wally Brown struggled himself out of the house he didn't really own, out into the yard (the yard like a child he lived with but hadn't adopted), and fired up the mower (his). It was a Lawn-Boy, the biggest of that brand's push-mowers and fairly new, and though the rains in May had gotten the lawn robust and tall, the grass did not figure to be a match for this machine. Wally muscled up and gave the cord a stout jerk and the mower fired. Almost enthusiastically then, he plunged in. He mowed first along the east fence in the backyard so close he wouldn't have to weed-whack it later. He ran it around the tractor-tire sand pile Becky seemed to have outgrown, around the birdbath with its cracked bowl, around the clothesline poles—all of these being installations from Carol's former marriage and the couple of years she'd lived alone after it ended—along the south fence by the alley, along the west fence bordering the driveway, around the PVC soccer goal he'd brought with him from his former life and put up for Stephen, along the sidewalk, then pushing in close beneath the hedges that bordered the back of the house. Then, after mowing the borders of the backyard and around the various barriers and obstacles, he plowed into the deep, fragrant, summer green of the middle of it. The lawnmower was cranked to full-throttle, creating white noise, and that and the systematic progress of this simple work did Wally good. He could think while he mowed. Reflect on the book he was writing, focus on other things he wanted to think about and not on things he didn't. When he started to think about things he didn't want to think about, he pushed faster and distracted himself with exertion until his face and shirt were wet, the rows efficient and straight.

Pretty soon, he was pleased to see that he was half-done with the back, and for a moment had visions of completing the entire backyard in what for him was record time, when suddenly there was a bang like a gunshot, and just like that the mower stopped. He'd only been working fifteen minutes. There was at least an hour to go, the rest of the back, the front yard, the parkway. Exhaust rose from beneath the machine. The entire town around him was quiet except for his ears ringing and the sound of one or maybe two other lawn mowers somewhere blocks away. He stood motionless, staring down at it. There was a shock in how fast the world went quiet. Apparently he'd hit something. He walked around the mower, bent down to look close. Everything seemed okay. He tipped it up to look underneath. Perhaps whatever he hit was still under there, maybe tangled up in the blade. Everything seemed okay at first. Whatever he hit, it was gone now. Maybe he could just fire it up again and finish this life-sucking task. But on closer look, kneeling in the grass with sweat dripping from the tip of his nose, Wally saw that the blade itself was bent and not just a little. He was done.

This was what he hated most about work around the house: that a project for which he planned to take some confined length of time, that he could delude himself into thinking was mind-clearing and thus rather healthy for him if it didn't take too long, would, because of the wrong tools or some unforeseen complication, suddenly drag him into the loss of a day or the annoyance of returning to his study with the job left, for all his efforts, ragged and unsatisfactory, with no way to finish short of turning it into a major Cecil B. DeMille ordeal.

And, of course, there was no way to concentrate on his real work, his reading, his writing, his thinking, while the interrupted chore teetered in the back of his mind.

Carol had an old mower in the garage, and it too was a Lawn-Boy, so Wally went onto the enclosed back porch and punched the garage door opener. The door didn't respond. Punched it again. Nothing. Held it high, nothing. Low, sideways, nothing nothing nothing. Batteries maybe. He stared at the garage door. It could be opened from the inside if he could find the key to the garage's side-door. And thus tasks piled up on tasks. The light in the garage was out, and wouldn't have lit much even if it worked, so he wanted to pull Carol's mower out and take a look at it in the light of day. Maybe he could cannibalize it for a blade. Maybe a couple of long bolts out and in, and he could get back to work. The garage was really a two-car attic, full of stored broken things and boxes of redundant items and defunct implements and upended rusted one-thing-or-anothers such that trying to get through it in the dark to manually open the big front door was impossible. So he looked for a working flashlight among the several that didn't work—in the utility drawer by the broom closet, under the downstairs bathroom sink, under the bedside table in his and Carol's room, on the top shelf of the hall closet, on Stephen's desk, in the piano bench in the front room. There was one flashlight Wally was sure worked, and that was the exact one he couldn't find. But it was okay, because he couldn't find the key to the garage's side-door anyway. One of these days he needed to get to the hardware store and get some keys made, and a nice orderly rack of some kind to always hang them on, and the tools to hang it with, and some batteries, triple and double As, Cs and Ds, and some air conditioning filters, too, and some gas for the grill, and spray paint for the patio chairs, and some sealant for the deck, and a pressure washer and a car vacuum and some inner-tube patching kits, a stretch of gutter, hedge clippers a hammer nails a saw an actual tool kit screwdrivers wrenches electric stapler some twelve gauge shotgun shells duct tape rope a red wheelbarrow and some fucking white chickens and maybe while he was at it he could get an actual life.

He thought for a moment he might yell the loudest he'd ever yelled in his life. His throat felt scratchy, as if he'd already yelled. Maybe he had. He stared out the front window. He wasn't going to cry. The grass was tall, but at least *all* of it in front was tall. It wasn't half mowed like in back. Lucky he didn't start in front, and then that would be what was only partially cut for all the world to see—but then he remembered that whatever he hit, of course, he wouldn't have hit if he mowed the front, because it, whatever it was, was in the back. Of course, maybe if he'd started in front, the bad thing hidden in the grass in the back would have been in the front, or he'd have hit something else that was in front, like the stump of the deceased Chinese elm invisibly lurking where he least expected, or it would have been something else, because if this, then that, *et cetera*, cause and effect hooked together with rubber bands.

It was Saturday morning. He went upstairs and took a long, hot shower. Someday, he was thinking, he'd like to build an addition on this house—*he* couldn't build it; he'd have someone else build it to his design—an addition that would feel like his. After his divorce, he came to like having nothing and leaving no trail on the earth. He liked living austere. He liked living withdrawn. He liked laying low. He liked owning nothing, including having no pot to piss in. Now he was over that. Now he was starting to long for something that could be home to him and feel like it. His grown son could come there and be his pal in a place where they both belonged. The addition would be two stories, a nice spacious master bedroom on the ground floor, where he and Carol could sleep together—not in the nest and rut where she slept with her first husband. He could have her in his space, or at least have the illusion of having her in the illusion of a space that was his. There would be a study on the second floor, with many bookshelves, the desk given to him by his father, maybe a small fireplace, space for an easy chair and a good reading light that Carol would allow nowhere in the current house, because it was all hers and not a bit his and she had an eye for creating her own continuity. A man's retreat is what Wally was dreaming of, the too-hot water pounding down on him, the steam filling the bathroom and fogging the mirror. The administration building over at the college had recently burned to the ground, and with it his faculty office and with that most of his scholarly life. In the long interim post-first-marriage time, that office had been his retreat. He needed a new one. The house phone rang and Wally stood under the water and didn't even consider getting it. He never answered this phone. It wasn't for him, and the answering machine would catch it. The shower was fiery hot. He dressed and felt better.

Out on the back porch, he tried the garage door opener again, and now the door lurched open. Grand. Perfect. There isn't a rational explanation for absolutely everything, he thought to himself. He went out to the garage to wrestle Carol's old mower out onto the driveway, but it wasn't there. He crashed around through the boxed or rusting detritus of two formerly separate lives, but no mower. He did lay eyes on his ten-speed mountain bike, fairly new and still functional. He'd forgotten it since last summer. He wheeled it out for a moment to look at it. Did he really own this? Had he bought it, eleven hundred dollars worth, ridden it last summer on a regular basis, and then entirely forgotten it with all else that was going on? He felt the sun on his wet hair. A plane was flying over. There was a time when he fantasized about getting a flying license. He had always liked flying, and now he scanned the sky to try to spot the plane he was hearing but it was behind a tree and anyway too high. He wiped off the bike seat, wheeled it a little and flexed the brakes. All good. Great. He might start biking again.

Right then, out of the corner of his eye, he noticed the soccer goal was sagging. He parked the bike against shelving where there were numerous gallon paint cans stored, the splash marks on their sides revealing mysterious colors nowhere to be found inside or outside the house. He approached and started analyzing the broken soccer goal.

The upright post on the left side was broken. Not *just* broken. It was missing about a foot of PVC, erased cleanly like it had been sawed away. The soccer goal was now useless. The way it was drooping to one side, why didn't he notice it earlier? He didn't notice anything anymore. He hated the goal being broken like this. It was an icon for him. It was his from a past life. Possibly it was in the backyard more for him than for Stephen, he realized now. Wally raised his son—his grown son, not Stephen—to compete head to head. Not like baseball, which was Wally's sport. He remembered how his son, in high school—his real son, mostly grown now and gone somewhere, the son from the other life, the other life that Wally'd ruined—he remembered watching his son receive a pass in soccer, then turn with the ball and face his defender. Wally had practiced this with him, and then Wally remembered seeing him do it in a high school game. Later there would be real life, and there would be a need for this skill, Wally told him, twelve years ago, standing in the other backyard in the other life, under this same PVC goal, now destroyed.

The cell phone rang. He dug it out of his pocket and looked at the number. It was his wife calling from Ohio. "Hey."

"Everything fine?" She was trying to talk real loud.

"Yes," he said.

"Kids?"

"Are you in the car or on Mount Everest?"

"Car."

"Hi to your mom."

"Yes, I'll tell her. I'm between venues at this time." The rest of Carol's family, apart from Carol, was all over Cincinnati, taking care of her mom.

"Right." He could hear the sound of her open window. "Where's your old lawnmower?"

"What?"

"Where's your old green lawnmower that used to be in the garage. I need it."

"Honey, it's been gone two years. Garage sale."

"I thought I'd just seen it recently."

"Nope. That wouldn't be my old lawnmower. Gone and good riddance. One time I was mowing with it and the back wheels both fell off simultaneously." She was attempting to talk above her car radio and the wind from the open window. "So the kids are at Margie's?" she said.

"Right. When do you think you'll get home?"

"What?"

"When do you think you'll be home?"

"You don't need my lawnmower anyway. What's wrong with yours?" she yelled.

"Oh dang, I hadn't thought of that. Using my own mower that actually works."

"You're breaking up."

Wally felt a wave of something, maybe it was just adrenaline, rise up, and he choked it back. "*When* do you *think* you'll be *home?*"

"You're breaking up and your mood doesn't seem all that great. Is that right?"

Wally scanned the yard, the phone up to his ear. He looked up at the sky, white fluffies on blue. Don't shout on the cell phone when talking in the yard. People can hear you for a block. It's one of the modern comedies.

"Are you there?" Carol said vacantly.

"Carol. How about you close the car windows and turn off the radio when you're calling somebody on the cell phone." He was talking through his teeth like he was getting mad, but he didn't really care about this. His annoyance was about the broken piece of his past that he was staring at.

"Sorry," she said, apparently the car window closed now. "Can you hear me okay?"

He looked toward the garage. He used to have an ax. A few years ago he chopped wood in the backyard, split logs for the fireplace, and for this mighty task he bought a hefty, all-business, double-edged ax. It was red and would leave red paint in the notches where he struck the logs. Now for some reason a big angry charge of something inside him rose up, and he wanted to destroy a few things in the backyard and general area with an ax. That ax would be perfect. He stared through the garage doorway looking for it in the mess. Surely in a moment he'd see that very satisfying blond ax-handle peeking out of somewhere in there. No. It seemed like everything in the whole garage had fallen over or was upside down. One box, full of old clothes, was half turned over and coming open. Spilling out of it was the ten-year-old blue jersey from some soccer team his son had been on back when he was nine. Somewhere Wally had the team picture, his son—not Stephen but his real son—wearing that jersey when it was new.

Carol barked into the phone, "Listen, come to think of it, I really think you shouldn't mow until I get home. There's stuff in the yard. The kids need to pick things up. Before you mow—okay?"

"When are you getting home, Carol? In fact, why are you gone even?"

"Listen, honey, I can tell you're upset. Does it seem like I'm gone a lot? Want me to come home now? Look, please, don't mow, and I'll be home tomorrow, late afternoon. Maybe we can mow then, after we pick up the yard or get Stephen to."

"What's in the yard?"

"Horseshoes."

Now Wally realized there was also a hole in the red plastic netting that draped the goal. He bent down and looked through it, lined it up with the gap in the goal's left upright, and there was his lawnmower where it had suddenly stopped.

Carol continued, "You don't wanna hit a darn horseshoe with the lawnmower, hon, trust me."

Wally turned about-face and looked further downrange, toward the seven-foot privacy fence between his backyard and the Fosters' next door. In the mowed grass at the base of the fence was a horseshoe worthy of a Clydesdale.

Carol said, "The kids were tossing horseshoes. A binge of it last week. I told them to clean it up. They pulled the posts, but I counted the horseshoes, and there's about three missing. So don't mow yet."

The day seemed dark to Wally, but when he looked up, it was sky-blue with white clouds and plenty of sunlight.

"You could hit one of those big heavy old things and it wouldn't be good at all."

"Yeah," he said.

"Of course, it would be easier to find them if you mowed more often, because the grass would be shorter."

"But what's…"

"But what's done is done," she said.

"Exactly," he said.

That afternoon, Wally roamed around the house. It settled in on him how lucky he was he didn't lose a foot. Or kill one of the kids. Random, thy name is a fast-ripping mower blade slinging a horseshoe. He ate a grilled cheese sandwich and had a Coke. He went in his study and stood. He had forgotten his meds that morning. Bathroom. He popped his pill, toasted himself in the mirror with his special St. Louis Cardinals bathroom water glass. "Prozac Nation," he said to the feckless weirdo who smiled at him and toasted him back.

If Wally could have drawn a picture of himself that day, he'd have used chalk and would have depicted a man in blue weather, suspended in a net that was hanging from above, from somewhere out of the frame, the sky. It would have been a lost little fellow who was not trying to escape the net but was resigned to it in some way. Was sort of lying in it, like in a hammock, a prisoner without knowing it. But whose net was it?

God's. It was God's net.

It occurred to him that there was extra PVC under the house. He wondered how big a project it would be to make the soccer goal right again, like it was before. He recalled long tubes of PVC, left over from a plumber's visit a few years ago. Maybe there was a section of it that was the right size. Hardware store: glue, PVC joints. He was outside and another plane was going over. He'd left the garage door open, and when he tried to close it using the remote, nothing. He whacked the remote against the doorjamb, not too hard, tried again. Nothing. He wandered out to the garage looking for the ax. Today he'd be one wild-ass medieval Paul Bunyan if he found that ax. He was rummaging and digging in the disaster they called the garage and didn't notice Lowell Wagner had come up the driveway.

"Hey, Wally. You in there?"

Wally looked up and laughed. "Hey, Lowell." Lowell was out for a run apparently. He was in his running clothes—a pair of black shorts and the usual sweated-up Lincoln State PE department t-shirt with the sleeves cut off. Lowell lifted the bike out of the garage, looked at it with the eye of an expert. "You gonna start biking again? Not a bad idea."

"I don't know. Maybe," Wally said, rummaging.

"Not a bad idea."

Wally skidded a pile of boxes a few inches, head down among boxes full of magazines, toward the back of the garage. There was a bookcase that had fallen over, and he was thinking the ax might be under it. "Look at this. A rat ate my ball glove. You believe that happy horseshit?" Wally tossed the glove out of the dim garage and onto the driveway.

"You need to keep your baseball glove in the house, man. It's a good one. Was."

Wally moved a few things so it was possible to walk without falling. He was wearing old Dockers; he felt lazy and fat when Mr. Exercise Man was hanging around.

Lowell said, "Don't forget, there's a 5k run next week down in Arcola. Broomcorn Festival."

"I know, Lowell."

"Want me to sign you up?" Lowell was sitting on Wally's bike. "I'm driving down there anyway."

"I don't know. I'm sort of slipping out of condition. I've got a few projects going."

"You're slipping all right." Lowell was astride the bike, wheeling it forward and back. "Back tire's low," he said.

"Ha," Wally said. He straightened up and looked at Lowell. He kept looking at him. He looked at him a long time, longer than either of them was comfortable with.

"Come on! Answer me. It's about three miles. It's nothing."

Lowell was sometimes so forthright about running. It was the foundation of mental health in his mind. Wally hated buckling under the pressure of his friend's purity and rigor. But he did. "Okay, sign me up. I'll reimburse. How much?" He could back out at the last minute, by phone or by simple omission.

"It's fifteen bucks counting the t-shirt."

Wally stared at the mess around him. "I've got a few projects going."

"I see that. You're frustrated."

Wally stood straight up and looked at him. "Stop being an active listener and getting on my nerves, okay?" Wally shoved some stuff with his foot, then pushed something else with his shoulder. Then he kicked something. "I've started about ten things today and don't seem to be able to finish any of them."

"Right." Lowell seemed to be staring at him waiting for the next thing to respond to responsively. He was applying his special kind of shrink's pressure. Didn't he have something to do on a Saturday? Gotta come over to Wally's when Wally's in a bad mood and looking for an ax?

"Carol's in Ohio at her mom's," Wally said, butt up, head down among the boxes. Arching over him was one end of a long defunct swingset. "Her mom's been slipping a little, you might say. *You* might say. So Carol's keeping an eye on her."

"And the kids are..."

"Margie's. Swimming."

"So..."

"So, you're annoying the fuck out of me right now, by the way. So, it's a good time to get some stuff done."

Lowell put the bike back by the paint cans, gently leaned it.

"So, you're doing okay otherwise?"

"Otherwise?"

"Bust your butt doing that, man."

Wally stood on a tricycle and got the burned-out light bulb unscrewed. Without event, he stepped down, light bulb in hand. He held it up to show victory over the odds. "Otherwise than what?"

"Everything going all right besides your ball glove?"

"Yes." Wally tossed the bulb over his shoulder and into whatever was back there. Then he picked up the steel tricycle, lofted it with a loud supremely satisfying crash into a pile of whatever was at the back of the garage, and turned toward his visitor. He stared at Lowell from the middle of his upside-down life. "How does that soccer goal look to you?" He looked around for something else noisy to heave. A rake. Holding it at the end of its handle, he wheeled around once, three-sixty and very fast, and slung it against the back wall, plenty of bam and rattle. He could feel his face go red, but he laughed anyway, too loud, and Lowell hesitantly laughed, too, but he didn't flinch. "Did Carol tell you to look in on me?"

Now Lowell was inspecting the goal's bad post. "This one we can't blame on the rats," he said.

"Did she?"

Lowell stood looking at Wally, like he was considering whether to answer the question or not, which meant the answer was "yes" as far as Wally was concerned.

"Veronica's got pizza for lunch today," Lowell said finally. "Smelled real good. Why don't you get out of your garage malaise and come on over."

Wally went back to stirring around, didn't answer. This wasn't a friendly visit. Carol must have phoned Lowell and asked him to come by and make sure things were okay.

"Little food wouldn't hurt," Lowell said to him.

The invitation hung there and died. Good enough for it, Wally was thinking.

"Okay, well—anything I can do?"

"How about you make like a tree and leave,"Wally offered, and though he regretted the wording immediately, it did make them both laugh.

"That's a really old one," Lowell said. "Look, actually it's probably a good time for somebody to be here. But okay." Lowell headed down the driveway, calling back, "Give me a call if you want some pizza this afternoon. Veronica and I are just hanging out. You'd be welcome to come over. Let's talk this week and we can coordinate the Arcola thing."

"Thanks for dropping by," Wally muttered in his direction, too quiet to be heard. "What a pal," he said, though Lowell was completely gone. "Have a good day, Lowell," Wally said to himself. "Thanks for caring, Mr. Perfecto."

On the side of the house, Wally kicked in the window-sized plywood piece that covered the opening to the crawlspace. Down on his hands and knees, he looked in. It took a moment for his eyes to adjust. What was the first thing he saw? The flashlight! The one that worked! It still did! It was under the house! What a weird day! He wondered if he could remember the details. With the flashlight, he could see the extra lengths of PVC pipe. There were plenty of pieces but the size was wrong and, besides, if he had to go to the store for the glue, why not get the exact length and size of pipe, the connector joints, and do this right. Of course. Wally was feeling better. There was not a chance in hell he'd find something to measure the goal with, but it was okay. Finding the missing flashlight was his reward for patience and for not losing his temper very much.

He replaced the crawlspace cover and went inside. He checked messages; there was one on the answering machine. Margie had called to say she was going to keep the kids overnight if Wally didn't mind. She'd be in touch tomorrow. Ah. Carol was working the system from a remote location. He sat in the leather chair in his study. The iron horseshoe was on his desk but he didn't remember putting it there. Probably had, though. Before long it was evening, and he realized he'd been reading. He looked at his watch. It was almost dark outside.

He felt okay but sometime in the past hour he'd sweated down his shirt. Where were the kids? He went in the kitchen. A burner on the stove glowed bright red. No harm. Do no harm. He turned it off. Maybe he'd fallen asleep. He'd lost some hours, he knew that. He looked in the backyard. Had someone smashed everything back there with an ax so that it looked like there'd been a Viking raid? No, everything looked fine except the soccer goal, and that was an act of God. The garage door was still gaping. From the enclosed back porch, right at dusk, he watched the garage door, pushed the little button on the remote, and the door obediently dropped down on its rails and closed. This was a torment and a mystery, one of the many. Another was that when Wally went back to the front of the house, he noticed through the front window a police car parked at the curb. He backed away from the window along the wall and slipped unseen into his study. He kept the lights off. The policeman was out of his car and standing at the front of the house staring in the study window. From his desk chair in the dark, Wally stared back.

•

Only the Lord knew what time it was when the next phone call came. Pitch black was in him and over him. The sudden noise of the house phone didn't faze him, nor did he move from his chair. It rang many times; he wasn't going to pick it up. What he might do, he was thinking, was stroll down the front sidewalk and have a chat with the constable. Do you know what was on his desk? His ax. Do you know when he found it? Neither did he. Do you know what was in the front yard? A stump. He should go out there and deal with it. The porch light would reach that far into the yard. He could chop out that stump, and maybe while he was at it he could go down and talk to the police officer at the curb. He could settle everything so that when the sun came up he could mow the lawn in front and the stump wouldn't hurt the lawnmower, if he ever got the lawnmower fixed one of these days, because of the horseshoe. Sleep was helping him see things clearly and in a more positive way.

The phone stopped ringing, and almost immediately his cell phone started squawking in his pocket. He writhed about in the leather chair trying to get at it. As he peered at the screen, he realized again that he was feeling better. Amazing how sometimes the weight could just be lifted.

The register said "Unknown Caller."

"Hello, this is Wally Brown." He tried to sound authoritative and business-like, even though most people who knew his cell phone number knew better about him.

"Hi, is this Wally? This is Rachel Crowley." How nice. Rachel, the beautiful neighbor across the street.

"Hi."

"You didn't sound like you, sorry."

"Well, I'm the one who's sorry. I'd like to always sound like me when you call, which is rarely."

"Is this Wally, really?"

"Well, is this really Rachel Crowley from across the street?"

"Haha."

"Nah," Wally said, trying to sound as friendly as he could.

"Hey, is Carol home? I wanted to talk to her for a second if I could catch her."

"Me, too." Wally looked at Rachel's house through the blinds of the study window. "Rachel, I was just thinking about you. I'm dazzled that you called right when I was mulling you over."

"Whatting me over?" she laughed.

"Mulling. Thinking, you know." He sat up straight in the dark. "It's a very surprising thing that you called right now. No, Carol's in Ohio at her mom's."

"Ah. Is her mom doing okay?"

Wally found he couldn't speak for a moment. Words were wedged and stuck.

"Hello?"

"She's slipping, Carol's mom is—but holding forth."

"Holding forth, or holding her own?"

"Yeah, holding her own."

"Listen," she said, "I can ask you this just as easy as I can ask your wife. I wanted to know if everything is okay, because there's a policeman out front and he's been parked there for quite some time."

"Really?"

"Yeah. Maybe something's up at the Fosters'."

"Lemme look," Wally said. And he went through the motion of looking.

He could tell somehow that she was looking, too—movement, maybe the sound of a blind at the window being moved. Finally, she said, "Maybe he's just parked there to slow people down. They go down Van Allen like bats from Hades."

"Did you just call on the other phone?"

"Yeah, but I know you don't pick it up. I got your cell from the campus directory."

"Why didn't you call Carol's?"

"Who says I didn't, smart boy? She didn't answer."

"Ah." Wally stood up. "Rachel, tell you what. I'll put on a shirt and go out and see what Sherlock Holmes is up to, and I'll call you back."

"Oh you don't need to do that. I can do it as easy as you can. I was just wondering if you knew anything I didn't."

"No, no, I'm going. I was going out there anyway. Some yard work."

"Very funny. It's two in the morning."

"Well, I've been planning on doing it for a long time."

"I see. The better the day, the better the deed sorta thing."

"What?" He had no idea what she was talking about. "Look, Rachel, I'm going out there. I'll call back after I find something out."

"Deal," she said. "Okay, I'm off then. Hope Carol's mom is okay."

"Thanks. Bye."

He went upstairs without turning on a single light and got his blue denim shirt and put it on. He loved this shirt. It was the best shirt he ever had. He went in the bathroom and, using the nightlight above the sink, wiped his face with a cool wet cloth, combed his hair a little with his fingers, washed out his mouth. Rachel was very pretty, everybody thought so. Sometimes it did one good to be in touch with the outer world. It was a fresh perspective on things. He wondered why his ex-wife intentionally got fat and wouldn't make love anymore. Even if she started hating him, still, that seemed like an extreme and self-destructive tactic. Life could be real convoluted first thing you know it. Back in the bedroom, he slipped into his top-siders. In the dark, he walked out the front door of the house, ax on his shoulder like a rifle and he was a soldier, down the front sidewalk to the mailbox, which was about fifteen feet from the front end of the parked cruiser. He hoped the mere presence of the large double-edged ax would send the message that he was out there to work on the stump. He looked up, as if to notice the police car for the first time, with the intention of walking over to the driver's side window and saying hi. But no one was in the car. From the foot of his driveway, Wally looked up and down the neighborhood, house by house, both sides of the street. Nothing, nobody. There had been some mail, though. Hands full of envelopes and papers, he turned toward Rachel's house and gave the "beats me" shoulder shrug in her general direction, figuring she was watching. On the front porch, he leaned the ax against the doorjamb, and then he walked back in the house.

In the dark he put the mail on the piano without giving it so much as a once-over, and went back into the study where his cell phone was. He sat down, and as he was redialing Rachel, he happened to glance out the front window in her direction. The police car was gone.

"Did you see that?" he said when she answered.

"See what," she said in a pleasant tone.

"Did you see Sherlock pull away?"

"No," she said. "I'm watching a tape in the bedroom. Why, d'you chase him off?" Rachel was a night owl, that's for sure.

"I don't know," he said.

She laughed. "Well, good work. He needed to haunt somebody else's curb, not ours. Glad everything seems okay in the 'hood."

After he hung up, he went upstairs and thought he might get in bed. Surely it was time. Instead he found himself taking another shower. He got all cleaned up. He was feeling okay. He was glad the policeman had shoved off. It was Saturday night, for God's sake. Didn't he have anything better to do than watch an empty house?

THE UNDERLIFE

Rachel had been staring across the street for some time. She had seen Wally leave for work at dawn, his usual habit, and then later Rachel's daughter, Hattie, had ridden off to school on her bike in a throng of raincoated neighborhood kids. Normally Rachel would have headed to the college shortly after that. But today she'd lingered at her kitchen table, in a kind of sleepy daze, looking out the bay window into the drizzle. She had the window cracked, and for a while she was noticing how the rain sounded different in each ear. In the left, it had a hushing, meshing sound, like wind in a dried cornfield. In the other, she could hear the sparkling, speckling, pecking sound of the individual drops of rain on the windowsill. Then she was looking out across the cool gray of the morning street, comparing distance vision with each eye. She would cover one eye, looking only with the other. She could see distance just a shade sharper with the left than the right.

It was during this experiment that she noticed Carol Brown cutting between her house and the Fosters' next door, bending down at the crawlspace entrance, climbing through the small window-sized opening into the area under her house. Watching this strange activity, across the street through a haze of damp, misty, morning air, Rachel was struck by how Carol moved. It was somehow obvious that she was on a private mission. In order to get in and out of this hole, a person had to get on all fours, push headfirst into the dark, leaving a blue-jeaned butt out in the daylight, then ease through the hole taking care not to scrape one's back or shins. Carol carried a flashlight and, after having disappeared through the little window, apparently turned around so that she could reach out and get the wood crawlspace cover and replace it.

This awkwardness was not Carol Brown's style—she was a lovely, graceful woman from New York, from a family tied to opera and politics. Before Carol remarried, she and Rachel were close friends for a couple of years. Back then, there wasn't anything they couldn't tell each other—they talked on the phone deep into the night, and they took care of each other's kids. Rachel wondered if enough of the old friendship still existed that she could ask Carol about the crawlspace thing. It was an idle thought and it passed. She locked up the house and went to work and eventually forgot about the whole episode.

A few months later—in fact, it was shortly after the first of the new year—Hattie came home ill from school, and Rachel left work early to be with her. After making her comfortable on the couch, with 7-Up and chicken soup and the well-worn DVD of *The Princess Bride*, Rachel ran out for groceries. As she backed out of the driveway, she noticed a movement in the corner of her eye (it was two in the afternoon, the winter shadows short and dim). Over at the Browns', the plywood crawlspace cover suddenly dropped open; then there was the long thinness of Carol's blue-shirted arm reaching out, next her head with her hair tied up in a red bandana, all this in a flash, in the moment of shifting gears. Rachel drove on up the street before she thought much of it.

•

Around that same time, over at the college, another scenario involving the Browns was unfolding. Wally—an emotional man known for his wit and wisdom, a history Ph.D. from Notre Dame who was past president of the faculty senate—had had a couple of episodes. In one he'd yelled "get out of here" at a student so loud that the classroom building, Faculty Hall floors three through five, had fallen silent in the various classrooms and offices, as teachers and students waited for the other shoe to drop. In another incident Wally had shoved the registrar, a white-haired old man who was defenseless. It was at about the time of the thing with the registrar that Rachel had noted Wally began seeing Lowell Wagner—the chair in the Department of Psychology, the well-loved psychological counselor for half the community. Wally wasn't seeing Wagner professionally, but he was a project of Lowell's and they did play racquetball, which had gone on for years. Rachel *was* going to Wagner. From time to time she'd see Wally in Lowell's waiting room. They never exchanged words. Both just looked down in deference, like fellow citizens encountering one another in the vestibule at Saturday evening confession.

•

But life went on. Winter passed, and with it Hattie's cold weather illnesses, real and imagined. Spring came and went, and with it Rachel's annual spring blues. In May a feeling kept coming in on her, that she needed something, needed it. She had a fondness and affinity for cops, historically. This time she bought cognac and started dating a chiropractor from Arcola. She looked forward to school being out and over the summer having the hottest affair she could muster.

In her last session with Wagner (they'd decided to give it a rest at the end of the academic year), she took the liberty of telling him about Carol and the crawlspace. It felt to her on the one hand like gossip, but on the other hand she seemed to have a need to say something.

"Do you know her fairly well?" she asked.

"Not too well, no," Lowell said, ever guarded. Rachel noted something in the eyes.

"She's an old friend of mine," Rachel said. She offered that Carol was a lovely woman, a pianist and artistic sort, and politically active with the League of Women Voters. She was aware that Wally would have discussed Carol in his unofficial sessions with Lowell and surely Carol would have discussed Wally in her actual sessions. She watched Lowell's eyes for some sign she was bringing him new information. "She's quite lovely, actually," Rachel said.

"Yes. People always say that about her." Wagner asked if Rachel ever socialized with the Browns, and she said that since her own divorce from her husband, Ken, she'd not socialized with many couples at all and hadn't been asked much, but in the past, before Carol married Wally, she and Carol had been pals. And Hattie still often played with Carol's kids, Stephen and Becky, and rode to and from school with them. Rachel offered that Wally and Carol as a couple were one of the handsomest pairs around and had been known to have great parties. It gave her a sense of warmth and expansive happiness to tell Wagner good things about the Browns. Like she was indirectly saying this to Carol herself.

And Wagner answered with his usual measured nod that seemed to be the opening to close the subject unless Rachel insisted, which she did.

"But I've noticed something," she said. "I feel bad telling you this, in a way. I mean, we both know you see Wally, right? But after all you're also *my* shrink." She laughed, watching to see if he'd laugh with her. Unreinforced, she soldiered on. "There is something kind of odd—Carol goes under her house sometimes. Crawls under. Mind you, I never see her working in the yard, in the garage, or doing anything outdoors with the place—yet there she is, on a nearly regular basis, crawling through this little window thing under her house. I keep wondering, what's going on?"

Wagner thought for a while. "Probably some logical explanation." He smiled. "What do you think? Part of this, you know, is about you—watching the movements of your neighbor and old friend across the street."

She stared at him. He was turning it around.

"Are you lonely?" he asked. "Do you want to be Carol's friend again?"

This caused Rachel to retreat, of course. Feeling chastised. For the moment. It was several weeks before she and Lowell Wagner talked about it again. But when they did, they revisited the matter with great curiosity and wonder.

•

Because one hot July Sunday morning that very summer Wally stabbed Carol nearly to death, right there in their house, right in front of their children. And then outside in the backyard he had a shotgun, and it seemed clear that he would have shot himself but Sheriff McArthur and the local police cornered him and disarmed him.

After a few days in jail, he was carted off to the psych ward at Vandalia, and Carol was many weeks in the local hospital in the painful process of recovering. She had very nearly died. The community carried this picture in its collective memory, the horror, Carol naked and unconscious, bleeding in what Rachel recalled as a cascade on the front porch of the house. Carol had made it that far trying to get away before her blood loss caught up with her. Wally, this wonderful, brilliant man, was corralled like a wild dog in the backyard. The police marched him to a car right past the frantically working EMTs on the porch. The Browns' children, hysterical—God, what a memory to carry—were being held at a distance by the Fosters, the older couple who lived next door to the Browns to the south—who had called the police, fire department, and ambulances from everywhere to make the horribleness stop, yet there it was, horrible.

It was a small town. A guy jogging by, this former professor at the college named Vasco Whirly, had magically appeared just as Carol fell down in front of her house, and he went right to work on her and at the same time raised the alarm and got people to the phone. Help arrived in less than five minutes. A crowd of the curious and amazed lingered through the afternoon, the blood still on the porch—at first a long gleaming river down the front sidewalk, gradually becoming a brown, wine-colored stain—and the police were going in and out of the house, hovering in the yard, talking, pointing. In shock, Rachel held Hattie and watched the activity from the window of her breakfast nook across the street.

In the following days, relatives and neighbors took charge of the things that needed doing. Rachel learned that the kids would be staying in Chicago with Carol's sister until Carol healed. The neighbors mowed, and offered up prayers, and got the house cleaned up, and so on. As part of that neighborly effort, Rachel got the job of taking Carol the mail every three or four days. Daily, she pulled the mail from the box and packaged it and, every few days, drove the swollen manila envelope up to the hospital. At the hospital, they had the first good talks they'd had since Carol married Wally. Carol was obsessive about getting the mail and told Rachel it was because she expected to hear from Wally—which seemed odd, but, Rachel thought to herself driving home, love is odd.

The events at the Browns were the talk of the town the rest of the summer. People would go by the dark house on their evening drives. At the store, people would conjecture what had gone on. It was more or less agreed that Wally had been psychologically erratic for many years, that pressure at the college and the financial hopelessness of being a full professor and still completely broke most of the time finally caused him to slip a gear. In all the talk there was the assumption that this was a fault, a flaw, a horrible thing waiting to happen, that had been inside Wally all along, like being a Red or having an underground life of pedophilia and peddling pornography. Murder had been in him. Inexplicably, the town seemed happy to let go of the other, quite fond, image everyone had of him. As they saw it, the truth about him was now out.

About a week after the Browns' bad scene, Rachel found herself unable to resist calling Lowell Wagner. It was a Saturday, and she called him at home.

"Hey," she said.

"Hey, Rachel."

"Whoa! You recognized my voice."

"Yes, I do. I guess I've been expecting your call." He was chuckling under his breath, knowing she knew what he meant.

"Got a second?"

"Yeah," he sighed. "Veronica just left for Champaign and I'm washing floors. Grudgingly but with a certain academic thoroughness." She could hear him working, some kind of mop maybe, probably holding his phone in the other hand.

"Well, I just wanted to find out what you make of it all."

"Uh-huh." He sort of laughed, exasperated. "Well, I can't figure it out. But I admit I did think of you when it happened."

"Pretty weird, wouldn't you say?"

"Yeah. I can't say much, you know, but…"

"I know you can't. I just…"

"…but it sounds very unWally to me, this thing, it really does." He seemed to mop for a minute. "But what about you? How has it affected you?"

"God, don't turn it around *yet*!" She laughed.

Lowell grunted, perhaps lifting the bucket. "You know all my moves, Rachel." She could hear him working. "I went up to the hospital to see Carol, but we didn't get a chance to talk. The priest, what's his name?"

"Kelleher."

"Yeah, Father Kelleher, yeah, he was there, and I kind of waved over his shoulder, just to let her know I was thinking of her."

She could hear him breathing as he squeezed out the sponge.

"Tell you what worries me, though," he said. "The kids. What do you know about them?"

"They're with relatives last I heard, up in Chicago. Carol's sister jumped right in. How's Wally?"

"I'm just hoping they get them some help. This could be permanent, life-altering stuff."

"Hell yeah!" Rachel barked. She watched Hattie go down the drive on her bike, out of the shade, into the summer sunlight.

"Wally. Wally's in a psych unit they've got over in the prison at Vandalia and will probably be moved soon. They're likely to move him to Marion. I'm supposed to see him next week."

"But also, don't forget this thing happened to me, too—I live across the street. Carol's blood was on the sidewalk all afternoon. I've got PTSD. You're *my* shrink, too—right?"

"Uh-huh. So now you're turning it around on yourself, right?"

"But…"

"But come on, you're surviving okay, Rachel. It was pretty terrible but you can handle it, right?" She could hear him moving a chair, perhaps sitting down to concentrate on the call. "Am I right?"

"Okay. Right."

"Yeah. And lucky, right?"

"But, so, I mean, do you ever think about Carol and that going-under-the-house business I told you?"

"I've thought plenty about that."

"Yes?"

"And I can't make anything add up on it."

He'd clammed up. No problem, she thought. He knew a few of her secrets, too, and she was glad he observed the rule of confidentiality. And, of course, there was always the possibility he knew as little about all this as she. He wouldn't have seen either Wally or Carol since the disaster.

"Okay, then," she said. "Doesn't hurt to ask. I don't want to come off as some leering old gossip." And that was pretty much that.

•

One night not long after that conversation, Rob Donahue, Rachel's chiropractor lover from Arcola, came over, and Hattie was at her latest inseparable friend Amber's for an overnight. Rachel and Rob settled in to an evening of dinner, rock 'n' roll, a little dope, and a few hours of athletic love. Rob was a great lover, active and interested and fun but always very careful with Rachel's spine, and his grass was homegrown and sweet. It was only recently, because of this relationship, that she had begun to see her spine as other. Her ears no longer heard the same, her eyes no longer saw the same, her ovaries alternately gave her identifiable periods each month, and now here was her back, always in need of adjustment and care, all by itself, completely apart from the rest of her. Rob, high on Rachel who was on her knees and face down, moved her this way and that, applying just the right pressure here, the proper twist there, and when she came, as she usually did three times per time with Rob, she could feel her individual parts rolling and pulling and tightening and releasing in a blessed array of individual and not quite coordinated spasms of quick, hot pleasure. Things used to hit all at once, she seemed to recall.

Anyway, after love, they relaxed into a long, sprawling conversation that finally looped around to the Browns. Down in Arcola, he'd heard about it. Rachel laid out the situation as she knew it, and they pondered aloud well into the night, smoking a little more dope and basking in their privacy. They explored the various corridors of detail and fragmented fact for a reason for Wally's snapping, for the stabbing, and for Carol's crawlspace sorties. It made for easy speculation but wasn't very satisfying since neither of them, in fact, knew a damn thing.

Later they found themselves dressed. Then they were an hour getting good batteries for two flashlights which involved a trip to Huck's, the twenty-four hour convenience store on the highway, and then later middle of the night, they were making their way across the street to Carol's empty house.

High as eagles on the wing, giggling and shushing each other, Rob and Rachel found themselves removing the plywood cover on the crawlspace, shining their lights under, crawling in, and replacing the crawlspace cover. They had to stay very flat except right at the opening, where they could sit almost straight up. They were both nervous and felt like burglars, but the togetherness and adventurous mischief of it spurred them on. They shined their beams in all directions—the under-area had rooms, it seemed—and following the flitting flashlight beams with their eyes made it all like a dream. You forget the under-area exists, down under your feet and general life—dark, dirt and gravel, the smell of mildew and cat piss, and something else, the echoes and sift of family life that finds its way down through the rugs and floorboards.

Rachel saw in the dirt the well-traveled trail of the previous crawler. It led toward the front of the house, through a break in one of the under-walls, into the pitch dark. The flashlight beams couldn't reach back there except in tantalizing glimpses. She began to crawl in that direction. Rob was over it. He urged her to stop. He said they better go. He told her she might find something she didn't want to find. He kept saying he thought he heard something. He warned her that someone might hear them under there, and how would they explain? Better go, he kept saying.

As Rachel crawled through the dirt, she could sense Carol's presence—she was seeing what Carol saw when she was down here, the dim far-back shadows, the looming cobwebbed floor beams; she was doing what Carol all alone seemed to frequently want and need to do. Rachel knew she was on the trail. She knew Carol well enough to know there was something really worth this odd journey, and she kept crawling. At the broken wall, she shined a light back into the last under-chamber. Webs and mounds of concrete obscured the view. But at last she spotted, against the brick foundation wall, a dark gray Samsonite suitcase. Now Rachel began to feel, even through the fog of Rob's good grass and her own curiosity, that she was on the brink of violating someone's most intimate privacy. She was at heart a good friend and civilized neighbor, and this guilt caused her to pause a full minute before she piled herself hellbent over the broken under-wall and crawled like a madwoman in the direction of the suitcase.

It wasn't latched. The contents of it were disheveled. They were love letters, to Carol, from a man named Nick, currently living in

Ohio. The letters had been coming to her for years, hundreds of letters dating back several years before her marriage to Wally; in fact, Rachel was amazed to note that by her calculations the earliest letters reached back well into Carol's previous marriage, had been sent to her previous address, in Moline. In the dishevelment, Rachel found a picture of Carol, sitting on a park bench with Nick. He had his arm around her. They were lovers. Staring at the picture, Rachel noted that, in some odd way, the woman didn't seem to be Carol exactly. It was some other version of Carol, an unknown other side of her, devoted to this secret man. On the back of the picture there was handwriting: "Tampa, FL, June."

Rob's flashlight beam flitted all around but Rachel was hidden in the shadows. "Did you find anything?" he called in a loud whisper.

"No," she said.

•

Over the next few days, Rachel was obsessed by the suitcase under the Browns' house. On a Saturday night, less than a week after the first foray, she went under again—this time alone. Since one needed a flashlight anyway, it was easy to go under at night. She imagined that Carol went under there far more at night than in the day, that the times she had actually observed Carol were only the tip of the iceberg. It was a long crawl, longer than she remembered. Once she reached the suitcase, she leaned up against the brick wall, set up her flashlight on a pile of broken bricks so she could see without holding it, and began reading randomly among the letters. Her heart pounded and her hands shook.

Nick was a Vietnam veteran. He'd taught at the college only a year, and though Rachel worked there, she'd never seen him before. He lived in Athens, Ohio now. The couple had had several rendezvous over the past six years. Nick apparently always supplied the money for these outings. How the occasions were arranged and explained was unclear. The letters were all very short, and they all said much the same thing, that he loved Carol, her love of adventure, her body, her music, her good soul. He said many times that he envied Wally. He said change was inevitable, and he could wait. He said he hoped if ever she was free again, that she would find him, that he'd be waiting. All of the letters were signed the same: All my love, Nick. What a heartbreaking love, what a beautiful, impossible, sad secret to carry.

Rachel's sneaking curiosity had landed her in a river of human complication. She found that she admired Carol. She was ashamed she had intruded, but now she couldn't un-intrude. In the process, she'd learned something, a strange clue to how things are and how people behave. Through the cool concrete brick wall of the foundation, Rachel could hear the night outside—birds, wind, somehow also an airy looming presence, the high clear sky of night. After a while she heard a car pass, slowly, and there was an intermittent slap accompanying it. The Sunday *News Gazette* was arriving. Sated, and anxious because soon it would be dawn, she piled the letters in something close to the way she had found them and took one more look at the secret picture of Nick and Carol. Then she closed the suitcase tight, reached her dimming flashlight, and crawled back to the plywood exit.

·

For several days, she moped around. Her earlier curiosity was now replaced with guilt at having invaded a strand of Carol's life. She hadn't felt guilt like this since she was a child. During all this, Rob the chiropractor was calling, and for some reason she kept putting him off. She didn't think she wanted to see him again. He reminded her of something. Finally she just had to say to him, "Look, stuff's happening with me right now—I'm not sure what. You're great, but I'm going to have to take a break. I'm sorry, I really am."

After that, Rob quit calling.

And the same approach-avoidance thing was happening with

regard to Carol. Because Rachel couldn't face her, she missed a couple of her regular trips to the hospital with the mail. Although she did, each day, collect the mail and package it. She was watching for a letter from Nick. She knew the handwriting, the various guises and letterheads of subterfuge he used. Nothing came. And nothing came from Wally either, of course.

Late the following week, the pressure became too much, and she took the mail to the hospital. That time and each time after, she sat with Carol and talked, at first in a distant but friendly way and later with increased comfort. Carol would be sitting up, and she might show Rachel her healing wounds, and they would talk about nothing in particular and perhaps would ask about each other's kids, and sometimes Father Kelleher would come and Rachel would wander down the hall by the nurse's station and kill time and let them talk. When her visits were over, she would leave Carol, down the long white linoleum hall, down the concrete-block stairwell, across the hotel-like lobby of the little community hospital, out into the sunlight, thinking about Carol's eyes, how she seemed so open, and how Rachel knew in many ways she was open but in one way at least she was not. It was interesting for Rachel to study those eyes knowing what she knew. But it was painful, too, realizing that there was a whole life beneath the surface, for Carol, for Rachel, maybe for everybody—an underlife that had to be dealt with or that, ignored, built steam and ultimately altered the terrain at the surface.

·

One day after work, the phone rang and startled her. She figured it was Rob, and just hearing his voice promised to plummet her into a state of confusion, but she answered anyway.

"Rachel, it's me." Carol, calling from the hospital.

"Hi. Is everything okay?"

"You alone?"

"Yeah. Everything okay?" Rachel heard something in the voice, foreboding.

"I need to talk with you."

Something in her voice made Rachel resist. "Now? I'm kind of tied up right this minute."

"I need you to come see me. Can you?"

There was no way out. Rachel said she could. She was shaking as she hung up the phone. How terrible, to be caught doing a terrible thing.

She drove to the hospital determined to face the music. Up the tunnel-like, yellow-bricked stairwell, down the white shining linoleum hall, into the room.

Carol was sitting up. She was very thin. She was wearing glasses, looked older. Her hair was pinned high on top of her head. "Rachel, I have something to discuss with you. It's very difficult."

"Okay." Rachel sat in the green plastic side chair. She forced herself to stare into Carol's eyes. She deserved this.

"I don't know how to start this, how to say this, except just to start."

"Okay."

"For years, I've been aware of you, across the street. We were good friends there for a while, it was a great consoling run we had—and then there was Wally, and we lost touch, sort of, right?"

"Yes," Rachel said.

"But we were, we were, we were, don't you think, awfully close, very good friends, before that? With much in common?"

"Okay, right." The build-up was almost too much for Rachel.

Carol stared at her. Her face seemed cold, stern. "I've been wanting to say this for a long time..."

Rachel braced herself. Now it would happen.

"...that I wish I'd done better with our friendship."

Rachel's face turned, her eyes went to the wall—she felt herself go pale as she realized she was safe. This stunned, turning gesture appeared appropriate even if it wasn't. "What a nice thing to say."

Carol looked down, embarrassed at the intimacy of the moment.

"I've felt the same," Rachel said, "but I did understand, you know. I know how things work. I knew you were still there. I'm sure that if I'd been married, we could have continued on."

"Well, yes I was, I was still there."

What now, Rachel thought.

"I've watched you over at your house," Carol said with a deep sigh. "Not spying, you know, but occasionally observing. How do you do it! Everything well-kept and never a missing beat. Hattie's such a nice girl. And I never hear even a single word. Such a quiet, calm, orderly existence."

"Well, I play like I'm on a desert island," Rachel said. "I play like I'm alone for good, except for Hattie and she keeps me going. I take in the sun in the backyard, get nourishment when I can. I listen to a lot of music. I go everywhere alone, except when this guy from Arcola shows up. It's pretty bad, actually."

They both laughed. But Rachel sensed it wasn't quite over.

"I want you to know," Carol said, changing vectors, "that I have always trusted you."

Rachel looked down, shifted on her plastic chair.

"Because we're old friends, and because we had a lot in common. *Have* a lot in common. Because I'm probably more like you than you even think. I don't know what I mean by that. Anyway. I trust you—I do. Of all the people I know."

Rachel tried not to slump in her seat, tried to hold the posture of a friend, a good person, worthy of trust, whatever posture that was.

After a moment, Carol looked at her and said, "I need your help, Rachel."

"Okay."

"There's this woman, a lifelong friend, who has been writing to me for many years. She's a very good friend. It's a personal correspondence. Wally didn't know about this—I never told him, and for years I've been hiding the letters."

"Hiding them?" Rachel asked in a moderate tone.

"I've got them hidden so well, in fact, that in my condition I can't get them—I can't get to them."

Rachel watched Carol's eyes closely. Steely gray, troubled, but direct. So this is how it looks when you know both sides.

"Actually, they're hidden in a pretty dumb place."

Rachel laughed. "Where on earth did you stash them?"

"Under the house."

Rachel laughed. "Under the house?" Quick, she reeled herself in.

"They're in a suitcase. All you have to do is get the suitcase and take it up to my bedroom. You can put it in the closet. I trust you, Rachel, not to read the letters or open the suitcase. I'll be home soon, and I can deal with it after that."

"Okay."

"Do you know how to get under there? There's a..."

"I think I do."

"Yeah. An opening thing, on the south side. Wear old clothes. You'll be in dirt. The suitcase is locked, and the key is right above it, on a floor beam. You'll need a flashlight. Once you're in, turn left and crawl until you hit the second wall. Watch out for nails. There are a few daddy longlegs, but it's not bad under there really." She laughed. "Once you get used to it."

Rachel looked at her.

"I know it's a lot to ask."

Rachel looked at Carol, at the hands Nick loved, jabbed with needles and tubes. She tried to see the *other* Carol Brown, the one in the Florida picture with Nick's arm around her. "Does this person, does she know what's happened to you?"

"Probably not. No way of knowing, really." Now Carol occupied herself by rummaging in her purse. With a reach, she handed Rachel the house key.

Rachel considered not asking the next question but couldn't stop herself. "Why all this intrigue over a correspondence with an old girlfriend?"

"I don't know. It made sense at the time—it evolved. The relationship has a kind of tradition of secrecy, something like that. We're very close, across a couple of husbands for each of us. We share so much. Nothing is held back. I don't know."

"Is she your lover?"

Suddenly there were tears.

Rachel pulled Kleenex, handed it over, watched and waited. She understood that Carol was asking her to back off, and indeed she didn't want to push too far. It was just that the alibi made so little sense. "Why haven't you called her? I don't get it."

"I felt guilty, maybe." Carol looked down at the hospital sheet covering her legs. "I don't know." She wiped more tears. "Just get the goddamn suitcase." She laughed through the crying, dabbing at her eyes.

Rachel laughed, too. A little tension left the room. She stood up to go. She touched Carol's shoulder, her hair, kissed the top of her head. There was a trace of their lies in the touch.

•

That evening, a little after dark, Rachel again crossed the street to Carol Brown's house. As she came between the Fosters' house and Carol's, she could see the old couple, Don Foster and his wife Ruthy, at their dinner table, which faced that direction a little too much and on the spur of the moment Rachel decided this wasn't the time. But she did have her flashlight and was wearing old jeans and finally had to try to act like she had some reason to be there. The Fosters were, after all, waving at her through their window. She smiled and waved back, and the old man got up. Rachel heard the scrape of the chair on the bare wood floor. He came out onto the front porch, leaned over the rail so he could talk to her in the sideyard.

"Hi, Don," she said. "Carol told me to take a walk around the place and see if it was okay."

"Yeah, great," he said. "I wanted to tell you there have been people around over there. I just never know whether to call the police." He was pointing. "The alley, the backyard—somebody was even under the house the other day—and we had some kids throwing rocks. I'll be glad when she gets back."

While he talked, Rachel opened Carol's crawlspace hatch. "You say someone crawled under here?"

"You bet, few nights ago."

Rachel practically dove into the dark space, her flashlight ahead of her. "Did they take anything? Did the Browns keep stuff under here?"

"Who knows?" he said, laughing. "You know how people are. Never enough storage." She heard him come off the porch and stand there in the little stretch of grass between the houses.

Underneath, Rachel slid her way to the west foundation wall. The suitcase was undisturbed since the last time she was there. She reached up and got the key, looked around for anything else. She made sure the suitcase was latched, then slid it ahead of her to the crawlspace opening and left it standing up against the foundation wall just inside. Then she stuck her head out.

"Find anything?" Don Foster said.

"Seems empty, actually." She climbed out and brushed off, taking care to be in the way of Mr. Foster if he wanted to look in. "Looked like some old plumbing work, or something, but that's it."

She replaced the plywood cover and bade Don good evening. She said she'd look around the rest of the place. She told him she had the key to the house and would be inside this evening making sure it was ready for Carol to get home, so not to worry if he or his wife saw lights.

Very late that evening, when the Fosters' lights were finally out, she slipped back to the crawlspace, reached in and got the suitcase. The interior of Carol and Wally's house was eerie to her. Even though the neighbors had cleaned it, the horror of that Sunday morning lingered in the odd spots on the floor, the wrinkled throw rugs, the magazine rack upset next to the easy chair, the dark shadows at the top of the stairs and in the rear rooms of the ground floor. Rachel was spooked. She locked the suitcase, put it in Carol and Wally's bedroom closet and shortly after that was out of there and back in her own blessed home.

•

The following Monday night, Carol Brown came home from the hospital, arriving with her mother, her sister, and the two kids. The amazing Vasco Whirly had power-washed the front walk and the porch. Carol's mother planned to stay a while. From the dark of her kitchen, Rachel watched the family re-gather, unloading in the driveway, climbing the steps of the front porch. Carol quietly stood on the lighted porch as her mother worked the lock. In a jumble, the little group disappeared inside. Cars arrived and left, food being brought, best wishes being wished, no one staying long. Rachel continued to watch the house. It was great seeing the porch light on and all the activity. Something felt like it was ending.

Suddenly her phone rang. It startled her. She figured it was Rob. "Let it ring," she called into the living room, where Hattie was watching TV and coloring. There was a phone in there, and Hattie often answered it first unless Rachel waved her off.

The old-style answering machine on the kitchen counter took the call. "Hey, I'm home," Carol said into the recorder. Rachel picked up.

"Carol! Is that you? Are you back?"

"I *thought* you were over there. I can see your car."

"How do you feel?"

"Well, for starters—Jesus, it's stuffy in this house. I think we're gonna have to sell it. I'll sleep on it, but right now I'm in the mood to get this thing out of my life."

Rachel stretched the cord into the living room, sat down. "I assume you know not to be too hasty."

"Right, right. Not one of my problems." They both laughed. "Listen. Mom's going to bed soon. Why don't you get Hattie down and come over for some brandy or something, ten or after, when things get quiet. We can raise a toast to a new life and surviving."

"Aren't you tired?"

"Mom'll be in bed. We can talk. If I fall asleep in the chair, you can leave. No big deal."

"Okay."

"Hey. The Fosters just came over with homemade ice cream. And Don said he saw you in the crawlspace."

Guilt and panic churned in Rachel's temples. "Yes, well, I..."

Now Carol spoke confidentially, away from whoever was close by. "I can't thank you enough. I'm sure you understand now that I couldn't have gone under there myself."

"Yeah."

"Okay? Sometime after ten? Brandy on the verandy?"

"Sure. Great."

•

Around nine, Hattie was asleep. Rachel stirred around, restless, and finally pulled a little of Rob's weed out of the freezer. She used it to get up her nerve. In the living room, she began working on the phone, calling a series of informations, finally getting a number that seemed right. And she dialed.

"Hello."

"Hi," she said. She liked his voice. Don't gush, she thought to herself. "How're you doin'?" She tried to sound familiar. Could he tell she was high?

"I'm asleep, actually. Who is this?"

"Is this Nick?"

"Yes it is. Who's calling."

"Nick of *the* Ohio University?"

"C'mon."

"C'mon, yeah right, sorry." She was disguising her voice, she suddenly realized—she'd arrived at a Southern country accent. "Nick, this is a secret and anonymous phone call, hon. From Illinois. I can't tell you very much, and it is important that you not share with Carol—you know Carol, right?—that you have received this communication, are we clear? I'm trying to do a favor to you both."

It was quiet on the other end for a moment. "Okay, talk," he said finally. His tone had changed, like he'd gotten up and gone into a different room, like now she had his full attention.

"Carol was attacked by her husband a few weeks ago, nearly killed—had you heard about this?"

He said nothing.

"Didn't think so. She's just out of the hospital. He's in jail somewhere."

"God." Rachel heard him breathe deep. "He was unstable—I knew it." He spoke quietly. He seemed to be talking to himself.

"Well. Something maybe made him that way," Rachel said. "We don't exactly know."

Rachel waited for him to respond. It took a few moments.

"He was scary, I'll tell you. Had been for a long time." He was now close to the phone, talking very directly into it. "Just tell me, is she okay?"

"Right, that's what I said."

"What did he do to her?"

"He stabbed the bejesus out of her, that's what, with a big-ass knife from the kitchen. She can tell you the rest. She's alive by a miracle, we all agree. I gotta get off the phone. I just wanted to notify you. So maybe you could do something, I don't know."

"Well, just so you understand—I'm staying clear now. I don't want to be why she dies."

Rachel suddenly felt unstoned. "I didn't expect chivalry, Nick. I know how this shit works. Maybe just let her know you know and show a smidgen of concern, okay hon?"

"Nah, I'm out."

"I read the letters, you fuck. Call her. She just got home. Her husband's locked up. Nobody's gonna gitchya. The bad shit happened to her, not you. I thought you were a soldier." It was quiet on the other end of the line. Her heart was hammering. "Jesus. Whatever," she said. "Good night, then."

"Goodbye," he said.

•

Around ten-thirty Rachel finally slipped out the garage door, locking it behind her, and walked across the street to Carol's. She thought of Hattie and rationalized that she'd be gone a short time. She was struck by how Carol reached out to her. After years of very little contact, now her neighbor was almost driven about it. Carol met her on the front porch, happy and welcoming, hugged her, and invited her in.

They sat in the den, a gouge mark from Wally's knife prominent in the wall above the easy chair where Rachel sat. Rachel felt very internal, Nick's voice still in her brain. Carol sat temporarily on the arm of the sofa.

"What do you think I could get for the place?"

"I don't know," Rachel said quietly, with a shrug. She looked around. She remembered walking through it alone in the middle of the night when she'd retrieved the suitcase. It was a scary place.

Carol reached up and ran her fingers across the damage in the paneling. "Sell it to out-of-towners who don't know about the hex it has on it."

"Ha. Fat chance."

"I know. Everybody's talking."

"I'd rather you stayed. Selfishly speaking." Right then, for a moment, Rachel meant it.

"Really? That's nice of you to say." Carol looked at her.

"You'll never get for it what it would have been worth, before the murder. The almost murder."

That didn't seem to register with Carol. "We could have fun maybe. Wouldn't it be swell to have some fucking fun for once?"

"Maybe," Rachel said. "You know... I've noticed that you seem to have become more subdued. Than in years past. It's like you can't *let go* anymore."

Carol went in the kitchen. Rachel could hear her pouring them each a glass of a wine, and Carol returned with a tawny port that Wally had kept around. She handed an over-full glass to Rachel. "Sorry. Brandy's gone." Carol settled on the couch, taking care not to spill the port. "I noticed the same thing about you. I keep wondering, what is it with you anyway? I noticed it when you were bringing me mail."

Rachel sat quietly. What is it with *me*? she was thinking.

"And God almighty thanks so much for bringing that mail and visiting me. What would I have done?"

Rachel smiled at her. "You know, I really don't think I'm subdued. I think it's just ordinary life, how it goes. Getting older maybe. Probably the same with you, at least until recently. We're grown up. We've got kids that are growing up." She held the eye contact.

"Well," Carol said, "after all this crap my antenna is way up. And I'm paranoid and worried and really I gotta get in and spill the beans to Dr. Wagner."

Rachel stared at her. She was barely in control. Would she suddenly blurt something? Carol! I've done something terrible and I must tell you! She rode it out, silent, staring. When the moment grew raw, she said: "Friendship doesn't come as natural to me as it used to, maybe. I'm in my own little cocoon over there. I've just terminated an affair with a guy from Arcola. I think I'm done."

"Well, let's fix that," Carol said. Her hand came up—seemed to reach for Rachel's wrist. "You've been there for me. Maybe I could..."

"No," Rachel said. "There's nothing." She suddenly wanted to hurry back across the street.

Carol looked down. "Okay."

Rachel stared at her. "We've both changed. There's no going back. You actually know this."

"Well, yes, but…"

"We've *both* changed, Carol."

"Change isn't all bad. You and me, we're at the top of our game." There was a creak in the ceiling, movement upstairs. Carol smiled, and added quietly, "Even though our mothers won't believe us." Carol seemed to want to share a conspiratorial laugh.

Rachel didn't laugh. She sipped the red syrup. Something was coming.

"Anyway, you don't have to talk about it," Carol said. "I probably can't handle it yet, anyway. I want to be friends, is all. I'll keep trying." Carol's hand was on the armrest of the chair, where it had come to rest when Rachel had pulled back from her.

Rachel was trying to contain everything, but it was coming. Here it came, up into her throat. And now there were tears. "Carol. I've spoken with your friend in Athens, Ohio," she said into the dark room. Oddly, she immediately felt strength come into her as she said it. She watched Carol sink back. "Is this the person from the letters in the suitcase?" She wiped her eyes. "I think so. I think it is."

Carol sat still.

"None of my business, but he sounded weak. If you'd bled to death on the porch and been buried out at the cemetery, he wouldn't have been here. He's a coward."

Carol was looking down.

"Maybe that's just the way these things go. The other person can't really ever be there for you, but in the meantime there's the illusion."

Carol looked at her hands in her lap, or pretended to.

"I think we all have secrets, one or two. It's okay." Rachel felt strong. Her dark veneer was coming off, as was Carol's light and friendly fakery. Now Rachel reached over and touched Carol's hand. "C'mon," she said. "Let's get it up here in the light of day." She waited. Nothing. "I looked in the suitcase and got the phone number. I read the letters, I saw the picture in Tampa, Florida. He needed to know what was up with you." She bent forward trying to get in range of Carol's averted eyes, but she was frozen in place, and that's how Rachel left her.

SCARS

FORTY MARTYRS

Carol never understood what happened. A year later, coming up the short, curving sidewalk to Forty Martyrs Catholic Church, still dressed in her yellow jogging suit from the morning run, Carol had one of her periodic flashbacks, this one of Wally's second lunge at her—it had come in from low, upward toward her face and she'd turned her shoulder into the blade to protect herself. Then she thought of that letter of Nick's in which he hauled out his most horrible ghost from the war, about the time he had to call artillery fire in on his own unit when his position was being overrun. Thirty-nine of some sixty were killed. That particular letter came to mind, when, for no reason, as sometimes happened, she suddenly recalled turning her shoulder into the knife. You do what you've got to do. Not to compare her shoulder wound to the deaths of thirty-nine young men, but anyway, this morning she suddenly saw the parallel.

Her morning run usually took her south, to the highway, then along Route 36 to the university, then up the campus sidewalks to the railroad, and then across to the old Eisner parking lot and down Central to home. This morning as she returned, she'd stopped at the church because Father Kelleher had called her and wanted her to drop by if she could.

The Forty Martyrs rectory was a block-shaped house in tan bricks matching the church next door. The drapes and shades were pulled. The front porch was a grotto of sorts, with a small pond, a statue of the Virgin, many hanging plants, now neglected, and what was once a fountain, now dry and cracking.

She rang the doorbell. Father Kelleher's dog, Bliss, woofed lazily on the other side of the door, and Carol heard the chain rattling. She pictured the shy priest at an upstairs window, slanting the shade to see who was there.

But, instead, immediately after she rang the doorbell, the door lurched partly open, and she could see his eyes through the crack, right at the level of the taut chain from the lock.

"It's me," she said to him.

"It's okay, girl," he murmured, his whisper dry and raspy.

"Glad to hear it," Carol said.

"No—I meant the dog." He closed the door to undo the chain lock, then opened it wide. He stood there looking at her. "Oh. You knew that." He smiled hesitantly but fondly, too. He was clearly happy she was there. He turned to lead the way, waving his heavy arm for her to come along. "C'm'ere, lass," he said. "I want to show you something. Tell me what you think."

She closed the door and followed him. Although Kelleher had been to her house many times, she hadn't been in the rectory in years. She and Wally often visited when the previous priest was there. Now the place had become a cave, smelling a little too heavily of both man and dog. The dullness of the rooms seemed to spread to the furnishings themselves, pale greens, stained and dusty browns. The ceiling light in the hallway was dimmed by a collection of dried moth carcasses silhouetted above the glass cover. The ceramic floor had a gritty feel under Carol's running shoes—she kept thinking she was tracking something in, but looked down and saw her own footprints in the dust. Kelleher was too private and embarrassed to have a housekeeper, too moody to do it himself. By now it was so far ahead of him that the job probably seemed intimidating and would require professionals.

"You got here quick," he said, his voice so low she wasn't sure if she was intended to hear. He cleared his throat.

He was fully dressed, all in black with the white Roman collar, but the jacket shoulders were dusted with a sprinkling of oily dandruff, and although he was fairly young, perhaps 60, he walked slumped like an old man, his large, heavy feet shuffling as though he were bone tired. His thick yellowish-gray hair was slicked back and matted. Bliss, a large, ancient Irish setter with scaling skin, lumbered behind him wherever he went, pausing sometimes to scratch or nip at her tail.

"The police are coming," he muttered as he walked ahead of Carol through the foyer and up the short hallway beside the stairs. "Should have gotten here before you did. I don't know."

"The police?"

"Well, yes," he said. "It seems I've been robbed." Now his voice shook, and in the added light from the office windows Carol was able to see that he was upset. The office had been ransacked. A safe door was visible under the bookshelf, open. On the desk, the lamp was overturned and broken, and papers covered the floor. The desk drawers had actually been thrown, slammed against the wall opposite the desk, and one was in splinters at their feet right next to the door. Carol saw incongruent things in her moment of looking, a black rosary and some dice, an old Bible and a copy of *Sports Illustrated*, a small plastic model airplane and an aged apple core.

"I got up at the Angelus and said mass before I noticed this. I came back over and found it and I was so mad, Carol. I thought someone had done it while I was over at the church." He wiped at his face with his jacket sleeve. "They had the place cased, seems like. Yesterday, I was in Springfield, seeing the Bishop again. They must have known." He seemed short of breath. "Maybe they were here when I got back last night—right here in the house with me."

He reached under his coat, toward the back, and pulled out a pistol.

"I've got this if they come back." His voice was shaking. Carol thought the gun looked like something John Wilkes Booth might have used—old, oddly shaped, like a child's cap gun, but there were actual bullets in the fat, round cylinder. She tried to think of something else. She stepped into the debris of the office and automatically moved to set the desk chair back up on its casters.

"Let's leave it," he said, his free hand coming up to stop her. "There may be fingerprints or something." She left it. Bliss was panting in the hallway, her chain clinking on the ceramic tiles.

"Some stuff is gone, far as I can tell. A couple of relics from the parish centennial. Small important things, you know, that collect. Over time." He smiled painfully.

He looked at her as if she might have an answer. She didn't.

"Yeah. Okay, let's go in the other room so we don't touch anything. I've got to sit down. This business has had me dizzy all morning."

He walked ahead of her as he talked, not looking back. He was carrying the gun in his right hand, holding it limply with the muzzle pointing mostly to the floor, except when he would gesture with that hand and Carol would see the barrel flash by. She noticed that his finger was actually on the trigger.

In the living room, he half-gestured with his gun-hand toward the empty TV stand in the far corner. "They got the VCR, too, of course. I hated the thing anyway, given to me by the Knights of Columbus. The VCR's all I lost from in here, I think." The sitting room seemed even dingier when he clicked on the table lamp, its shade closed at the top by a haze of cobwebs. The room had two enormous windows, completely closed off by heavy, dark green drapes.

"I thought this kind of thing only happened in cities."

"Did you really? Amazing." She laughed. "Did they get any money?"

He looked down. "They got Sunday's collection." He rubbed his eyes. "Probably a couple thousand dollars. Completely uncounted. There would have been a lot of checks though."

Father Kelleher looked at her. "The missing stuff from the safe is what worries me. A lot of it can't be replaced. It means nothing to anybody else but to us it's priceless. There's a centennial relic—a lump of gold from the old church that burned. How would you even recognize what it was, sitting there in the safe? I wonder if it was maybe somebody we know."

He sat down heavily in a big beige easy chair next to the lamp. "Who'd do this?" he said. He set the gun on the table and ran his big hands through his hair. "Who would do this to me?"

He was looking down, talking so quietly that he seemed to be talking to himself.

"Father," Carol said, "I don't think whoever did it will be back this morning. If you'd like to put the gun away somewhere."

Kelleher looked at it, and then at Carol, and then back. He cleared his throat. "I s'pose," he said. "I suppose that makes sense." He was looking at it. "I don't know. A man's alone all the time—I always think they'll find me a week later, you know. Decomposing in my chair in the kitchen." He tossed "decomposing" out like it was silly to think it, but there was distant thunder in his voice, the undertone of a man terrified by the idea. "I don't know. I don't know what I mean. Anyway, I get you. I'll just—" He struggled up out of the chair, pushing with his arms as though he were ninety and the chair wouldn't let him up. "I'll put it away. I see that it bothers you. I'll put it upstairs." He started in that direction, then stopped and turned around and looked at her. His arms were out, the gun in one hand. "I was so mad. You know what I mean? This morning?"

"You're taking it personally, Father. It's a burglary. Sooner or later it happens to everybody."

"Well, I guess." He looked at her a moment. "Think it was a parishioner?"

"It could have been anybody. Anyway, give thanks. Somebody up there was looking after you. There was no violence. You're just fine this morning."

"Well," he said. "You're my parish expert on that—you're probably right."

She didn't know why that whole thing made her an expert on violence, but people would, from time to time, make a reference like

147

that, and she'd learned to expect it. She had a job at the college now, a secretary position in the Education Dean's office, and all Wally's faculty friends had dropped in one by one to puzzle on these events and communicate their grief or surprise. It had been almost twelve months, and Carol was still healing in many ways. For instance, the low throbbing aches in her shoulder as she talked with Father Kelleher. Her shoulder always acted up after a morning run.

"Okay, I'll put it away," he said.

She sat down in the dim light of the sitting room watching Kelleher head off toward the stairs. Gun in hand, hanging from his index finger, pointing toward the floor. He stopped to peek out the curtain for the police.

Kelleher had been in the town a long time, twenty years. He was a part of the community, even as Protestant as it was. He visited her every day during her recovery, both at the hospital and when she came home. He would walk over in the late afternoon, sometimes with the dog—he would sit in the shade on the porch with her, talking to her and the kids. They would pray together, and he'd tell the kids their guardian angels were protecting them and wouldn't let anything bad happen again. Kelleher was a good and generous man, working hard to be a good priest.

"How did they get in?" Carol called after him.

"Broke in," she heard him mumble, lumbering up the stairs to put the gun away. Bliss was following him, also lumbering. He was petting her and Carol could hear the dog responding, claws clicking and sliding on the hardwood floor somewhere above, then pausing to scratch, the chain clinking in that rapid-fire way. Otherwise the house was quiet—the dim religious paintings muted in the clutter, framed prints of Christ appearing, brave men kneeling astonished and humbled before Him, and the Virgin ascending. She imagined Bliss and Father Kelleher in the evenings, whiling away their time.

In the library off the front room there was a phone, and while Kelleher was upstairs, Carol presumed to use it. Her four-year-old answered.

"Hi, Becky, get Stephen will you?"

"Who is this please?"

"This is your—"

"We have to go to the baseball game and after that to Show-Biz Pizza so you better go home now because I have to put on my beautiful coat."

"Becky. This is Mom."

"Hi, Mama—guess what."

"Becky, you aren't to answer the phone when I'm not home. Get Stephen, please."

"Guess what, Stephen's fighting with me."

"Do you remember, I told you to behave?"

"Mah-am, I *am* being haved. Stephen—"

"It doesn't sound like it."

"Guess what. Stephen ate all the Raisin Bran. He didn't share and he didn't say I'm sorry."

"Well, are you—"

"He hit me with a toothbrush."

"Well, you get him to the phone."

She could hear Stephen grab the receiver from his sister, a loud "ouch" in the background. "Mom—I didn't eat all the Raisin Bran—there was only a bowl left from yesterday."

"Did you eat it all? Will you turn down the TV—I can't hear a word."

He turned it down. "Yeah, I ate it all, but there wasn't much. Not a great deal anyway."

"I see. Well, I called to ask if everything was okay, and it appears you have things well under control."

"Right. No prob."

"I was being ironic."

He spelled "ironic" for her.

"Good. Fix your sister some breakfast, can you?"

"There's nothing left."

"Fix her a great deal of toast."

"Mom," he said in his best complaining voice. "When are you coming home? Don't forget my game."

"I'm over at the church—I'm helping Father Kelleher. Now Stevie, I'm having him over for lunch so I'd appreciate it if at least the downstairs were picked up. Dig? The game's not till four, dear. Can I count on you?"

"Aaaugh. Becky made these messes. I've been watching TV."

"I'll be home in half an hour, and Father will be with me. Please. The vacuum's in the—"

"Broom closet. Can Mark come in the house?"

"Not until I get home. Straighten up the downstairs, Stevie—this is a small step for mankind, and call me here if there's a problem. Father's number's—"

"On the fridge. Mark's already in the house. Should I throw him out?"

"Half an hour. Okay?"

"Okay," Stephen said, with mountains of hesitation.

"Great. I love ya. Bye." Carol hung up. She stared at the wall a moment, thinking about him. Fifth grade, and last week a girl had called to speak to him.

Carol had been watching him closely. Her bad day with Wally had also been an unspeakably awful day for Stephen. He sat on the living room couch watching TV that morning, huddled in a blanket with a bowl of cereal on his lap. His stepfather was stirring around, brooding as usual. First he was out in the garage, then in the study, and finally in the kitchen. Stephen told her he remembered half-noticing Wally coming out of the kitchen carrying a rolled up newspaper.

"I have to give your mother the book section," he may have said to Stephen as he passed through the living room, heading upstairs.

He went into the master bedroom and waited for Carol, who soon came into the room from the shower dressed only in a towel. He said, "I brought you the book section," and pulled out the knife. The first lunge caught her in the chest, slightly to the right and pretty high—she heard it go through bones before she felt pain at all. Blood went everywhere. Luckily, in order to stab her again, he had to pull the knife back out, and the body had a way of holding on somehow.

"Goddamn it, Wally, I'm bleeding!" she shrieked at him.

Carol remembered the spit flying and the blood and the surprise of hearing these completely inane words come out of her mouth. She thought they were her last words, and already she heard them with a kind of embarrassed objectivity, body and soul in the first stages of separation, Carol already sinking out of existence. She tried to get to the door. She remembered knowing she was hurt badly. But what she remembered clearest was the fierce anger that came up out of her. Wally's second lunge was at her face, which was stopped by her shoulder when she turned away. She shoved him back, and he fell to his knees at the edge of the bed. They were two large animals, a vicious fight to the death. Blood was everywhere. Wally looked confused, like she was supposed to be dead already. The knife was on the floor, in the folds of the skidded blue throw rug. He was down on his knees getting it, crying. She remembers looking down on him, his face up and frightened. She went out the bedroom door and down the stairs.

"Stephen!" she was shouting, screaming, the sound of her voice leaving her like an echo. "Get Becky out of here! Run next door, quick!"

Stephen stood up in the TV room. White pajamas with firemen on them. His mother, naked and covered with blood, stumbled into the room from the stairs. Carol remembered this as a noisy scene, but she couldn't recall what the noise was. She also remembered it taking several minutes, but doctors said the whole thing must have taken about forty-five seconds or she'd have lost consciousness and never gotten downstairs at all. Wally stormed into the room right after her. Carol was reaching for the phone. Stephen, dragging Becky, was already going out the door. Wally left them alone, actually passed them, came right for Carol, determined to finish it. How could he show her no mercy, his wife, seeing her hurt like this? His knife was raised high this time, and she raised her good arm to shield herself— and the knife pinned her forearm to the paneling. She didn't even feel it. Carol pulled the knife out of her forearm and the wall, and faced her husband, who was by then braying and yelling at her. She couldn't remember what he was saying, even under hypnosis, but his face had a green cast to it, and there was blood and everything was coming loose. Now she had the knife, but was too weak to use it—dizzy, she collapsed to her hands and knees. She didn't even remember crawling all the way onto the front porch, dropping the knife between the boards down into the dark below, safe.

Father Kelleher was back in the sitting room. "No police yet?"

"Nope," she said. She was now sitting by the window, parting the curtains to check. "And I don't know how much longer I can stay, Father. Things seem to be breaking down on the home front. How long ago did you call them?"

"The sheriff lives down the street four houses!"

"Sheriff won't come. He's county. You're gonna get the city." She smiled at him, but Father Kelleher wasn't with her—he was looking down and away.

Carol took the liberty of opening the curtains. The sun streamed in with enormous brilliance. When she looked at Kelleher in this light, she was reminded of an old pirate, maybe Ben Gunn. There was a day's growth of stubble on the man's face and when his teeth showed, the gums were red, the teeth gray. His lips were cracked. He seemed like one of those pale white bugs you see scurrying for a hole when you lift a rock.

"There," she said.

He seemed very soft in this light. "What do you think, Carol—what do you think the church council will do about this?" He sat down.

Carol was the head of the church council, had been for three years. "Well. If I want these curtains open, my bet is the council will vote with me."

He grunted, then laughed grudgingly. "The burglary."

"We need you here, Father. People love you. The kids are crazy about you."

"Bah. Be my friend and tell the truth. People think I'm a dump." He laughed at his own term for it. So did she. "A big dump," he said. They both laughed. "They do," he said. "So. What will the council think about this? Really."

"Well. I think they'll have a few comments to make about how long it's taking the police to respond." She looked out the front window, shook her head. "And I think they'll use their clout—they don't have much, you might have noticed, but they'd try—to find whoever did it. And I don't concede your point about how you are viewed in this community. A lot of people will help you on this. You didn't burglarize your own place, and obviously whoever did this had to tear the place apart to find what they wanted. So stuff was secured properly, the collection and all that. They took the VCR. Common burglars, Father."

Just at that time, the police car pulled up in front.

"Ah," she said, pointing, and he got up to look. Then he went to the door.

Orson Morrell, the chief of police, was hurrying up the walk, dressed in a black uniform, badge and shoes gleaming on this Saturday morning. He was perhaps sixty-five, and had been for about fifteen years. In Carol's mind he looked exactly the same as he always had.

"Good morning, sir," he said, doffing his cap but leaving it on. "Sorry to take so long. Weekends are..." When he entered the foyer, he saw Carol. "Ah, good morning." He smiled. "How're you doing?" She could sense in the question the weight of Orson's own memories of her stretched out naked and bleeding on the front sidewalk of her home. Not so very long ago.

"Great," she said. She nodded cordially. He was wiping his feet on the bristly pad in the foyer. "Have you and Father Kelleher met?"

"Oh sure. The Reverend comes over to the jail, time to time—right, sir? Shoot, he heard Wally's—er...your husband's—confession right there in the jail, when all that happened, you know."

Even hearing Wally's name was disorienting to her. Wally and

Carol had known each other a long time. They'd been good friends in the many years before their marriage. They'd been married to each other four years, the second marriage for both of them. Now he was gone, and his name had shadows on it. Truthfully, until this moment she hadn't known, hadn't even thought of, Wally's experience immediately after the scene at the house. Now she got a picture of him in jail, blood-covered, remorseful, going to confession to Father Kelleher in a cell. Father Kelleher had never mentioned a confession to Carol. She pictured them taking his shoes, belt, and wallet, and putting him on suicide watch.

Orson stared at her, and when she did nothing but stare back, he followed Kelleher on up the foyer toward the office. Bliss trailed along behind.

"So. What we got here—a burglary someone said?"

Kelleher gestured for him to behold the mess.

"Did you touch anything in this room, sir?" Morrell asked, his notepad already out of his pocket.

"Not lately," Kelleher said. "Except—I was looking to see if they got some things I was…"

"I did," Carol said. "I touched the chair—then Father said to leave it in case of fingerprints."

"Okay, that's good," Morrell said. He looked in the office a moment and then turned and looked at the rest of the house. He almost ran into Carol as he turned.

"And the VCR's missing from that room," Father Kelleher said, pointing.

"Happened last night, did it?"

"Right," Kelleher said, following him. "Between yesterday at four and this morning around two, when I got home."

"Between four and two." He noted this. "Found it when you got home, did you? You were not home, is that it?"

Kelleher nodded. "Right. Er. Actually, it was this morning that I found it, after mass. Last night I just sort of went to bed. I mean, maybe they were still here, do you think?"

The policeman was writing in his notebook. Finally he looked up again. "Were you at someone's house or something?"

"I was in Springfield, an appointment with the Bishop'."

"Where's the Bishop live?"

"Springfield."

"Ah. Way over there?" Morrell said, but he was only half listening. He was eyeing the ceiling light in the foyer. Father Kelleher looked up there, too, and when he looked back down, Morrell was in the kitchen, leaning over to examine the window sills, his hands back so as not to touch anything. "You got a list of what's disappeared?"

"No sir, but I can. Make one."

"Yeah, well, you'll need to make one then. Any big valuables gone?"

"The Sunday collection, for one thing," Kelleher said. "I was saying to Mrs. Brown—I was saying that much of that was probably checks—but we hadn't counted it yet so we don't know for sure. And there was this gold rosary—maybe it's under something, but I haven't seen it.

"Manny's gone, yeah. I thought about that. He counts the collections. I knew that. What do you think? Estimate?" He poised to write in his notebook, at the kitchen counter.

"Well, like I say, it wasn't counted, and..."

"Ballpark it, Father."

"Maybe five hundred in cash—probably not more. That's confidential, right?"

"Of course. You know, Manny helps at the jail sometimes— feeding prisoners and such, during the holidays. I knew he was gone. Funny how things work, around and around. And it wasn't counted yet, am I right on that, because Manny is out of town presently, correct?"

"He counts the collections, yes."

"Okay." Morrell wrote in his notebook, at the kitchen table. Looked around the room from where he stood. Wrote some more.

"Wonder how they got in," he said after a moment.

"Kicked in the basement window," Kelleher said.

Carol was amazed at this, amazed Father hadn't mentioned it before.

"They got in down in the basement—there's an extra bedroom down there."

The policeman was writing. No guarantees he was getting it all down. "What was that again?" he asked. "Hold it. The basement? Can I see that?"

Father Kelleher took him down the narrow steps. He explained, "See, I had this door open here, from the basement into the kitchen, for the dog."

"So, is that your usual practice, or is that the first time you ever did that? How'd they get the safe open?"

Because of a shortage of space in the little church hall across Central Street, the fourth-grade religion classes were held in the rectory basement—Carol remembered when Stephen attended catechism down there. She didn't go down the steps, but through the floor she could hear Morrell and Father Kelleher mumbling and occasionally pointing things out, and a little broken glass skitter on the linoleum of the basement floor.

"If that don't beat all," Morrell was saying as they came back up the stairs. He was laughing.

"What's that?" Carol said when the two men were back up and standing in the kitchen.

Morrell said, "Well, you remember old Father Hubbard, right? Or was that before your time?"

Carol knew the name, the priest of the parish in the fifties. Three priests ago.

"Well, Father Hubbard's got a solid gold—what do you call it?"

Father Kelleher sighed, embarrassed. "It's called a chalice, but I..."

"Chalice, yes—Father Hubbard's chalice is on a bed stand down there, in the extra bedroom the assailants entered into, but the old chalice is under Father Hubbard's wig. Being employed there as a wig stand has apparently saved this chalice from the burglary." He was bent over, smiling rosy-faced and writing in his notebook. "A chalice worthy of a Pope," he said, "under this ratty old gray and brown wig. Whoooeee."

Kelleher was agitated. "I'd prefer that not be spread."

"Now don't be so all-fired defensive here, Father. Think about it. If you'd had that thing locked up in the safe, it'd be history. This here was a good move, from a strictly criminology point of thinking."

"Yes, but you understand, word of that, if you don't mind, it could be embarrassing to the church here," Kelleher said. He was upset, a little out of breath, trying to keep good humor in a tough moment. He leaned against the doorway to get his balance. He looked at Carol. "It's no longer consecrated, and it's among effects we are gathering to ship to his nieces up in Cedar Falls."

"Well, Father, I would hope you aren't sending them Father Hubbard's wig. Are you? The man's been dead twenty-five years."

Morrell sat down from laughing and removed his glasses. He wiped them with a gleaming white cotton handkerchief. "Whooboy, that's a good one." His eyes went down to his notepad, but for a few moments he was still laughing even as he read what he'd written thus far in the investigation.

"Anybody check for tracks outside that basement window?" Morrell asked, proud of his idea when he saw that no one had thought of it. "Okay—you make your list and just leave it on the counter—either I'll get it or the boys from the lab will. Anything else you can think of?"

"No, I—"

"Oh yeah, one other thing. About the dust all over the place."

"I know," Kelleher said regretfully, "I'm sorry. I just—"

"Fingerprinting dust. I mean to say. Nasty stuff. I apologize in advance, but listen, on your insurance, charge a cleaning person to come in and scrub the place down after our boys are gone. It really is disgusting, don't say I didn't warn you." Morrell looked right at him. "And also, you got a gun?"

"Yes, I..."

"Well, make sure they didn't steal that, and be careful. Just be careful. Some night you'll sit up in bed and start blazin' away at the ghost of poor harmless Father Hubbard, just back to retrieve his wig."

Cordially, Morrell stood back up and patted Father Kelleher on the shoulder as he came by him heading for the door. "Handling this with good humor, Father—it's an inspiration, truly. I'll check for those tracks on my way out. And I'll be back later, okay? Oh, and by the way, we have about one chance in—pardon the expression—hell of catching anybody on this. You know that, right?"

•

Half an hour later Carol and Father Kelleher were discussing Realtors as Bliss towed them up the front sidewalk of Carol's home. They had walked over, leaving the church rectory to the fingerprint crew. Carol's place had been for sale since she came home from the hospital, but houses weren't moving very well. Father Kelleher tethered Bliss in the shade by the front porch, and they walked in—Becky was there.

"Hiya, Becky m'girl," Father said in his best Irish. And then he coughed. She shied away from him, unaccustomed to the heaviness and rumble of an adult male in the house.

"Where's Steve?" Carol asked.

"He's in the kitchen eating toast."

"Mom," Stephen called from the kitchen. "I fixed toast but she wouldn't eat it."

"Mom," Becky said, "I've been hicking up. Guess what. Stephen let Robby come in the house and play."

"She's got the hiccups," Stephen called.

Carol noted that the house appeared to have been straightened up. Father Kelleher sat in the TV room in Wally's old recliner. Just above his head, the gouge mark from the knife in the paneling.

"Father, can I get you some iced tea?" Carol called from the kitchen.

"Got any scotch?"

"Yes, I think so," she said. She bent down and pulled it from a lower cabinet in the kitchen.

"Got brandy?—that'd be better."

"Fresh out," she said.

"You know," he said, "that policeman, what's-his-name?"

"Orson Morrell."

"Manny told me he's pretty sharp. He seemed slow and dull to me. What did you think?"

They rehashed the police work a while, Carol working in the kitchen, Kelleher back and forth between the easy chair and the kitchen doorway. He was in the chair when she finished pouring the drink on ice and brought it to him. She saw him looking around.

"I've been thinking of hanging a picture on that poor paneling— to hide the hole," Carol said, handing him scotch and water. "Maybe Dali's 'The Last Supper.'"

"Yeah, Dali'd be about right for that wall," he said. "You poor girl, I swear I can't believe you still live here. You're one of the strongest people I know."

Father Kelleher sipped his drink.

"Well. It wasn't the house that did it," she said, from the kitchen. "And we have to live somewhere." She was fixing sandwiches. Stephen took his and went out the back door. Becky left hers on the table and brought a book for Father to read to her—*Charlie the Broken Steam Shovel*. Carol listened to the story, told in the low rumbling brogue that sounded like the voice he used when giving out penance. Becky wasn't quite ready to sit on his lap, and instead stood and leaned on the chair arm. When he was finished, Becky asked him, "Father, is your dog mean or nice?"

"Don't you remember Bliss, my girl?" Kelleher said. The dog had often come with him on his visits during the bad days. Carol hoped Becky had put the bad days away in her mind. "She's a real nice dog, Becky."

"Is she used to little girls?"

"She'll like you, but you're pretty big, really. Scratch her on the head, up there between the ears."

So Becky went outside and petted the old dog tied in the yard. Both Kelleher and Carol watched the clock so Father would be sure to be back at the rectory about when the police were finished.

Eating the sandwich off a paper plate, his second scotch on the floor next to him, Father Kelleher chatted on. "Do you think of remarrying, Carol?" This was the kind of personal question priests were known to ask abruptly.

"No. I'm not really divorced, you know." A central life question, answered easily as can be. Carol was amazed, standing there at the counter, cleaning up the lunch. Her mind flashed to that last time she'd met Nick, in that dingy hotel in Coal Grove, his smile and strong hands, the photo in that terrible parking lot, the bundle of letters she'd hidden, so sweet and artful and never once did he ask her to leave Wally.

"Well, I know—but marriage, my dear. That's a formality really in this situation. Everyone would understand. Wally's…"

"Sick," she said.

"Yes. He's…"

"Absent," she inserted.

"Well, he is—he's gone, gone for good. You're a young woman and you have a right to move on."

She pictured Wally confessing in jail, this man hearing the confession. "I guess."

"Of course you do. There are steps we should take. We should begin right away."

Carol wasn't into annulments and other shufflings of the deck chairs.

Suddenly Kelleher was saying, "I should have married." His tongue was loosening now.

"Well." She stared at him a moment. "Marriage isn't any easier than what you've got now, do you think?"

"For God's sake, lass, I'm not expecting easier. I'm expecting…"

"Debt? Financial stress? Four-ply frustration, the evaporation of your best years? Endless self-denial, children causing not the postponement but rather the absolute negation of your own needs, and so on?"

They both laughed at her negativity. She kept going. "A gradual emptying out? And then you end up alone anyhow? Is this the sacrament you wish for yourself? Hey. It's Dali all the way," she said. "And most married couples I know who know anything are walking the thin line."

"What thin line is that?" he asked. "What's more important than raising your children the best you can? What thin line?"

"The thin line between walking the thin line and jumping off of it."

"But these people, these couples, have no idea what being really alone is like."

Again she stared at him. "Trust me on this. Let's not talk about it."

Carol was standing in the doorway of the kitchen, staring off, trying to think of something different to discuss.

"Anyway," Kelleher said, "well, okay. But do you think Wally felt alone? Do you try to think of reasons why this happened?"

She thought about it, but she didn't like thinking about it. "Well, I just think Wally was mental," she said. "That's about it. He had secrets I'll never know."

"Yeah."

"You feel what you feel and you do what you have to," Carol told him. She hesitated a moment. "And you keep it a secret as long as you can. I cheated. A couple of years ago." It came out easily, this shadow in her life, not as a full and accurate confession but more in the spirit of instruction. She was standing in the kitchen door wiping her hands. She glanced back toward the back door, making sure Stephen was outside. Maybe she'd been wanting to tell somebody this. She felt it literally lift off of her. "It was a guy I knew from high school. He taught at the University of Illinois and a few other places and suddenly he was teaching here. One night he called—I hadn't seen him in many years, and in the meantime he'd been to Vietnam, of course. He was a little sad, maybe. A little crazy, too. And Wally and I were…"

"Were what?"

"Sideways. Flat as a pancake." Carol thought of the long strange days that had made up those few short years. Getting letters in the mail—waiting for opportunities when no one was home to slip through the little wooden window into the dark of the crawlspace, a grown woman otherwise relatively dignified, crawling in dirt under her pipes and floorboards to hide the love letters in a bundle in the dark. She thought of how circumstances could evolve that would, for a while, make that behavior seem normal. She recalled the deliciousness of her secret love.

"And you made him happier?" the priest was asking.

"What?"

"You made this sad man happier?"

Carol had no answer for that. She doubted it, actually.

"It's all over?" Kelleher asked after a few moments. Here again, the directness of the parish priest. She wasn't about to tell him the full duration and impact of the affair. It was enough to mention it at all, to admit it existed.

"Yes, Father, it's over," she said. "Wally never knew about it. He had plenty going on. We hadn't been married very long, but it was like we'd been married a lot longer. Deep in adult crap, numbing routine." She deconstructed it all. There must have been some reason why the affair happened. Many reasons, probably, including her own flaws as a wife. She wasn't sure she could even remember the numbing routine. She watched the priest's face, to make sure he could handle something this big. "He had a thing about veterans, Wally did. A sort of in-between kind of thing. A kind of male rite-of-passage fantasy about having missed Vietnam— even though he ran from it feverishly back when he was eligible for the draft. Got somebody to testify in writing that he was colorblind."

She felt Father Kelleher looking at her. Finally he said, "So. Carol Brown had an affair."

There it was, the word. She looked down and waited for the priest to give her penance.

"Well," Kelleher said after a moment, "does this man, your friend—does he know what's happened to you? Has he come to you, since it happened? Since you were nearly murdered?" He coughed.

"He was pretty far away for the most part, and by then," she lied, "we hadn't seen each other for a year. Mostly we wrote letters. I talked to him on the phone once, after. I just don't think he had the energy for my personal disaster. He was still working on his." She flicked at her hair.

She looked at the old priest. Somehow she sensed that a priest couldn't quite grasp the approach-avoidance aspect of things between men and women. On the other hand, maybe priests were masters at it.

"I guess I don't really think you'd ever understand, Father. In a million years."

Unexpectedly, Kelleher laughed.

"I mean," she said, "I don't think this is your world, this trafficking in relationships."

"Trafficking. My God," he said, still laughing.

"I mean—"

"For Chrissake, stop. I know what you mean," he said. He was still laughing—maybe it was the scotch. "What a wonderful thing for you to say," he said. "You really are my friend."

Carol didn't quite get it. Kelleher went into the kitchen, tore himself a paper towel, and wiped his face. His laugh went into a cough again. He poured a little scotch, tossed it down, rinsed the glass and filled it with water. "Mercy," he said, still laughing a little, "that was a good one." Carrying the glass, he went out of the kitchen then, lumbered to the front door of the house, still chuckling. Carol followed him. They looked out where Becky was playing. A cool breeze blew through the front screen door.

"You know, for years I was a pretty good pastor, in the St. Louis area. East St. Louis. Hard to imagine, I know."

She was relieved to have him talking about himself.

"And then I thought about other things and went through—you know—one of these priestly crises." He rubbed his eyes, wandered back into the den, sat down heavily in Wally's chair. "Essentially, I went through the motions for a few years. And I'll tell you, we have some *motions* in this church, if you just want to go through 'em. You can look very busy and very holy with motions like these. Acquired over centuries, you know."

Carol noticed how unnatural he seemed in the sunlight from the window, his eyes pale and squinting, his skin blotchy white.

"And then finally I went down on the ice, as we say in the profession. And the Bishop put me in Moline, and then Murdock, and then here. He'd like, what he'd really like, is to spiral me right out the bottom of the diocese." He walked back into the kitchen for more water. "Things the Bishop could never tell you."

"The Bishop figures you can get yourself together here?"

"Figures I'll die, Mrs. Brown." He put ice in his water glass. "You're my friend. We're just talking here. I've been robbed recently. I feel bad, so I'm running off at the mouth." He laughed to himself. He wandered back to the front door, the fresh air breezing in. "You've told me a Carol Brown secret. Not to be trading stories, but the Bishop figures I'll croak. Hopes so, I think. That's that." He was staring off.

Right then there was a yelp from outside, then another. The first one was Bliss, the second Becky. At the door Carol saw that the dog was leaning against the tug of the leash, staring down the street.

"What's this white stuff on her?" Becky asked.

"Just dry skin, honey. You pet her real nice."

"She's got a big tongue!" Becky shouted. "Yuck!"

"You wash your hands before you eat that sandwich," Carol called to her, her voice reminding her of her own mom. "You hear me?"

"Watch this, Mom," Becky shouted after realizing the potential audience watching from the front screen door. She did her well-practiced back-walkover, and Carol noticed yet again and proudly that Becky's snappy cartwheel demonstrated some very real athletic ability even at her young age.

Father Kelleher was watching out the screen door. "Bravo!" he called when she perfectly executed her trick.

Carol watched with him. "Becky just started taking gymnastics."

"She's catching on pretty fast, it looks like." He toasted her with the last of his water, and sighed. "Well, Mrs. Carol Brown. I've enjoyed our chat. And all I can say is, there's a message in all this somewhere."

Carol smiled. "Well, Father Randall M. Kelleher," she said, "I'm sure there is."

•

It was about a two-minute drive to the rectory from Carol's. Stephen and Robby were enlisted to play with Becky and the dog in the backyard while Carol was gone. Later they would have to walk Bliss over to the rectory. Kelleher insisted on driving, although they went in Carol's two-door, army green Chevy Monte Carlo. Carol hadn't ridden in the passenger seat of her own car in long time.

They went by the rectory, but the fingerprint crew was still there—they could see that the window wasn't repaired yet, and no one appeared to have arrived to do it, so they decided to drive up through town and through the park. The priest didn't seem ready to go home just yet, and the drive seemed to hit the spot. He had a light sweat going—he was in direct afternoon sun, wearing all black, and Carol hadn't put freon in the car since Wally—so the air conditioning wasn't particularly cooling them. But Kelleher might have sweated anyway, in those clothes. He wasn't all that accustomed to sunlight.

"Well, I'll tell you, it's lucky for them I wasn't home," the priest mused, feeling a little more robust on three scotches. "I do have a pistol, as you know, and I would use it, too. Shooting low, of course."

Carol smiled at him. He turned into the park, and they paraded down the long, shaded one-lane drive. "It's fifteen miles an hour in here," Carol said. They were doing twenty-five, Kelleher engrossed in his fantasies of vengeance.

"If you introduce a gun, Father, they might shoot you."

"Then I'd have to shoot back. You have to take chances. You have to," he said. "Or maybe I'd just shoot a lot, and confuse them. Pop, pop, pop!"

"Confuse them into shooting you," Carol said. "They're probably just kids."

"Well, sure. But think of your Vietnam friend," Kelleher said. "Calling in bombs and rockets on his own men. You have to act sometimes. In certain situations. Take your chances. We forget that until we're in a situation."

Carol's mind whirled. Something was odd here. They came out of the park and turned down Main Street, heading back to the rectory. She kept looking at him. Something was odd.

"How do you know about that, Father?" He kept his eyes straight ahead. "Father? How do you know about what my friend did in the army?"

They rumbled on the brick street, south. The priest was frozen in place.

Finally he said, "Let me tell you, a man has to take action. *That's* my point. A man has to act. I've been *robbed*. There's pride in this, the male way, standing up for himself."

He was agitated. The sweat rolled down his face.

"Don't change the subject," Carol said.

"I'm a peaceful man," he said, wiping his face with his sleeve. "Don't people like me in this town?" He produced a dingy gray handkerchief and dabbed at his forehead. "Somebody should think about what the Jesuits are doing in Central America. They're heroes down there—heroes of the poor."

He looked at her, his eyes red.

"I think you might owe me an explanation, Father," Carol said. She leaned back in the seat, looked away from him, out the opposite window. He turned onto Van Allen, nearly home.

They rolled to a stop in front of the rectory. Two men were bent over the basement window in the side bushes, and Morrell's police car was in the back driveway. Father Kelleher turned off the car, handed her the keys and climbed out. He slumped around the front of the car and started up the front sidewalk. She rolled down the window.

"Father Kelleher," Carol called. "I need to know everything you know. You know I do." The priest kept walking toward his front door. "Look at my life," she said.

Morrell came out of the rectory and met him halfway on the sidewalk. He had his notepad and was asking more questions, and together the two men went inside. Carol sat still, in the passenger seat of her old car. A cloud of blood-pounding, ear-ringing guilt set in on her. Wally knew.

BOTTOM

On a rainy Tuesday night in April, around nine-twenty by his running watch, Lowell left Carol Brown's home by the back door, leaving her naked in her bed. Drunk, he shambled down the back steps, stumbled through her backyard gate into the dark yards across the alley, heading south to the next block where his Corolla was parked—but Gene Skolnick was on his screened back porch smoking reefer, and Lowell had to duck him by pausing behind a silver maple. Gene was one of his clients. After a while, Gene's wife Mary came out, and they talked for a time, both staring out into the dark, both smoking. Lowell couldn't hear what they were talking about. He resisted taking a peek around the tree. Then Mary and Gene receded back into their home, and Lowell saw their upstairs bedroom light click on. Then falling not once but twice over the same downed limb, he scrambled to his car, drove around a while on the quiet streets trying to settle himself down, and eventually parked in the alley behind Forty Martyrs Catholic Church. He parked in the shadows among bushes where the car wouldn't likely be seen, hurried crookedly along the west side, out of sight of the rectory, careened up the steps in shadows, stumbling only once, tested and found the door unlocked, pulled it wide and went into the vestibule. Catholic churches were almost always open, inviting in anyone who needed quiet. Astonishing how few actually came. Up by the altar, candles flickered, and it was so quiet it was almost possible to hear them flutter. It seemed there was a draft across the front of the church—a window open maybe. He moved to the front pew, slid in, pulled down the kneeler, sat for a moment. When Lowell was a kid, he came to this very altar from time to time, in some kind of peculiar mood or situation—at twelve he was the most neurotic kid he knew, though back then he wouldn't have put it that way. Therefore on this night he couldn't come here unselfconsciously. He turned out the way he turned out, and that was that. Dizzy, he kneeled down and drifted off his solemn prayer and stared emptily at the altar.

The floors were matrix marble in the aisles and wood beneath the pews, and everything creaked. He heard shifting and thumping, and it seemed almost certain someone was in the choir loft behind him, but he decided not to turn around and look, and anyway it was too dark up there to see. Shadows from the flickering candles gave life to the statues of Mary and Joseph right in front of him and to the giant Christ hanging on the cross centered above the glittering altar. The crucifix was an icon in the Roman Catholic Church. The cross wasn't quite enough as a symbol of Christ's martyrdom, so there had to be a dead body hanging from it. He stared at it a while. Before long, he was reliving the evening. He was very sorry that it happened, but she was as beautiful as he knew she would be.

He slumped, leaned back, his butt now against the seat of the pew, and he may have slept, head down on his arms. It was chilly in the church. Each time he awakened, he caught himself tipping over. At one point, he heard a commotion as Father Kelleher came in through the vestry. After some throat clearing and some clicking and clacking, the priest left by the same door, taking the short sidewalk back to the rectory; there was indeed a small window open next to his pew, and Lowell heard Kelleher working the locks. While the nave was open to anyone who might need to come there, the back doors were locked. The chalice, after all, was made of gold. Lowell watched the motion detection lights come on and go off through stained glass. He heard the shuffling footsteps of Kelleher. Lowell dozed again, deeply enough that when he woke someone had walked up the center aisle and kneeled behind him.

A hand clamped onto his shoulder and he turned to see who was there. It was Vasco Macon Whirly. "Hey, you okay?" Vasco whispered.

Lowell looked at him but said nothing because he knew he couldn't talk well and his breath stank.

"You okay?" Vasco whispered, sitting back in the pew.

Lowell said nothing, turned back to the altar.

"Drunk?" Vasco waited for a reply. "Or even more trouble than that?" Vasco asked, almost as though he knew all the things he couldn't possibly know. "Mind if I sit here a while?" Vasco rattled his rosary. Lowell put his head back down on his arms. Vasco ran through the monotony of prayers in a low, vibrating rumble that hypnotized Lowell into a netherworld of almost sleep.

Next time he nodded awake, Vasco wasn't behind him anymore. Instead he was back in the choir loft. "I'm still here," he said. "I like it up here. Perspective." He began to pray the rosary aloud again. A low hum, steady like the monks' chants in prayer calls at the Trappist.

Around ten-thirty, not much more sober than when he arrived, Lowell got up and headed for the front of the church. It was quiet upstairs, and he thought maybe he would make it to the car without even having to break into a run. He wondered if he would remember this in the morning. There was a chance not. Upstairs, Vasco hopped up fast and clambered down the narrow wood stairs into the vestibule. He caught Lowell by the shirt. "You planning on driving home?"

Heading out the front doors, towing his friend, who still had a grip on his shirt sleeve, Lowell said nothing. It was a warm, muggy night after the rain. Skim of clouds rushing past a waning moon. Wind churning the tops of maples on the courthouse lawn across the street. It would be a beautiful spring. "Hey. I'll drive ya. I can walk back." Vasco lived two blocks from Forty Martyrs. Lowell lived ten blocks away, on the northwest side. Next thing he knew, Vasco was in the driver's seat. Lowell handed him the keys.

Lowell imagined Veronica at the door of the carport, the car pulling in with Vasco at the wheel.

"Where have you been," she'd ask.

"Found him in the church," Vasco would say.

"Thanks," she would reply. "Want some coffee?"

"Nah. But he needs aspirin and a tankard of water."

"I know," she'd say. "We do this a lot. But can't you stay a bit?"

"I should go," Vasco would say.

"Okay," Veronica would say.

"Nice night," Vasco would offer.

"If you say so," Veronica would whisper back. "Listen, can't you stay a few minutes? Help me."

"Help you what," he said.

"Plan," Lowell thought he heard her say.

·

Veronica dropped two Alka-Seltzer tablets in a big plastic St. Louis Cardinals cup and handed them to Lowell, who was already on the bed fully dressed, including shoes. She pulled off the shoes.

Then Veronica went to the kitchen and Lowell heard her start a pot of coffee, even though Vasco was never known to drink the stuff. Lowell could picture her rubbing her eyes and running her fingers through her hair. "He owns a gun," he heard her say. She spoke quietly, as if she knew Lowell was listening. "I'm afraid he'll use it," she said in a rushed whisper.

"On himself?"

"Who knows. It's all random around here right now."

"Is Misty here?" Lowell pictured Vasco on the front edge of the kitchen chair. Lowell, still drunk, was struggling to focus on the conversation.

"Yes. She's in her room."

Misty was a senior now but preferred her childhood bedroom to her dorm.

"Where's the gun?"

"In our bedroom closet in a shoebox."

"What kind?"

"Nike."

He laughed. "What kind of gun?"

"Fuck if I know, Vasco—Jesus!" Veronica barked. She coughed. "Sorry. I don't know what kind of motherfucking gun. It's a pistol. Rifles don't fit in shoeboxes."

"Neither do a lot of pistols," Vasco said. "Sorry. But do you know, is it loaded? Is the ammunition in the box with it?"

"I don't know. He likes thinking it's keeping us safe. I've never liked having it in the house."

"Let's wait until he's asleep and you can bring me the box."

Lowell was looking out the bedroom window, waiting for Vasco to leave. He knew the gun was on borrowed time.

Lowell heard Veronica stand up and pour herself more coffee. "Good. Thank you. I really want it out of here." It was quiet in the kitchen for a moment. "He's probably asleep now."

Lowell hopped into bed, and Veronica padded her way to the bedroom in bare feet. Lowell pretended to sleep, feigning a couple snorts when he sensed Veronica in the doorway. He could smell her coffee, which helped keep him from actually falling asleep.

He heard her say, "He's still half awake. We'll have to give it a few minutes." She set her coffee cup on the kitchen table. Lowell could smell it. "Sorry. You didn't really intend to stay for hours, am I right?"

"It's fine," Vasco said. "I'd like to help you make a plan."

Veronica's voice faded as she headed back to the kitchen: "How're the girls? Do you see them much?"

Vasco replied, "I assume they're okay. I don't like the thought of them in the Mattoon schools, but I'm not in charge anymore. Someday, maybe they'll come stay with me again."

"I thought things might have improved."

"Takes time."

Lowell imagined Vasco smiling and staring at her. In Lowell's mind, Veronica stared back.

"Well, there's been plenty of time, don't you think?" Veronica took a big breath and dove into how the day went for her and Misty. "Anyway, it was shitty around here today. Misty's furious with Lowell. He showed up drunk at her softball game this afternoon, and then he never came home this evening. Loud and stumbling around out at the park, she said. She wanted him to come and see her pitch. Embarrassed her in front of the whole college, is what she said. She came home angrier than I've ever seen her. Went in her room and slammed the door. Didn't come out for dinner. Not that there was much of one."

"Can't he get himself through this?"

"We've been here before. Can't dig himself out of it. We think it's genetic. This was a problem his father had."

They sat quiet under the fluorescents. Before long they were talking about other stuff. It was close to eleven-thirty when Veronica assumed Lowell was asleep. She would get the gun, and Vasco could take it away. She quietly walked down the hall again.

In a moment she was back, and what she said was garbled. "Oh my God, the gun's not in there."

Lowell heard Vasco say, "Maybe he hid it."

"I doubt it."

"Was the gun gone or the whole box?"

"Box and all."

"We'll find it," he said. "Maybe you should check on Misty."

"Better to leave her alone right now, I think." Truth was, and Lowell knew this: Veronica didn't want to barge in on Misty. She might be asleep, or she might be settling down at least.

"Well, I should go. My girlfriend's at the house. I hate leaving you like this. We could get Misty and you could stay at my place," he said. "Plenty of room."

Lowell jealously listened to the two of them whisper in the kitchen.

"Give your girlfriend a call, why don't you. Let her know what's holding you up."

"What about you coming over. We could make a plan in my kitchen and we wouldn't even have to whisper." He laughed.

"You're the best guy I know," Veronica said. "You're our safe house. I've got your phone number." They stood up, and Lowell imagined her hugging Vasco.

"And I've got yours," he said. "I wish we'd have made a plan tonight. I don't like thinking of the gun floating around somewhere."

"Well," Veronica said, "couldn't we just throw a net over him and haul his ass off somewhere to dry out? Don't you guys do that sometimes?"

"I'll work on it. I'll let you know." He went out the door into the carport.

Lowell was at the window again, watching Vasco depart.

"Good night," Vasco said to Veronica. "Please do check on Misty and make sure she's okay. If she was that upset, no telling what's going on in that bedroom." He headed down the sidewalk and back toward Scott Street. Lowell watched him until he disappeared south over the railroad tracks and then he faded out of view because of trees, but he was headed in the direction of Forty Martyrs and home.

Lowell could relax now that Vasco was gone. He lay back in bed and tried to recall bits of the conversation that just occurred, but he couldn't really keep anything straight. Instead, he listened to the faint sound of Veronica shuffling around the kitchen and, before he knew it, fell into a deep sleep. Veronica never did come to the bedroom that night.

•

She didn't check on Misty. Instead she stretched out on the couch and tried to sleep. For a while she did. At 1:07 AM according to the TV cable box, there was a spectacular noise in the carport. It was the firing of a gun, repeatedly, ten shots, probably more. Heart pounding, Veronica rushed to the backdoor and looked out. Lights in the neighborhood went on, porch lights lit up, and people hovered near their windows to see what was going on. Misty was in the carport with the gun. Gun powder was in the damp night air, the tires on the Corolla were all flat, and there were two dramatic holes in the windshield. On the hood of the car, a bottle of Jack Daniel's was destroyed and booze dripped down the bullet-riddled fender. Oil and antifreeze dripped into the gravel.

"I found his stash under the driver's seat," Misty said.

"Honey," her mother said. "Gently put the gun on the ground."

Misty did that.

"Leave it there so you don't hurt yourself," Veronica said.

Middle of the night, she dialed Vasco to tell him she found the gun. Sirens rose up, and in moments Orson Morrell, Chief of Police, arrived. Orson, uniformed in impeccable black and silver, climbed out of the car and put on his policeman's cap, and for the first time in probably ten years he might have drawn his revolver, but Veronica met him halfway on the front sidewalk. She walked him around to the carport. Misty was taken in on a charge of firing a weapon within the city limits and being stoned, and the police collected the gun from the gravel using rubber gloves, removed the clip, cleared it, and impounded it for evidence. Misty spent the rest of the night in jail, so far as Veronica knew. Orson insisted and Veronica went along with it. Lowell slept through it all, and Veronica as usual handled everything, then didn't sleep until dawn. Lowell would find all this out the hard way, or the easy way depending on how you thought about it.

When Lowell was up in the morning, limping, hair wild, whiskery, bags under his eyes, Veronica let him discover their shot-up Corolla on his own. Even hours later, the carport still smelled like the O.K. Corral.

Lowell was very upset. "Where'd she learn to shoot?"

"She's a woman now. Angry and resourceful. Besides it doesn't take a fucking genius."

"Well, she could have shot herself. The car's totaled. There's a bullet in the motor."

Veronica stared at him. "The car was just a metaphor. You know that, right? You really pissed her off."

Lowell, in his robe, fixed himself Cheerios and poured some seven-hour-old coffee. "How'd she even know we have a gun?"

"It's a little house. Snoops around while we're gone. Probably knows where the lubricant is, too." She stood very close to him. "You better get right on this and apologize your ass off. This is the stuff of permanent damage."

"Yeah," Lowell said. He started down the hallway toward Misty's room. He opened the door.

"She's in the county jail," Veronica called to him. "You may be the only person in the neighborhood who slept through it. Bail's four hundred. We had about fifty people plus WCIA and the *Tuscola Review* in the front yard last night. P.S. She was high when they handcuffed her."

Lowell was dizzy.

"So what's going to happen?" Veronica asked, aiming her voice down the hall. "Think fast. We're coming apart, in case you care."

He stood in the hallway, staring into Misty's room. There was a stuffed puppy, a giant stuffed panda, and the Nike shoebox with the nine-millimeter clips in it.

•

Showered, dressed, heading for the jail, walking east on Houghton, Lowell called Carol Brown.

"Good morning," she said. "How're you feeling?"

"Not real great," he said.

She seemed to stretch as she spoke. "That's what it looked like on TV." Quiet a moment. "Anyway, I'm okay. Thanks for calling."

"I'm going over to the jail to bail out Misty."

"Yeah. I saw that. It was horrifying. What the hell happened?"

"Long story. You were not involved. Well. Just wanted to make sure things were holding together on your end. Today is dedicated to squaring things away. I'll call back later."

"Okay, Lowell. Listen, be good to yourself. Nothing's all anybody's fault."

"Right." The call was just a bit off, disturbing his paranoia. Like Carol and Lowell were now on the same side of some secret line. He was relieved to end it. This was all his fault, and he damn well knew it.

When he arrived at the jail, he steeled himself and bounded up the front steps. The front part of the jail was one of the oldest houses in town. The jail was attached to the rear. The front foyer of the house was now an office. The sheriff's wife was behind the desk. "She's with Vasco," the woman said to him before he'd said a word. "He bailed her out three hours ago."

Lowell, out of breath, sat down in a chair.

"He said she had no business being in the jail because she's almost a minor, so he coughed up the four hundred bucks and took her to his place. Said his girlfriend would be there to talk her down."

Lowell stared at the woman, whose name was Marguerite McArthur. "Where's Bud?" he asked.

"He had to go over to Oakland, so he's out in the county somewhere. Want him to call you?"

"Don't parents have to sign off if you're releasing a minor into somebody else's care?"

"Yeah, but you know Vasco. We all trust him, and we know you do, too. You totally trust him, right?"

"Do we really have to pay bail even if she's not supposed to be in custody in the first place?"

"You'll have to ask Bud or Orson about that. I don't know the technicalities."

"Ah."

"Well, like I say, I don't know the technicalities. But don't think for a second, Dr. Wagner, that everybody doesn't know what upset your daughter. It's probably you who should have been in the clink. Right?"

As he was going out, Marguerite called after him, toasting him with orange juice and a bagel: "Here's to holding it together, Professor."

Vasco's home was just two blocks east. It took him less than five minutes, and he was on the front porch. Gloria Steinem answered his knock. Gloria Steinem wasn't her real name, but that's what everyone called her. Like Vasco, she was a do-gooder—gentle, pretty, and, like a lot of librarians, had an independent authority in her bearing. "She's feeling better now. I'll go up and get her—just have a seat."

"Where's Vasco?"

"He's gone over to Forty Martyrs to talk with Father Kelleher. I can have him call you. Aren't I good enough for this?"

"I owe him some money."

"Oh, no, I doubt that very much, but I'll have him call you. Okay, I'll be right down with Monique." She turned on the stairs. "FYI, she insists on being called that."

Misty came down the stairs in bare feet, jeans, and a black Grateful Dead t-shirt Lowell and Veronica had given her for her sixteenth birthday. Gloria Steinem remained upstairs, ostensibly to give father and daughter a little time together, but Lowell could hear her talking real low on the phone to Vasco.

"We won the game, five to two," Misty said to him. She told him about the game and how she'd gotten a couple of hits. "Sorry you missed it." She was looking at him level and serious. She *was* a woman now.

"Me, too," he said. He put his arm around her. "Misty, I'm sorry. I caused this. I'm a giant hunk of pooh."

"Very funny. Dad, it's Monique," she said. "It's the new me." She looked at him.

He smiled. "Monique will take some getting used to."

"*Tell* me about it," she said. "You and Mom *named* me that."

"True." He laughed. "We like the name."

She gave him a hug. "I'm sorry I ruined our car. Please don't ever do that again. You embarrassed me in front of everybody. I'm so used to being proud of you, and you… I was so angry I went crazy."

"Well."

"And the police have your gun."

"Okay. They can keep it." He smiled at her. "It's not registered anyway. It'll be a relief to have it gone. I don't want to be next, after the Corolla."

"Stop it. I was crazy, I told you. Why isn't the damn thing registered?"

"I bought it before guns were being registered. Never fired it. Never took it out of the box."

"You bought it in a Nike shoebox? Weird. Well, you apparently loaded it, because it was damn sure loaded. My ears are still ringing."

"Do you want to go home yet?"

"It was great that Mr. Whirly brought me here. Jail was awful. Gloria Steinem has been wonderful to me. We had donuts and coffee at five this morning."

"Did you sleep?"

"Not really."

"Where did you get the weed?"

"You know, it isn't really characteristic of a person on marijuana to shoot up her father's car. It's a very peaceful drug."

"You were upset."

"Upset? I was out of my mind. Did you see the news on TV?"

"No. I never want to see it."

"I didn't even recognize myself. Anyway, I got the stuff from Buddy." Ah. The boyfriend. "After the game he said I probably needed it more than he did. He thought it would settle me down."

"Is it all gone?"

"I think so." She stared at the floor. "Well, of course, there's more where it came from."

"Was it your first time smoking dope?"

"No."

In a mental ditch after yesterday's drunk, he couldn't get himself to lecture her on marijuana.

"You don't even know me, do you?" she said, tears streaming down her face.

"I know you, honey," Lowell said.

Vasco suddenly appeared in the room.

"Hey," Lowell said. "What do I owe you for getting Misty out?"

"Monique," she said.

"Nothing," Vasco said. "Lowell, we're going to get you out of town for a while. We, you and me, are taking a flight to St. Louis out of Champaign. Veronica knows about it. So does Misty."

"Monique," she said.

"Father Kelleher's waiting outside in his car. Veronica packed a bag for you."

Orson Morrell stepped into the room, shiny silver handcuffs hanging from his belt.

"How long would I be gone if I agree to this nutty idea?"

"Depends how you do," Vasco said. "Four weeks max."

"A month. That's a long time."

Vasco said, "Yeah. And we gotta go if we're gonna make the plane."

"Bye, Dad," Misty offered.

"Anyway, honey, I'm sorry about yesterday." Lowell couldn't hide tears then. He stood up. "Look, fellas," he said, wiping his eyes, "I'm fine, and I'm not going on this little trip you've cooked up."

Vasco and Orson Morrell came up close to him, Lowell pushed them away, and in two shakes he was on the floor of Vasco's front room being handcuffed. His face was smashed into the rug, and somebody's knee was on his back. Misty was shouting, "Get off of him!" He could almost breathe. His heart was bam-bam-bamming, the mortification in front of his daughter. This was payback for the ballgame, no doubt about it. He had a rug-burn on his cheek. His arm was twisted in a way that arms aren't meant to twist, a famous cop trick.

"Get the fuck off me," he said. "Pardon my French, Monique." And as he said it, he thought, I was wondering what the bottom looks like. This is the motherfucking bottom. He understood they were trying to help him, that this is what friendship looks like in the extreme, and he decided since there wasn't a choice, he would lean in and make a break for it at the first opportunity.

Together Morrell and Vasco got him upright, and Lowell had no energy to push back anymore and get thrown around Vasco's house like a handcuffed beanbag.

One on either side of him, they marched him out to Morrell's squad car. Orson drove, of course. Kelleher rode in the front passenger seat, with Vasco and Lowell in the back seat, which was really a wire cage with the door locks controlled by the driver. It was a twenty-minute mad rush on the interstate, going 90 mph with the police lights flashing. This was the only way they could catch the plane. Nobody said anything. Lowell's friends were determined not to crack smiles or lighten up in any way.

Lowell squirmed in the handcuffs, which held his arms behind him and made sitting a contortion and a chore. "This is an over-reaction," Lowell said.

"Give me your cell phone," Vasco replied.

"Why?"

"C'mon, give it to me."

"Get the cuffs off me so I can get it." Lowell realized the phone had several calls to Carol in the register. "I'd like to text Veronica, before it goes off."

"We're almost to the airport," said Orson Morrell.

Orson produced the key, and Vasco unlocked the cuffs.

Lowell scanned the register and removed calls to Carol Brown. He changed the security code so no one could get in. He texted Veronica: *I've been abducted by Vasco, Kelleher, Morrell. Back in a few weeks. When they did this with my father, it wasn't possible to text and we didn't know where he went. I'm sorry for all. Feel free to buy a car before I get back. Love, L.*

He handed Vasco the phone. "I locked it," he said.

Yes, this was something that happened to Lowell's father when Lowell was fifteen. His father never told him about it, but it probably wasn't much different. In a way, Lowell was fine with this forced trip, something he'd never managed to do for himself. He was following in his father's footsteps, not entirely by choice but at least by genetic script. He wouldn't soon forget his chat with Misty, her earnest, mature plea to him to get control of himself and step up to being her father. It was true she had more or less grown up while he was looking some other direction. It was time to get himself together.

Southwest Airlines. Soon they were sailing down Illini-Willard's longest runway in a 737, en route to Lambert in St. Louis. The jet lifted off and gained altitude fast, as though the noise would bother the corn. At the level of the clouds they banked left and went all the way around the airport. From his window seat, Lowell saw Orson Morrell's car, police lights still flashing, departing the lot enroute to Tuscola with Father Kelleher. There was no one in the middle seat and Vasco, earnest, far from feckless, sat on the aisle. It was over. Lowell thought of Veronica. He hoped she remembered to pack his notebooks. He would do a full dump in his notebooks over these coming weeks, sort it all out. He would once again read the literature of AA and drink the Kool-Aid. He would go to mass. He would purify—run, drop weight, detox. He would think, he would work, reconsider, get ahold of himself. He would step away from people who were trouble and recommit to a responsible life. He would be dry forever because he had no handle on alcohol and hated himself for all that had happened. He would read *The Stranger* again. Why did he suddenly think that, high up above the clouds? It wasn't long and he was asleep in his seat, his head leaning against the window. He was emotionally exhausted and couldn't control all things at home anymore. Instead, he gave himself over to it, all of it.

•

On the approach into St. Louis, people on the plane stirred with anticipation and Lowell woke up, not exactly refreshed but feeling better. The plane was bumpily descending and outside his window there was another plane also on its approach, apparently parallel runways. He woke up Vasco and asked him what was next.

Vasco was groggy. He hadn't slept much either. "A van from the White House will pick us up. That's the name of the facility we're going to. It's on the Mississippi, an old retreat place that because of the economy they've started using as a drying out facility. It's south of St. Louis someplace. I've never been there. Kelleher suggested it."

"Three weeks?" Lowell asked.

"Four." Vasco remained serious, staring straight ahead.

"What happens during these many weeks?"

"I understand that three hours a day you're either with a counselor or in an AA meeting or doing some menial task to keep the place afloat. The counselor one to two in the afternoon—he's who will pick us up at the airport. The meeting eight to ten nightly for your whole time here. Seven days a week. There are others there drying out. I think it's a bit like basic training. KP, working in the fields, the whole schmeer."

"What else?"

"No talking otherwise. You can read in your room, take walks. No talking at all. There's a mass early morning each day. It's not a monastery with prayer calls all the time, anything like that. You'll have a lot of time to think. The rooms all have showers, and you're expected to keep the room clean and yourself too. Hopefully Veronica packed other clothes for you and your shaving kit."

"You're saying I'm dressed shitty?" Lowell looked at him. "I'd have dressed up if I knew I was traveling." There was a laugh or two from that. "Are you staying for the duration?"

"I want to monitor how you're doing and make sure you give over to it. Forty Martyrs is paying for both of us to be there. We all want this to work, for you, the family, the community. You're important, and you're losing it."

The plane touched down, taxied, lurched to a stop at the gate. There was a little ding, and everyone was up and wading into the overhead bins. Lowell and Vasco remained in their seats. "They pick us up at eleven," Vasco said, eyeing his watch, "and it's just now ten, so we've got time for some breakfast." They went to breakfast in the airport and found their bags at baggage claim, then met the White House van driven by a Jesuit named James David Cavanaugh. He was a tall guy, silver-haired, a psychiatrist in addition to being a priest. He had a hard New York way of talking, everything very pointed and quick.

"So you're Wagner?"

Lowell nodded.

"Been here before?"

"No."

"You'll love it. Who knows, you might come back under improved circumstances." He laughed. "Bring your work clothes?"

Vasco said, "He doesn't know what he brought. His wife packed for him."

"Well, no wives here. We do it all. We cook, we clean, we maintain, we repair, we build. We sleep eight hours. Ever drive a tractor?"

"In high school, yes. Baled hay."

"That's good work. If you liked that, we've got plenty of it here. There's some livestock. There's painting, maintenance, that kinda stuff. Do any of that?"

"In the Army."

"In the Army. Okay then. You been in the Army, you paid some dues already. When was the last time you slept eight hours?"

Lowell had no answer for that.

Lowell saw that Cavanaugh was imagining an infantryman in Vietnam, delayed PTSD. He'd leave it like that for a while, until the question was asked directly. In fact, Lowell was a clerk in Germany, a cushy job while the rest of his generation was fighting Charlie. Still, it was the Army's choice to draft him and then send him to Germany, and it was two years of his life and that was not nothing.

They found their way to the beltway and were quiet for a while.

"I work with a lot of drinkers and junkies," Cavanaugh said. "One of the things I notice is that they are dishonest. They lie their asses off, and many of them don't even know they're doing it. Part of what you're here for is to get honest, with others and, more importantly, with yourself. You and I will meet after lunch today for an hour, my office. It's easy to find. You are probably living with a number of lies, and it's important to dispose of all that as soon as possible."

They drove for an hour, took an exit, and drove another forty-five minutes. They turned up a green lane, stone buildings in the distance. Cavanaugh gave them each keys to their cells, which to Lowell's dismay were adjacent. Vasco was apparently his jailer. "Okay, men. Your silence starts now. Oh, and it's lunch time." He pointed out the cafeteria, the chapel, the walking gardens. He shook their hands, and said to Lowell, "See you at one sharp."

There was something foreboding in how Cavanaugh said this. As in the Army, a cost was promised for lateness. At any rate, they were finally where they were going. It was April, high spring, flowers sprouting and leaves sprouting in a new green. In bright noon sun, they wheeled their bags over blacktop to the dorm facility, attached to the chapel, and took the elevator to the third floor. Saying nothing, they each unlocked their rooms and stepped in.

•

No surprise, Veronica had read his mind. There was a handwritten love letter in the bag, and a nice note from Monique—it was signed "Monique"—and his leather-bound notebooks were in there along with plenty of pens. There was a sheaf of writing paper, envelopes, stamps. There was a box of instant hot chocolate and his favorite coffee cup. The clothes she packed were right, casual and also work shirts, and pants, including favorite jeans and t-shirts. Tons of socks and underwear. Also his running clothes and shoes. And his laptop.

The room was sweet, especially with the view of the river his window provided, a view of the Mississippi far below. The writing desk was substantial, not a token thing like in hotels—good sized, with a worthy desk chair. The single bed was firm and perfect, and next to it was a chair for reading, with a small ottoman and a good strong floor lamp that served both the bed and chair. An alarm clock was on the desk. On the wall above the door, a crucifix that Lowell would have photographed if he had his camera. The walls were construction block, painted tan, but the room was full of color, from the scarlet wool blanket on the bed to the royal blue curtains to the large framed print of *The Sacrament of the Last Supper* by Dali on the common wall between Lowell's and Vasco's rooms. The whole building was quiet even though it didn't seem like it could be with all the concrete block and hard tile flooring. Since there was no talking, all you heard was the occasional sneeze or cough, a clearing of the throat, a hard short screech as a chair was moved. That afternoon Lowell noticed people in the hall were at special pains to go quietly, to close the door to the stairwell carefully. Because his window faced east over the river, with no retreat property in between, there was the very real sense of being alone. A hawk would circle. A murder of crows would come flapping in from Illinois. Boats, big and little, would steam by, and watching them Lowell could discern the main channel.

He unpacked and stacked everything on open shelves. A black curtain could be drawn across the shelves to keep it all private, but what was the sense of that since all here was private anyway? Four weeks of quiet stretched before him, and within the confusion about the future he was relieved and happy in spite of himself. He stared out the window and let go of worrying about home.

At one in the afternoon, he found Cavanaugh's office and was invited in. It was a professor's office, books open and closed everywhere. A high ceiling and big windows and amazing light gave the room a comfortable feel, and Cavanaugh embarked on a mission of getting to know Lowell, whom he called Wagner. During their visit, Cavanaugh defined "alcoholic" as a person whose drinking had begun to be a problem in his family and his work. This consoled Lowell, because he realized he didn't have it bad if he had it at all. The slip at the ballgame was serious, but it was the first one he'd had, perhaps the first sign that he was on the slippery slope.

"So, Wagner, were you in Vietnam?"

Lowell told him he'd been in Germany, very lucky.

"Yes, lucky—same with me," he said. "I benefited from the favorable outcome of the lottery."

"I was drafted before the lottery," Lowell told him.

Cavanaugh was reviewing a file in front of him. "Well, I understand you are a psychologist in your town, and have been for a long time. Do you have other interests? Do you have an avocation?"

"Teaching perhaps."

"Yes, yes, well that actually is a job you must do, as I understand it. I mean something that drives you, captures your passion when you are not involved at the college."

Lowell thought a while. "I have a family, a wife and daughter."

"Is that all going well?"

"Not lately, but overall yes." Lowell immediately questioned the veracity of his answer.

On the wall behind Cavanaugh was a black crucifix with an attached gold chain. Lowell asked about it.

"Oh, that's a gift from a professor of mine, a Precious Blood Father who mentored me in college and who was present at my ordination. He's died and they passed the cross on to me." Cavanaugh stared at it a moment. "It's part of the garb for that order. Quite dramatic when they wear it."

It was quiet for a few moments.

"But we were talking about avocations. Do you ever think about returning to school and getting another degree?"

"I did that actually," Lowell said. "For a number of years I worked on a doctorate in Anthropology."

Cavanaugh was enthusiastic about that, saying that it complimented the work of counselors, filled in the cracks left by training in psychology. "Any other driving interests?" he asked.

"I like silent retreats," Lowell said. "And baseball."

"Don't we all!" Cavanaugh got up and went to the window. "You will agree then that you aren't the only lucky person in the room. So what has precipitated your friends forcing you to come here?"

Lowell told him the whole story in the least self-serving manner he could. He said that Vasco was a good man and had known for a long time that this, all this, needed to happen. Cavanaugh agreed that Vasco was a good man, one of the best. Lowell talked about Misty and Veronica, the town, the college, the counseling practice, the drinking, his affair with Carol Brown, the fire in the administration building, made it all sound like a hectic roil of tasks and busyness and exhaustion that had caused him to lose who he is. He talked quite a while and Cavanaugh sat back down and took notes on a pad on a clipboard. Cavanaugh asked follow-up questions, about Carol, about Lowell's health, about anything going on in town at that time that might be preoccupying him. The time flew by, and finally Cavanaugh indicated the time was up. "I really like this idea of yours, anthropology," he said as they were walking to the door. "You may think all your time is accounted for. You'll be amazed how much more time you'll have once you get off the sauce." There was a pat on the back and a handshake. "Nice to meet you, Wagner," he said. "We'll make this real good for you and send you home well." As Lowell departed down a long hall, he realized his initial impression of Cavanaugh as a ball-buster was wrong. Why didn't he know that first impressions were never right?

It was a sunny day and after that meeting Lowell walked in the garden. Vasco joined him out of nowhere, exactly like at Forty Martyrs that last night, and they walked together in silence. Vasco's presence next to him seemed to be a conversation and a comfort. When he thought back on the walk they took, Lowell felt the communication was crystal clear, and they hadn't said a word. They walked nearly a mile on the bluff above the river, and finally Vasco tapped his shoulder and indicated they should begin walking back. Otherwise Lowell might have walked all the way to Arkansas. It was a Tuesday, the first day of a long, long stay.

By Saturday, Lowell was feeling much better. Rested, his mind refreshed and alert, and his system cleared of alcohol. Why couldn't he live this way at home? He could feel pure rest behind the eyes and in his legs, shoulders, and back. Across the highway from the White House there were running paths, and Lowell ran there, became familiar with them. It was a forest, and among the trees there were benches and small venues almost like chapels, each with its own imposing statue of a saint. Sometimes Lowell would sit awhile to cool off before returning to his cell. He preferred the small area dedicated to St. Paul. The statue of Paul was particularly relatable, how his arms were open to passers-by. Others would jog by from the White House, some alone, some in twos or threes, all silent, and Lowell noticed the sounds of them running together, the rhythmic breath, the footfalls. None of them glanced his way as they passed. Somehow these runners had become friends, even without talking.

Vasco would sit with Lowell at the meals in the cafeteria. The cafeteria intercom played a recording of Hal Holbrook reading Mark Twain's *Life on the Mississippi.* Other than that, the sound was of plates and silverware clinking. Lowell found himself looking forward to meals because of the recording and because it gave him a chance to get some eye contact with Vasco, who was deep in his own reflections. Because of this retreat and Vasco's strong interest in everything working out, Lowell knew theirs was a friendship that would last forever.

In the middle of the night, in the middle of the second week, Lowell was awake and reading when he heard someone outside his door. He went to the door and put his ear to it. Whoever it was was just outside. He slowly opened it. It was Veronica. She was smiling and she handed him a bundle of flowers and a box of ginger snaps. There was a nice card attached to the box from Veronica and Monique—saying "Come home soon." Then she took his hand and wanted to walk him outside. He slid into his jeans, and they sneaked down the stairs instead of causing the elevator to rattle. She'd driven to St. Louis in their new car, a royal blue Toyota Camry, appropriately humble but symbolizing renewal. She was all smiles. Not a word was said. How had she found him?

Back in the room, in silence, they immediately went to bed. The bed was small but they didn't need any extra space. Even a whisper would travel through the halls, they knew. Veronica frequently did this, a rescue, a touching of base. She had an instinct not only for survival but for renewal. And what a beauty. When Lowell popped awake at sunrise she was gone again, and except for the flowers and the ginger snaps and the lingering scent of Veronica herself, it could have been the best of dreams. Many more days to go at the White House, one day at a time, and Lowell was rising off the bottom. That morning at breakfast, Vasco smiled at him and said in a whisper, breaking the rule of silence, "So, how was your evening, bro?"

•

Lowell fell into a routine of running the trails in the morning when it was still cool. He didn't eat breakfast, ran instead. He was fascinated by the silence. In the afternoons he walked with Vasco. The shaman. Former lit prof denied tenure. Former miner. Seer of the Virgin Mary. And so in some ways it was like having a holy man to retreat with. They walked on the bluff high above the Mississippi and wandered in the woods wherever the paths went. Shoulder to shoulder they walked and, mysteriously, when he remembered it later it wasn't like they were silent but more like they were conversing. Lowell thought about how communication had become so dependent on talk. But somehow it was silence that was needed, silence that couldn't be misunderstood. Lowell had used it as a technique in therapy sometimes. He'd come into the room, his client sitting across from him. He'd pull out the drawer on his desk, put his foot on it, keep the clipboard on his thigh. He'd stare at the client without a word. There was a period of discomfort, but finally the person sitting across from him would find some forward momentum and begin to tell a story. Or she wouldn't. She might sit there for the hour and stare back. But that was a different situation. Lowell was a counselor, getting paid to say a few things. Two people walking in silence at the White House south of St. Louis could arrive on the same wavelength as they walked, could relax and truly be together. Somehow their souls would converse, without any real talk.

In the cafeteria the tapes were played during the meals, Lowell realized, to muffle the sound of silverware and plates and cups tinking in the silence. Once Holbrook's reading of *Life on the Mississippi* was finished, another recording played, of the great Trappist monk Thomas Merton giving a lecture on some excerpt from scripture. You never knew what you'd get at dinner time. Sometimes it was Gregorian chant, or prayers put to song; through the windows the music went, out across the bluff, and down into the gardens and into the forest along the walking paths. A failed Catholic, Lowell was hit hard by nostalgia, remembrance of his parents and mass at the old Forty Martyrs Catholic Church.

Rehab, it turned out, was a gift. Cavanaugh was genuinely good and seriously bright. Lowell learned from him. Never once did Lowell think of leaving or of wanting a drink. Of course, everything was different at the White House—the pressures were off, from family, work at the college, and the dark lure of Carol Brown. Reflecting on those events, that one night with Carol might have weighed the heaviest. No amount of running or silence could suppress it.

The one and only evening Lowell was with Carol and their clothes were piled next to the bed, a street light shined through a crack in the curtains, like a lightning flash darting across the bed, and Lowell stared at the damage the stabbing had done. A large deep purple scar in her right chest above the breast, and a terrible tear in her forearm where Wally pinned her arm to the paneling in the den. Lowell wanted to talk about it, but Carol didn't care to, and so, both drunk, they made love, then made love again, and an hour later he guiltily dressed and, without saying much, went out her back door into the black of the damp, windy, wooded night. When he remembered back, her beauty was still with him, but it was the scars he recalled in detail, how vicious the attack was and how surprising that Carol had recovered. The story had sunk into the swamp of rumor and wonder among the people of the town even though most of them didn't know much about it—they just had to talk—but Lowell had traced along the length of the scars with his fingers, and, for him, the attack became even more real than it already was. The miracle of her recovery became even more of a miracle. A miracle that Vasco presided over. A Vietnam vet, a combat medic, he stopped the bleeding right there on the sidewalk outside her house, and in moments an ambulance was there to transport her to the emergency room where surgeons waited. Lowell thought about Vasco. Vietnam was in him, in his hands, in the look in his eye. Vasco had seen plenty. Lowell saw that it was still there, the war, inside him.

All the nights Lowell spent there were quiet. The AA meetings revealed to him, once again, how lucky he was to have been saved from bottoming, really bottoming, as so many of these men had. That too was a miracle Vasco had presided over, in the best of spirits, with the best of intentions, tackling Lowell, handcuffing him, breaking down his resistance. Sometimes rehab was very emotional. Lowell cried in the AA meetings. The emotion came from the stories of the other men, how bad it could get, how far gone someone could be on drugs or alcohol—so far that the flesh on their faces began to change as their liver gave out and gradually they were out of control, then abusive, then mortifying for their loved ones. Their own children dodged them, their wives left with the kids and hid from them in safe houses. Family life was torn by strife and words were said that could never be taken back. Lowell thought of Wally, who went violent on his normal prescription. Lowell had seen him have Prozac episodes at the college, and when he heard what had happened to Carol, he knew that was what it was. Lowell had dropped the ball. He'd intended to call John Landen, Wally's physician, and report the strangeness in Wally's behavior, and to suggest a different prescription. Landen would have acted immediately, and Wally wouldn't be in prison and Carol wouldn't have been cut to the quick with a chef's knife.

But they were instructed in the daily morning homilies to let the past go, because nothing could be done about it. They learned to change the things they could change, let go of the things they couldn't, and to have the wisdom to know the difference. Lowell was gaining the wisdom to know the difference, and he could feel his blood pressure go down. Perspective arrived. He wanted his marriage to Veronica. He wanted his relationship with his daughter. He even tried to pray alone in the deafening silence of the chapel sometimes. He prayed that things would be fine when he got home, and that Veronica would accept him back. Part of the assignment for returning was to do Retribution. To find those he'd hurt with his behavior and ask for forgiveness. The walk to and from the chapel, night or day, was peaceful. Lowell would walk at night, under a big moon, and yes, it was on the other side of the earth during the day. One night by the light of the moon Lowell spotted a small silver stone on the asphalt, and he picked it up, handled it, and put it in his pocket. On the walk back the wind blew hard against the bluffs, but the windswept clouds spread across the moon like thin fibers of cotton. Lowell encountered Cavanaugh striding across the yard in his Jesuit robes. A silent wave passed between them. In his room, he pulled out the stone and examined it. It didn't seem of this earth, and he chose to think of it as a gift from someone somewhere else.

SCARS

owell's sudden disappearance from the town threw his clients. Veronica put a message on his answering machine that said, "Hello. Thank you for calling our office. Dr. Wagner is out of town for a few weeks, due to a family emergency. Please watch his website for the announcement of his return, so you can resume your appointments. Have a good day." Then she went on the website and posted a big sign on it that said, "Under (re) construction and (re) newal. Check here often for status updates."

Veronica had to explain at some length to Monique the principle of anonymity in AA, because Lowell had lapsed in his long-time AA association, and Vasco Whirly had emailed Veronica that Lowell would have to go back to serious AA when he returned, whenever that might be. A few days after he was gone, she received the insurance money for the car Monique had destroyed on that bad night and bought a spanking new royal blue Toyota Camry. Their first new car ever. In that same frame of mind, she cleaned the house top to bottom and went on a search for a handyman to repaint the interior. Howie Packer, a client of Lowell's and an old Marine from the Vietnam era, was suggested. He worked at the homeless shelter on a volunteer basis, helping out returning veterans from that war and all our subsequent wars. Because Howie was dirt poor, he didn't have a phone, but one day Veronica saw him leaving the shelter. A stocky guy, weightlifter type, about Veronica's height, with a stride like he was still in uniform. He was square-jawed and battle-ready and wore his hair short under a Seattle Mariners baseball cap. She decided not to approach him when she saw him because it seemed like he was on some kind of mission, but she would catch him the next day.

The next morning, she found out where he lived and parked down the street. At one point he came bursting out his screen door, whirled and locked up, then hurried along Buckner all the way to Main, then a left on Main and the business district was hoving into sight. Fifteen-minute walk at his speed. It was a small town. In her new blue car, Veronica hung back a ways, perhaps a block. On Main she pulled alongside him and accessed the nice new button to roll down the passenger window. She called to him, "Are you Mr. Packer?"

As he walked he looked over at her. He didn't seem to get it that she was talking to him. For one thing, he was listening to music in his headphones. And maybe people didn't talk to him much.

"Are you Howie Packer?" she said again.

He stopped, then walked over to her car, lifting off his headphones as he came. Stepping off the curb, he leaned down to look in at her. "Yes, ma'am, I'm Howard Packer." He had a friendly smile.

"I heard that you sometimes do handy work."

"Yes, I do."

"I've done some research and people speak highly of you. By the way, I'm Lowell Wagner's wife—Veronica." She reached over and shook his hand. "Lowell's out of town at this time, you might have heard, and I was wanting to get the interior of the house painted before he came back. Maybe some lively new colors, so it's different and fresh. I don't know exactly when he'll be back, so it would probably mean starting right away. Could that happen?"

"Yes, ma'am."

"Well, why don't you hop in, and we'll go for a ride and talk about it. I'll show you the place, and maybe you can give me an estimate."

"Can we drop by the shelter so I can let them know what's up?"

"Of course," she said.

With a click the door was unlocked on the passenger side and Howie hopped in. "It's nice to meet you," he said. "It's great that you caught me, because I was just thinking about this. I'm fresh out of cash." He had broken a sweat on his fast walk. Now he wiped his face with his sleeve. "And I owe some people."

"I know the feeling. There's never enough money." She smiled at him. "Do you mind taking a drive up to Champaign? There's a great coffee shop up there. I haven't been there in ages." Though her new blue car was still unfamiliar in town, Veronica didn't want to be seen with Howie while Lowell was away. She wouldn't admit to herself why this was.

"Can we be back in three hours?"

"Oh sure," she said.

"Sounds good."

She parked diagonally in front of the shelter and Howie ran in. She watched him through the front window, talking to somebody. Then he was back out. He strapped in and they were off.

They slowly cruised by the Wagners' house, an uncomplicated little bungalow that Veronica called home and loved. Howie commented that the place was not unlike his own rental, though the Wagners' was in better condition. He estimated that painting it might run Veronica fifteen hundred dollars, which was considerably lower than she expected. The drive to Champaign on Route 45 was less than half an hour, but not as quick as on I-57. Problem was that the interstate skirted Champaign, requiring a drive across town to the Café Kopi. Veronica did know what she was up to. Entering on the south side by the old highway and progressing into the center of the town on the city streets got them there quicker. They found a parking spot within a block. It was about ten in the morning.

The Kopi was in an old storefront, facing east. Its floors were hardwood, and the ceiling was tin in the fashion of the old department stores of the Midwest. Nora, the owner, was tirelessly devoted to the place. It was set up so that customers ordered at the counter, and then carried their order on a tray to a table. When they were leaving, customers were kindly asked to clear their own tables and put the dirty dishes in gray bins. Nora would gladly handle that task herself if a customer forgot. The piped-in music was vintage rock, and the interior was sophisticated and relaxing. Students from the University of Illinois frequented the place to get online, and attorneys and local office workers flowed in on the way to work or for a quick lunch. A large print of Hopper's "Nighthawks" was framed and placed in the restroom alcove.

Once they were settled, Veronica asked him a few questions. "Where do you come from?"

"Idaho," he replied. "Boise."

That surprised her. "What brought you here?"

"I wanted to start school at the college, but I have to save some money. The GI Bill won't handle it all. Old as I am, I can't seem to give up hope about going to college." He smiled.

"Majoring in what?" she asked.

His eyes stared down at the table. He was shy about this, the presumption of it. "I'm really not sure," he said.

"You like the town then?"

"Oh yeah, I'm good here," he said.

She was back to the task. "I'll pay you fifteen hundred dollars," she said, "and together we can go buy the paint—I'll put it on a credit card, so the materials money doesn't come out of your pay."

"Perfect," he said. "Really, that's perfect."

"What all do you do at the shelter?"

"I fix lunches and keep the place clean," he said. "I've painted it a couple of times, and I fix stuff when things break down. The place is full of donated appliances, most of them on their last legs."

They talked for a while, and Veronica found him interesting. He was resourceful and energetic, and his mood seemed very good. Of course he was hardcore Vietnam, in the old way she remembered from many years ago. He was in war before women were in war. His eyes were clear, and it was mysterious what his problem was, what he was seeing Lowell about, but PTSD had a way of hiding and she allowed that that could be what was holding him back. Something was holding him back, because otherwise he gave off the vibe of a stalwart citizen. Maybe he was just in a suspended moment of his life, a quiet pattern, pulling together money for school. He was older than most of the college faculty. He didn't need college, but he felt he did, so he did.

"I was a mess when I got back," he said. "I'd been shot while I was over there—I didn't process it very well. I'm not the only one—there are a lot of walking wounded around."

"Do you know Nick Bellinger?" she asked. "He's a vet."

"Yes, ma'am," Howie said, "but he isn't one of us. He was never in Vietnam. It's a big lie he used to tell."

"Oh my," she said. "Seriously?"

"He came to a meeting of the vets out at Squeak's, a project Dr. Wagner helped us pull together. Nick told his usual story and we asked him questions. This story he was telling is a cliché, right down to the number of guys he says got killed, thirty-nine, one survivor—Nick himself. He didn't have the imagination to change it even a little. And he couldn't recall his own combat unit. Most of us, we know the Vietnam combat units in the Army, where they fought. We know what units went into Cambodia. We know the war. We damn sure know our own combat unit. He broke into a big sweat when we started asking questions. We all knew what we were talking about, and clearly he didn't."

"Yikes," she said. "Poor Nick." Veronica never thought for a moment that all Nick's war talk was untrue. This meant he was a good liar, and that meant he was probably lying about a lot of stuff.

"Poor Nick? Are you kidding? He's lying about being in the war. He's appropriating other guys' war experiences and pain. It's sick."

"Sorry," Veronica said. "I didn't mean it that way."

"Seriously, this is one of the worst lies a man can tell. Anyway,"

Howie said. He stared out the front window of the Café Kopi.

Hours passed in the Kopi as they sat and talked. Howie said he really didn't need to be home in three hours, now that he had a job to do and a notion of what he'd be paid. As time passed, Veronica started to feel guilty and she wasn't sure why. They talked about a lot of people in the town and how small a town it was. Nearly everyone who came up had seen Lowell at one point or another. He was their common bond, though Howie seemed to avoid talking about his shrink. Like everyone else in town, Veronica brought up what happened between Wally and Carol, but Howie didn't seem all that interested. Howie seemed to go quiet at the mention of Carol Brown, but Veronica pressed him on it this time.

"Well," Howie said. "There might be some bad news about Lowell and Carol Brown."

Veronica braced herself. "What."

"That the two of them got together."

Veronica gulped, turned away in her chair. "How do you know that?"

"I'm sorry—I figured you knew."

"Where did you hear this?"

"I watched them. Back before the building burned, up there in Dr. Wagner's waiting area. It looked like something was going on."

"So it's just a suspicion?" she asked.

"I think it's real," he said to her.

Veronica got up and went into the ladies room. She stood at the sink and stared into the mirror. What was she doing here, out in Champaign? Did she really want Lowell to come home? She remained in there for fifteen minutes, splashed her face with water. Why would Howie tell her this? Didn't he like her? Or was he just odd? She unlocked the door and returned to their table.

Late afternoon, they put their dishes in the gray bins and, high on black coffee, they found themselves walking hand in hand down the street to the Inman Hotel where they got a room on the top floor of the building. The elevator ride to the sixth floor would haunt her for years, how she was on the cusp of a decision, how in Howie's mind that decision was probably already made. Once they were locked in the room, they held each other. She kissed him. He was different from Lowell—shorter for one thing, but also whiskered and solid in the neck and shoulders. His crewcut was bristly, whereas Lowell's hair was always longish and soft. Howie was a different sort, a different man. He began to remove her clothes, lifting her top over her head, unhooking her bra. She pulled his shirt over his head and there they stood, skin to skin. While he was in the bathroom, she took off her jeans and slipped under the covers. When he came out, he slid off his boots and a small pistol fell out onto the floor.

"What's that?" she said.

"I have a license to carry a concealed weapon," he said.

"Would you mind putting it back in the boot? It's disturbing."

He did. Then he took off his jeans, revealing pure white boxers, and joined her in the bed. "Do you mind if I ask a question?" he said.

"What," she responded, rolling toward him. She wasn't sure she wanted to hear this question. It was quiet a moment.

"Never mind."

Veronica noticed that he lost his nerve. Maybe he wouldn't go through with it. She realized she could. With the news of Carol and Lowell, she damn sure would—she might have done it anyway. Over the years she'd passed on a number of opportunities, and she was not in the mood to pass again. Sex in some ways was consolation for her. It was a power she contained, an option she was proud she still had.

She found Howie's terrible scars, a small entrance wound at his right shoulder blade, a blast hole out his right pectoral. She traced the scar with her fingers, front and back. Vietnam was not theory, not some Nick Bellinger war story, not merely ancient history. Vietnam still lived; the scars were still deep in people. People were shooting and killing each other back then, and they still were. She rolled Howie onto his back, climbed on top, and kissed his scars.

•

Howie painted all the rooms, including all the woodwork a crisp glossy white. It took him one week, it was such a modest little house, and he worked with steadiness and ease. He said it gave him the idea to paint his own place, far more ramshackle but about the same size. Veronica told him he could use whatever paint was left over. He was a clean, neat painter. Veronica imagined he'd have coffee with her from time to time, take a break to discuss colors or see what furniture needed to be moved to clear the way for him, but Howie solved all those problems himself, brought his own coffee, which he kept on his own ladder. He spackled over the wall cracks and sanded them smooth. He was good with color. He suggested ceiling fans in the master bedroom and Monique's room, and Veronica was fine with that. In a single morning, the big dark wood fans were up. She enjoyed having someone else in the house over that third week without Lowell. She would wander down the hall—with his headphones on and Creedence Clearwater Revival rocking, he didn't know she was standing in the doorway watching him work. It was turning into a good summer.

When the work was done, Veronica paid him two thousand dollars out of savings and lavishly thanked him. Lowell would love the changes and would know what Veronica was up to: a new beginning.

Veronica had high hopes that it would all work out, and from time to time she got reports from Vasco via email. "He's embraced this journey, and he's doing great here," Vasco would write. "He likes his counselor, Father Cavanaugh. By the way, it is now certain Lowell will be gone four weeks."

After Howie finished, the house was quiet. It smelled new, but the drying paint gave Veronica a headache, so the new fans were on high, the air conditioner was working to clear the air, and Veronica set up camp in the carport at a picnic table. She didn't know why she hadn't done it before. If it rained, the car could sit in the driveway and form a sort of privacy barrier, and the whole carport, breezy and dry, sheltered her. She began to imagine getting Howie back to pave the carport's gravel floor. It was wide enough for two cars, but in such a small town Lowell was fine with walking to the college and payments on a second car would have buried them. Because Howie didn't have a phone, she drove around town watching for him steaming down the sidewalk at an almost obsessive clip, heading to the shelter.

On the Monday of the fourth and last week of Lowell's absence, around ten thirty in the morning, Veronica found Howie in the park on the north side of town, stretched out in the sun on a concrete bench in the park's amphitheater. She drove across the grass, as close to him as she could get. A freight train was going by on the nearby Illinois Central tracks, and with that and his headphones, he didn't hear her pull up. She honked, one light beep, and swung the passenger side door open. He raised his head, saw her, sat up, and walked to her car.

"What's up?" he said to her, smiling his warm smile. He reached in and touched her hand.

"I've got another job for you if you have time."

"Oh yeah? What's that?"

"Hop in and let's go talk about it."

He did.

"You got a couple of hours?"

"Sure."

"Did you eat yet?"

"Nah."

He swung the door closed, and they were on their way to Champaign on Route 45. They caught up to the freight train that passed while they were in the park. There was almost no one in the Kopi, as it was still too early for the lunch crowd and too late for those who came in for a bagel before work. In the back, there were the usual four or five students on their laptops, alone at their own tables. It was fascinating for Veronica to watch Nora and the college girls who helped out as they moved around the room in the most cordial, happy moods. Nora took joy in the Kopi. It was a going concern. She didn't know Veronica, even as often as Veronica came in. Veronica could see that Nora preferred to let it be a place where people could meet, anonymously if they wished.

Howie carried their coffee to the back of the room and found a table. Veronica followed him. Students were close around them so they talked quietly.

"Have you ever poured concrete?" she said, as they pulled out their chairs and sat down.

"Sure," he said.

"What would it cost me if we paved the driveway and the carport?"

"Maybe twenty five hundred, including the concrete, sand, gravel. Maybe three. I forget how big the carport is."

Veronica gave him the measurements. "I got word Lowell will be gone another week. That's a week from today. Can the job be done by then, concrete dry and all that?"

"Sure. I'll have to do some prep of the ground. I could pour concrete on Wednesday. Might get one of the guys from the shelter to help me, if it's all right. It'll go quicker that way." He looked at her.

She said, "That's fine, whatever you need. It's crazy that this isn't already done. I don't think I ever thought about it before. To me the place simply is how it is." She laughed to herself. "I'd just like things to be different when Lowell gets back."

"Makes sense," Howie said.

As they talked, they sipped coffee. It was a beautiful day. Nora, moving table to table, came and poured them more. When Nora moved to the next table and her back was turned, Veronica reached across and placed her hands on Howie's. His hands were cool; hers were clammy. She held his gaze, her eyes watering. It was one o'clock on a summer afternoon. "Truth is, I didn't bring you here because of the carport."

"Ah," he said. "I didn't think so."

She shifted in her chair. "Is that so bad?" She was clearly nervous.

She could see herself sitting there. This wasn't who she was. "But I still want you to do the job, and of course I'll pay you and your friend when you're done, split it however you want me to." Still looking into his eyes, she said, "I'd like this all to work out well for you."

He pulled his hands away. "I appreciate it," he said. "Even though I don't know how to take this, I appreciate all of it." He brought out his pencil and did some math on a napkin. "I'll need some cash up front to purchase materials. Five hundred maybe."

"I'll go with you to buy all that. We'll use a charge card like we did with the paint." She leaned back in her chair. "We could do it all tomorrow, couldn't we?"

"Tomorrow's good."

She smiled at him. It had been inevitable. Veronica knew this is where it would go since that first day she'd flagged Howie down on Main Street.

Howie backtracked a little about Lowell and Carol. He whispered his regret. Maybe he didn't know as much as he thought. This made Veronica dark again. She was wondering who was feeding Howie these specifics. Somebody out there knew a lot.

Without a word about it, they paid Nora and walked down the street to the Inman. They booked a room on the top floor, paying cash. The room was great though the hotel was on to hard times. The carpet in the halls on the top floors was all rolled up, as though it was being replaced, but that wasn't it. The rolling up of the carpet was the beginning of the end. The curtains in the room were pure white and let the indirect afternoon light through. It was an old-style city hotel room, with the dresser, desk, and side chairs directly out of a Hopper painting, 1941. The headboard of the bed, too, was right out of Hopper. There was a mirror on the closet door. They showered and went to bed with their hair wet. Veronica paid attention this time, noting Howie's body, his Marine tattoo, and how gentle he was being, which seemed opposite of his soldier psychology. Their love-making was carefree. Afterwards, they lingered there for hours and talked. They made more coffee in the pot the hotel provided and guzzled water. They brushed their teeth. They looked at themselves in the bathroom mirror, the closet mirror. The room's window looked north and they could see the charcoal gray awning of the Kopi and Veronica's spanking new Camry parked across the street.

In bed, she asked, "What about Rachel Crowley? Did she tell you?"

"Nah," Howie said. "I don't know her. I really don't know a lot of people around town."

"Who told you? Tell me the truth."

"Sorry, I don't think it would be good if I told you."

They stared at the ceiling as they talked.

"Vasco Whirly."

"Fuck no."

"What—you don't like Vasco?"

"He's okay, I just don't know him. Please stop guessing. I can't tell you."

"Who else knows about all this? Who have you been talking to?"

"I really can't say. How do we ever know who else knows?"

"Tell me how you know."

"Sorry," he said. Everybody in that town knew stuff and talked. This was especially true out at the college. She saw that Howie didn't want to make a worse mess, so she left it at that.

The sun was setting when they left. Veronica liked this room, 601, made a mental note as if they'd ever be back. She heard the latch click as they left. She'd never be back. Arm in arm they walked up the street to the car. Rachel Crowley, probably in town to score some weed, happened to see them as she passed by in her car, because that's how things work sometimes.

They were quiet on the drive home. At one point, Howie told her Lowell was a really good guy. "Sometimes people just slip into what comes natural."

This did not affect Veronica, who had slipped for the second time only a few hours before. She smiled at Howie. "You don't have to tell me that."

"Just saying, I'm pretty sure it's over now."

"Ha. Well. I'm sure we'll see," she said.

"Of course, after once, who knows if it keeps on. Look at you and me. People know how to sneak around."

Veronica volunteered that if they continued to talk about it she might have to pull over and throw up.

"Sorry," he said.

In Tuscola, she dropped him at his house. They touched hands, but no kisses in the car. It wasn't dark yet. "Thanks," he said, as he climbed out. She drove home short of breath. What had she done?

·

A week before Lowell got back, Veronica sat down with Rachel at the Cafe Kopi.

"How's the summer going?" Rachel asked. She may already have known what this chat was going to be about.

Veronica rolled her eyes. "I've had better."

"Oh, have you?" Rachel smiled. "I know Lowell's been gone, and you've been doing some work on the house. Is that going well?"

Veronica, something else on her mind, nodded yes.

"How's Misty?"

Veronica said, "We're instructed to call her Monique."

"Ah. Sorry." Rachel smiled. "Hell will freeze over when Hattie asks to be called Harriet."

"Tell me about it." Veronica stared into Rachel's eyes. "I've been a bit worried, if you must know. About Lowell and Carol."

"Carol Brown?"

"Uh-huh."

"What are you worried about?"

"Maybe that they've been fucking."

"Hmmm. I don't think so. She's been fucking somebody, but not Lowell."

"Who?"

"Nobody I can actually mention to you." Without taking a moment to secure assurances, Rachel, like the gossip Veronica knew she was, proceeded to dump the bucket. "Nick Bellinger—you know? The Vietnam vet who moved away a couple of years ago? He used to work at the college and suddenly left? Got a job in Athens, Ohio. They take little trips together. Don't say anything about it. I think it's over since Wally went off the deep end." Rachel smiled at her. "Look, I don't blame you for being worried. She's slutty and she's been going to Lowell even longer than I have. But I don't think Lowell would cross that particular line."

"I think he has."

"Where did you get this information?" Rachel asked her.

"It's grapevine shit, but it's haunting me. When I heard it, it seemed to make sense. It's hard to believe she's keeping to herself while Wally's down in Marion."

"Well, you know, he's not just locked up. That marriage is toast." Rachel sipped the coffee. "Still, it's hard to believe she'd continue to sneak around after getting knifed because of her infidelities." Rachel and Veronica sat quietly for a moment. "It's a hard habit to break, maybe."

"God, I don't want to hear this." Veronica covered her ears, looked toward the front of the Kopi. The summer sun made all things flash and shine.

"When is Lowell due back?"

"Next week," Veronica whispered. "I've got to find out about this before he's home."

"Do you really?" Rachel sipped more coffee, buttered a bagel, looked out the window. "Why not let it go? He's got a rough road ahead, and going after him about this will just make it tougher for him and then worse for you."

"Could *you* let it go?"

"Probably not." They laughed. "So call Carol. She's a liar, be ready for that. She's really good at it. She's hidden a second life for years."

"In a lot of ways, I don't really want to know, I guess. I know if I do know, it will affect things."

"Of course you don't *want* to know. When he gets back you want to resume your good life. You'll never be able to get it out of your head if you know."

"It's true. But I can be fairly strong if I have to be."

"I know that."

"I mean, I could confront her." Veronica was staring into her cold coffee. "There's no turn off like this. It's the most awful thing ever. It threatens everything."

"Oh yeah, I know it. Do it then. Carol really needs a confrontation, face to face." Rachel stared into her coffee. "Goodness me, to be a fly on the wall."

That night Veronica contacted Carol and asked if they could meet out at Squeak's. At eight o'clock Carol came flying into Squeak's and spotted Veronica in a back booth.

"I'm sorry," she said, about being late, but Veronica wasn't worried about it at all. She was far more worried about the conversation they were about to have. Carol sat down, and Veronica realized they'd never really sat across from one another before. Carol was beautiful, a nice level look in her eye, her hair dark and long, her skin near perfect, a light blue bow in her hair. Her fingers were thin and long, the nails hard and red. She was a pianist, very good, and often did recitals in the studios in the Music Department. Classically trained, in New York City, so the rumor went, upper-class attractive and very nicely pulled together. Somewhere under those clothes were the knife scars from Wally's attack, one in the chest and one in the forearm. It was one of the most famous scenes in the history of Tuscola. She wasn't dead, she was just pissed off about her multiple stab wounds and all this blood in front of her kids. She'd survived. She made it to the front door and dropped the knife through a crack in the decking of the front porch, then collapsed naked down the steps onto the sidewalk. Then the local shaman, Vasco Whirly, out for a run, happened along to save her life. He was a medic in Vietnam. This was a mere two years ago.

"How's your summer been going?" Veronica asked.

"It's been kind of blah," Carol replied. "Thanks for asking."

"Are you lonely?"

"I get lonely," she said. "Our awful house torments me, but the kids keep me busy."

"Of course," Veronica replied.

"How is Lowell doing?" Carol asked.

"He'll be home before long. I assume you know what's going on with him."

"Not really. Is he off somewhere drying out?"

"Yeah, that's it. How did you know?"

"If Vasco's involved, that's probably it," Carol said.

It was a quiet evening at Squeak's, so the wait staff wasn't there and the bartender brought the drinks.

"I took the liberty of ordering you a Stella. You probably drink wine," Veronica said.

"Beer's fine."

They sat quiet for a while, sipped the cold beer. Veronica could tell that Carol didn't know why they were meeting. She didn't know how to get into it.

Carol sighed finally. "Look, I'm very nervous. Tell me what's on your mind."

"It's about Lowell and you and fucking." Veronica stared straight into her face.

Carol turned red.

Veronica said, "I don't want you fucking him anymore. He was drunk that night, but if I had my way you'd move on to another counselor in some other state, like Ohio for instance." Veronica went too far with that one, she realized. "Somebody else's husband, not mine. You are trouble for our family." She felt herself coming loose from her pins. She almost stood up in the booth. "I won't stand for it if it happens again. I'll raise holy hell and ruin you."

People in the bar looked in their direction.

"Well, I—"

"I don't care whose fault it was." She was whispering loudly. "He was drunk. Just stay the hell away from Lowell when he gets back."

Carol looked her in the eye. "I'll try, Veronica."

Veronica stared into her beer. "Nice. You know my name. You know who you're fucking over."

"I'm just saying it's a small town, and there aren't that many counselors."

"Well, you've been seeing Lowell for a number of years, and I think it's time to pronounce yourself healed from whatever the hell your neurotic little problem was."

Carol didn't blink at the insult. "It's true, I'm feeling better."

"How do you think *I* feel?"

"My guess is you're feeling pretty good. I can see it in you. A nice blush in your skin. You seem taken care of, I must say. Lowell will come home and you'll have a newly painted house, and Misty will be feeling better because the two of you are, and you'll have a new start."

"Stay the fuck away from my family."

"You're strong. You're muscling through it." Carol, too, eyed the bar. "I didn't want to hurt anybody. I wanted it all to be secret, one time, and like it never happened."

"Yeah, right."

"That's rarely how things play out, though. I rationalized because I wanted to go through with it. I really wanted to. There's something broken in me."

"So now what."

Carol reached across and touched Veronica's hands. Veronica snatched her hands back.

"I'm sorry. Do you hear me?" Then Carol pulled her hands back and wiped her tears with a napkin. "You've made your point very well." She looked around for her purse. "Are we done?"

"Yes, I think so."

"Great. It was really fun." Carol gathered her things, tossing her hair from her eyes. She tried to clear herself. "So go back to your perfect lives. Press on and relax. Oh. One more thing. I've been meaning to say: You're not perfect either, are you?" Carol was sliding out of the booth. "You aren't perfect either, Mrs. Wagner, are you? No, I don't think so. I don't think you're perfect either." She smiled like they were co-conspirators. "Are you?"

Veronica stared at her, not acknowledging the question. Very pretty, Carol, without another word, went out the open front door.

•

The morning of the Monday Lowell was due home, Veronica was nervous. Vasco and Lowell would go to a Cardinal ballgame and wouldn't be home until around twelve that night. By then Monique would be home to greet him. Veronica scrubbed and worked in the kitchen and bathrooms with Creedence Clearwater Revival banging off the walls all through the house. Starting around nine in the evening, she listened to the ballgame on the radio, hoping they had stayed for the whole game. It was a two and a half hour drive home. The night was like a bell ringing, a clear fine tolling of a bell. The moon was crystal white—full, it was a new month. She stood in the backyard, looked in the windows at the beautiful colors, a new vibe in the house. She hoped he would be happy with what she'd done.

In the middle of Lowell's absence, Veronica had driven over to the retreat in the new Camry, with Vasco's help had found his room, knocked on his door, lured him out to the parking lot to show him the car, made love to him in his room at four in the morning, all of it without saying a word and departed before the crack of dawn. Driving home on two-lane highways, she cried and the sun was in her eyes. She stopped to buy sunglasses in an all-night Walgreen's.

Yesterday, Sunday, she'd gone to mass to try to purge the feelings she had. That night, she found Howie walking home from the shelter and asked him to sit with her in the car a few minutes. She let him know that Lowell would be coming home and so it was over. He thanked her for the work she'd asked him to do, and he thanked her on behalf of Jed Penny, the old vet who had helped Howie with the driveway. Veronica felt her life had gone off-center, but Howie was pragmatic about it, like war can make a person. He'd killed people in his life, so this probably wasn't the worst thing he'd ever done. She was scattered. She knew this might be how Lowell would feel about Carol Brown—tormented, possibly a temptation to go over again.

"I'll miss you," Howie said, looking at her even if she wasn't looking back. "If you ever think of me, just know that I'm somewhere out here missing you."

They kissed, because it was dark out and they could.

The Cardinals were ahead two runs. Veronica sat at the kitchen table a while, savoring her beer and sinking into the music. The rest of the liquor cabinet had been handed off to friends. She got up and strolled through the house trying to see it through Lowell's eyes. She took a long hot shower for purification. She wore his favorite dress. Lowell had always described her as a dark-haired beauty. Now there were streaks of gray, and her eyes were tired. Nothing to be done about any of it. Who was she before and how could she find her way back to that person? Though her heritage was French, she knew Greek because her father was Greek. She loved music, she kept a journal— and knew what to put in it and what not to—and she drank one beer a day, something she would have to give up since Lowell was for sure on the wagon again. What if Lowell sensed what all had happened?

Back in the kitchen, she grabbed another beer. Her hand shook as she raised the icy beer glass to her lips. She switched from CCR to Wilco, "Misunderstood" on repeat. "Nothing, nothing, nothing..." The strong drums, delicate touches of the guitar, the understated bluesy lyrics. She was restless. Another beer and she'd settle, she imagined, and poured a last one. They would kiss and Lowell would pick up the alcohol on her breath.

She walked out the front door, looked up in the sky. Stars bright even with the brilliant moon. Bats flitting as though it were dusk. An owl in a tree across the street, and off somewhere the *eeeeeek* of a hawk brooding in the top of a dying tree. An occasional car would sizzle by on the damp street. The town did have a night life; people moved in the shadowy business district like cats, and unknown cars prowled the avenues. Adulteries and subsequent intrigues did take place; there was almost nothing else to do. Police parked in alleys and monitored who was out. The light in the homeless shelter stayed on all night. The Dairy Queen stayed open late, and the late movie at the Strand, "Reds," went until one in the morning. Squeak's and the other bars in the area closed at two on weeknights, midnight on the weekends by ordinance. Late at night new couples found their way to bed.

She thought of getting in the Camry and driving the streets for a while. Maybe Howie was out there, but she reeled herself in. Now the owl was on a telephone wire, staring at her. She stared back. She walked across the street to view the house from there, and with that the owl took flight, its amazing wing span, its silence. Veronica was proud of the changes she'd made. The house was fundamentally improved. She took a couple of deep breaths, and in a moment her throat tightened and tears streamed down. She crossed back to her house and went into the carport, sat down at the picnic table. A car came by and deposited Monique at the curb. She ran into the house, her greeting trailing behind.

At the stroke of midnight, a cab pulled in the driveway and a very skinny Lowell got out with his duffel bag. Veronica ran out the front door to him. He was thinner and somehow holier. They hugged and kissed, and then he pointed to the driveway, smiled, and said, "What's this?"

"It's concrete," she said to him. "Like real people's houses."

TRUTH

In a night that registered the rhythmic coos of birds and the dripping of dew from the gutters, a night when cats padded across the dark streets without a sound and stray dogs roamed the downtown alleys banging over garbage cans in search of food, in a night when the night trains came through with their lonesome whistles on the approach and then faded away quickly down the long tracks into the dark, in a night when truth weighed on Veronica, and Lowell was back at last and in deep sleep, a night a few weeks after his return when nothing much was expected, Veronica turned on her bedside lamp and sat up, waiting for Lowell to awaken. She listened to his even breathing. She looked at his face. Whatever was dogging her, she could no longer resist it. When Lowell did wake up, she spilled all: "While you were gone, because I knew you'd slept with Carol, I fucked Howie Packer—twice in fact, in the Inman Hotel in Champaign. At the Kopi, we sat and talked, and planned the paint and the concrete, and then, without a word of discussion, we went to the hotel. It was odd. We didn't talk about going, we just went. It was what I wanted."

Lowell, suddenly wide awake, didn't say anything.

"So," Veronica said. "There it is." This level of frankness was more their style than the long silences, which had taken over after Lowell's return from rehab and were, in effect, lies. She loved Lowell and didn't want the whole thing to blow up. Still, she did mean to push hard, to tell the truth brutally, which was how brutal truths needed to be told.

"Okay," Lowell said. He rolled onto his side and turned on his light. Rolled back onto his back and took a big breath.

She stared at him. "Okay? That's all you've got?"

He was quiet a moment. Then he whispered: "I saw her scars." He stared into his bedside light. "He really cut her up."

"Why did he do it?"

"We'll probably never know." Lowell yawned. "The theory is, he did it because she was fucking Nick Bellinger, and he deduced that from her phone calls. Or maybe Rachel Crowley told him—how she knew we'll never know. Also of course Wally was prone to going off his rocker and, here's where I come in, he was a poor match for the Prozac Doc Landen had prescribed for him at my request."

"So you think you figured in the stabbing scenario."

"Yeah. I saw there was a problem with the Prozac, but I didn't call Landen to get Wally on something else. I had too much going on. I kept putting it off, never dreaming that something really awful would happen. I never called him." He tossed himself over, flipped a pillow. "I never called Landen about the Prozac."

Veronica considered at what level of detail these truths should come out. There was such a thing as too much. "Interesting," she said, "because I had a chance to see Howie's scars, too. He was shot in the back in Vietnam. Through his shoulder blade, then a huge exit wound out the front."

Lowell nodded. "Yeah." He turned his head to look at her. "He told me all about it. I'm his shrink."

"Used to be." Howie had also recently begun ducking Veronica.

"What?"

"You used to be his counselor. I doubt he'll be back."

Lowell sighed. "Ah. Yeah. Probably not. I noticed I haven't heard from him to get started up again." Lowell thought for a minute. "If you're behind him when he's running, talking Howie here, you can tell something's up with that shoulder."

"In my experience, he can work circles around about anybody. He paints perfectly with both hands. He can paint a straight line, steady as can be, without tape. And he's good with concrete, too."

"Yeah." Lowell sighed again. "He's a good guy, many talents. He's trying to raise enough money to pay tuition at the college. I never know how to tell him being a volunteer at the homeless shelter doesn't raise a lot of cash. A pure soul, for sure." Lowell took in a huge breath. "I'm glad the two of you hit it off."

"What?"

"I said I'm glad the two of you hit it off."

"We did one whole helluva lot more than just hit it off. Don't be glad I was unfaithful." She was near tears for a moment, and then the moment passed. "Anyway. He painted the interior of the house in a week, which was a new land record. He worked with his headphones on, without saying a thing to me."

"Did you fuck him in our house?"

"No. It crossed my mind, but no." She'd reckoned that was going too far. She rolled away from him. "I wanted him to seduce me in our bedroom, but he was all business with the painting, and also I think he thought—though he never said anything about it—that he'd done enough damage. I doubt if he'll be able to face you again. Just remember, I was the aggressor."

Lowell chuckled. "Yeah. How could he resist?"

"I mean to say, don't blame him."

"I know what you *mean to say*, Veronica. I'll make it easy. I won't let him know I know."

"Yeah, well, okay, just so you know, that never works."

"Why did you tell me all this now?"

"I wanted to. The truth has its way with us. Somehow it's mathematical, like gravity." She was staring at the wall. "I couldn't sleep. I decided to try to control when you found out."

He flipped his pillow again. "I can stand you. I love you, but... Jesus."

"What bothers you? The Howie part or the Carol part or the me-knowing-everything part?"

"All of it," he said. "Though, as you must suspect, you don't quite know everything."

"Will you at some point think 'What the fuck have I done to my marriage?' or 'Oh well, what can it hurt to betray her again?'"

"Most likely both." Lowell stared at the ceiling. "But I'd never do anything like that again. It's serious trouble, and I'm messed up about it. I'm phobic about it."

"I don't know everything?"

"You don't seem to have internalized how horrible I felt afterwards. You seem to have forgotten that I felt bad about it. I have a feeling you didn't feel as bad as I did once it was over."

"Well, you're right about that. I felt justified. Do you love her and want to marry her?"

Lowell laughed. "No. I didn't have control. As you will recall." He laughed again. "You want to marry Howie Packer?"

"Not really." Veronica had known for a long time that he was vulnerable to Carol Brown. "Did I just hear you blame the alcohol?"

"Oh no, I'm not doing that. I own what I did. I'm not pushing it off on anybody or any one thing."

The bedroom was full of tension. The curtains at the open window stirred. Even the lights flickered. Lowell got up for a drink of water, then slid back into bed, turning off his light.

"And it only happened once with Carol? I find that hard to believe."

"Of course you do," he said sleepily. "You thought it was going on for years." He looked her in the eye.

Veronica slid down into the covers so she was lying flat.

Lowell put his arm behind his head. "But we got through it," he said.

"Yes," she said. They got through it because of her, because she soldiered on no matter what happened, because she loved Lowell and Monique and wanted everything to turn out fine. This Howie behavior wasn't who Veronica was.

But, as Carol said, she was far from perfect.

How they'd actually got to making love was unclear to Veronica. Maybe they just did it because it was a ritual they understood and there was nothing else to do. After sex they slept. It was mid-morning by the time they showered and made coffee. Very late that night, Monique's friends had picked her up and she went back out to the college. She didn't know any of this was going on.

Around noon, an unusual thing happened. Carol called. Veronica recognized the number. Lowell probably did, too. He picked up.

"Hello."

"Hi, it's Carol. Hope you're fine. Could I please speak to Veronica?" She was being all bubbly and bouncy. It was the first he'd heard her voice since the call before he was kidnapped into rehab.

Lowell was quiet a moment. Veronica could tell there was something he wanted to say, but with her in earshot it couldn't happen. Finally he said "Sure" and waved at his wife, pointing to the phone.

Veronica picked up in the kitchen. Carol jumped right in. "I wanted to tell you that I got a letter from Wally. He and I don't talk on the phone because phone calls are monitored in the pen, so this letter is precious rare communication. First, he told me that he has colon cancer, probably terminal since it's all through his system, and they are going to release him from prison. Good behavior, he says, because he wrote his book in their rather marginal psych ward and was never a problem for anybody and his meds are squared away. He said when he gets out he'd like to see me."

"I'm sorry to hear Wally's sick," Veronica said. "That's one of the worst things I've ever heard."

"Well, I…"

"Will you see him?"

Carol kept going. "But there's also news. He has a letter from Ben Carlyle, sent before he shot himself. Ben apparently died a few hours after putting the letter in the mail. Ben's dead, you know."

"I didn't know, no." She spoke to Lowell. "Hey, did you know Ben shot himself?"

"I heard," Lowell said. "Did it at his ex-wife's house."

Carol went on: "Anyway, Ben wrote Wally from up in Rockford to confess to burning down the administration building. It was a giant accident, he said, having something to do with a ritual Ben was conducting in his office, something perverted and private with the filing cabinet in front of the door and pictures of Barbi Benton he'd gotten on eBay taped on all three walls and the window. Wally knew something was going on because he and Ben were in their offices, next door to each other, and Wally smelled smoke. Wally knocked on Ben's door, tried to open it, but couldn't because of the filing cabinet. You know the whole town thought Wally burned the building down. He said Ben apologized for letting Wally take the fall. He said Ben knew he'd been an asshole his whole life, and that was why Barbi Benton was his only true love—*Playboy*, January, 1970." Carol was jumpy, sounded like a squirrel. "Isn't that about as sick a thing as you ever heard? I wanted you to know, because you're my friend now."

"Well, I'm glad Ben fessed up before he shot himself," Veronica said. "Wally's not a bad guy and he never would have set that fire. Does he know you think he's a good guy, you having fucked him over a few times with your old pal and lover Nick Bellinger in Ohio?"

"How do you know about that?"

"I never thought Wally was a bad guy."

"Did Rachel tell you?"

"Oh, so Rachel knows about it? Never mind, Carol. The word's out, just so ya know." Veronica sighed. "I always thought you were a bit of a slut. I could never put you and Wally together. It makes sense to me that you drove Wally over the edge and that he's the one in prison with a fatal disease that will put an end to him in the middle of his life."

"Well, I just wanted you to know."

"I don't really want to know everything anymore," Veronica said. "So stop telling me stuff. You will always know more than I do about everything in this town, and you don't need to call me up and tell me. I'm done with the soft underbelly of this fucking town."

"I suppose." Carol chuckled, then changed gears. "Well, so okay, I don't want to argue. I've remembered almost fondly our, to your great credit, humane conversation at Squeak's. Like we're friends. I just wanted to give you a call, and pass along this info about Wally being very sick and Ben and the administration building. Maybe pass it along to Lowell."

"Yeah, well, Carol, you can fucking forget that."

"Sorry to have caught you in a bad mood this morning. Okay, I have to go."

"Carol, are you on pills?"

"No." She sucked in her breath. "I mean yes."

"Seems like it."

"I might have called you even without drugs. I might call again. I feel close to you now, maybe closer than to anyone else. We're sisters. We're bad in the same ways."

Veronica felt Carol working to get under her skin. "Don't call anymore, Carol. If you please."

"I might. If I want to. We're sisters. We have a certain behavior in common. We pass each other on the streets. We meet up in a local bar. We do Come-To-Jesus. We're potential good friends, but we just haven't gotten there quite yet."

"We'll never be friends, Carol." Veronica took a sip of cold coffee, tossed it in the sink. "Seriously, don't call. Something might happen."

"Nothing that hasn't happened to me before. I suggest you think about being my friend. I'm not afraid of your anger. I'll stare it down, fly right into it, I'll eat it for lunch. I'm not afraid of you. You don't have me over a barrel. We both know what I'm talking about. Let's be friends. We can meet up from time to time, have a beer and talk. You probably need it as much as I do. We've got a buncha shit in common."

"I thought you had to get off the phone."

Carol was quiet for a second, settling down. "Nah. I just said that. I actually don't, but while I've got you I need to say a few things to you. You threaten. You're mean. You call me names. You think I can handle anything, being called a slut and about anything else. You're wrong. I'm not made of granite. I'm not made of granite, Veronica. With you my guard is down. I'm not stupid or oblivious. I've said I'm sorry for what I've done. Clearly you hate me and aren't inclined to treat me like a human being. I want to be your friend. Say yes."

"Unthinkable."

Carol said, "I could be dead right now."

"That's an interesting thought," Veronica replied.

"I don't know how I ended up in this godforsaken shithole."

"You followed your first husband here."

"Maybe I think we could be friends. You just need to soften a bit and think about it. Would you like to meet me at Squeak's again sometime in the near future? We could have a great chat."

Veronica concluded the pills were making Carol crazy and hung up on her.

Lowell put down his coffee cup. "Wow."

"Wow what?"

"That phone call was a thrill a minute."

"She said she wants to be friends." Veronica poured herself more coffee. "How does she think that's ever gonna happen?"

"I have no idea. She does need friends though."

"There's Rachel."

"Carol knows Rachel's watching her from across the street and spreading rumors. If she had the dough, Carol would move to Champaign."

Veronica fired back, "I won't ask how you happen to know that. Maybe we should provide financial assistance for the move if we're so friendly."

Lowell said, "You're being mean, honey. It's not like you."

"Okay, well. Truth is, I haven't been *like me* for quite some time, case you haven't noticed." She sipped her coffee, suddenly slammed down the cup. "Hell with it. I'm going back to bed." Instead of shuffling down the hall, Veronica, tears streaming, broke into a run.

•

A month later, after many of Carol's phone calls, Veronica caved and met her at Squeak's. For Veronica the seven miles out there was a long drive, on ice and snow. But the cool air was good. In Illinois, in the flatlands, the wind is strong and unrelenting. Tuscola is the county seat of Douglas County, the flattest county in Illinois, and so there's not much cover unless you stand behind a building or hunker down in your car. In the gravel parking lot, Veronica hopped out and ran for the front door, her winter coat tightly wrapped around her all the way to her chin. She went immediately to the back booth, in honor of their first face-to-face.

Carol was not far behind, and came in the front door, spotted Veronica and hurried to the booth in her snowboots. "Wow, this is very interesting," Carol said, her opening salvo as she removed her coat. "The same booth. Nice!" She shook the snow off her boots. "It is big of you to join me here and be my friend. You're really a class act."

Veronica smiled at her. "Whatever, Carol."

"Well, neither of us is perfect. Geeez, could you get off that? It's wearing me out. You may or may not know it, but you've made your fucking point." Carol smiled a hard smile.

Veronica removed her own coat but held the eye contact. "Is Wally out of the slammer?"

"Should be soon. His illness is holding things up—hard to figure, I know. I keep saying they just need to airlift him out of there and get him up to Champaign where there's proper medical treatment available, but it's not that easy to get out once you're in. Paperwork, they say. I'll bet Wally's going crazy, knowing his days are numbered and being lashed to the penitentiary."

"Will you talk to him?"

Carol looked toward the bar, wanting to order a Stella for old time's sake. "I will, yes."

"Glad to hear it."

"I hope we can get somebody, a third party, to be there, too. Some kind of protection, or maybe not protection but at least somebody objective."

Veronica knew Carol really did mean protection, and she was probably implying Lowell. "Lowell likes Wally and is really sorry he's sick. Of course, Kelleher could play the objective third party role, or Vasco Whirly."

"I thought maybe we could all meet up at the Kopi, or at Forty Martyrs."

"Well, don't turn it into a canasta party. Forty Martyrs makes sense. You don't want Wally driving all over Central Illinois, delaying the meeting even further when his time is short. Do it on the home ground."

"Good advice. But it's a tough one for me," Carol said.

"Why?"

"I really don't have a home ground in this town. It's difficult."

"I'm sure it is, but you have to give him a chance to say what he has to say. He can't die without that."

Carol looked at her. "Yeah, I know."

"I'm sure it's plenty awkward for you."

"Very awkward."

Two draft Stellas arrived at the table. Veronica had thought ahead.

Carol and Veronica toasted with their chilly beer mugs. "Here's to friendship," Carol said.

"Whatever," Veronica replied, and their beer mugs clacked. "By the way, I just want to say you were right on the phone. I've been nasty, particularly to you—I'm just so damned angry about everything. I'm sorry. It's not like me—calling you names and all this other business. There's no end to what all I wanted to say to you, emptying both barrels. But when we're together I never can think of all of it. It won't happen anymore."

"Does that mean we're friends now?"

Veronica replied, "Hell no!" She sipped her beer. "Stop it, bitch."

They both laughed.

By arrangement with Carol, though she denied it repeatedly,

an old fellow sat at the bar with a big camera, a long lens, and the toast was photographed. The next week it played in the very popular photography section of the *Tuscola Journal*. This, after all, is how Carol operated, stretching heaven and hell for witnesses to her new friendship with Veronica.

•

And so winter locked down on the town, and people retreated indoors. January, a dark, hopeless month, sat on Tuscola like a boulder. A drive on the night streets during the week was reliably quiet but for the tires crackling on the icy snow and the low hum of the car's heater. Few people would be out late. Instead, families were huddled indoors, the furnace on, the fireplace crackling, dinner dishes in the sink. Teenagers, and certain adults prone to closet fever, went out late at night on weeknights and on the weekends, prowled the town's streets, gathered with friends in drafty booths at the Dairy Queen, or Squeak's out on the township line, or sat in their cars at Mel's Drive-in—yes, there was a Mel's Drive-in. The whole panoply of human behavior, though, didn't pause for winter. Babies were made. The college was bustling. The administration put a new administration building on the drawing board, one that paid homage in size and grandeur to the one that burned, including a five-story atrium (but not the spiral stairs behind Lowell's desk). The faculty offices would of course be smaller, thinner doors, lower ceilings. Part of the reduction of expectations so characteristic of the times. Real materials were expensive.

That winter was dim, long, and cold. At Forty Martyrs one evening in February, Wally and Carol sat down, with Father Kelleher and Vasco Whirly nearby (Lowell didn't show). Wally, who was failing, made his peace with his wife. In the Forty Martyrs elementary school gym, they sat at a folding table, across from each other, and they whispered so the witnesses wouldn't hear. Wally had grown old in prison. His hair was long and gray, and he had a beard and a tattoo on one arm that read "On the Stoics."

"I don't even remember what happened," Wally told her, and she believed him. "But I'm very sorry, in fact I'm horrified that I'd do you harm and not even know I was doing it. So prison was probably right for me."

"Well," Carol said, taking a breath and attempting to match Wally's level of frankness. "Your meds were all wrong."

Wally offered, "I love you—that's all I wanted to say."

"Okay," she said. "I love you, too, and I wish you weren't so ill."

"Would you accept me back?"

"I don't think so, Wally. I've been on my own for a while and am learning to prefer it."

"Okay," he said. He looked away. "I knew that would be your answer. Why would you ever let me back in?"

They tearfully touched hands, hugged goodbye, knowing it would be the last time they'd see each other or speak this intimately.

That spring Vasco and hospice attended to Wally in a little apartment on Green Street in downtown Urbana. Wally passed quietly on a big dose of morphine, and by April first he was buried. His book, *On the Stoics*, came out that May and did well, but he was gone and never knew it.

Carol moved to Church Street in Champaign. She signed up for yoga classes at the YMCA nearby. Initially, Veronica and she met sometimes at the Café Kopi, but as time went by that happened less and less. Three years after Wally, Carol remarried in a subdued ceremony in a side-chapel of St. Matthew's Catholic Church in Champaign, and not long after, disappeared into the north suburbs of Chicago.

In May, Lowell received a letter from Carol. "I promised Veronica you and I wouldn't be in touch, but I wish you would write or call. Here's a little reminder of us." It was a full frontal nude picture of Carol taken in a bathroom mirror, her big nasty scars on full display.

Lowell stashed the letter and picture deep in his private files at the office, and started up a correspondence with Carol.

He continued to run and play racquetball. He counseled a growing number of clients because the town was growing. He and Veronica remained together in their good marriage, and the new trees around their little bungalow grew tall and thick. One of them, an oak, had such robust roots it began to lift the sidewalk in front of the house.

From time to time on her meandering winter drives while Lowell taught his night class, Veronica would spot Howie Packer motating down Main Street toward the homeless shelter. It seemed to Veronica that nothing ever got over, not really. She had no idea how right she was. Things festered and gnawed at her. And there was Howie, headphones on over his stocking cap and ever the Marine, staring down at the snow and hellbent to get where he was going. Though he never noticed, she would always wave.

And with that, the facts in the matter sank into the dank, mossy, unspeakable history of the town's people and its walking wounded.

ACKNOWLEDGEMENTS

These stories were written over the last thirty-one years, 1984-2015.

"The Underlife" was published in *Crazyhorse* and was listed among the "100 Most Distinguished Stories of 1994" in *The Pushcart Prize: Best of the Small Presses, XX, 1995.* "Coal Grove" appeared in different form in the inaugural issue of the Kyle Minor's *FrostProof Review.* "Vasco and the Virgin" appeared in *Tamaqua* and was reprinted in different form in *Provo Canyon Review* in 2013. "Lowell and the Rolling Thunder" appeared in the *Kenyon Review* along with an author interview with Nancy Zafris (then the fiction editor of the *Kenyon Review*) in the online archives. "Projects" in a different form was selected for distribution online by Dan Wickett's *Emerging Writers Network*, Christmas, 2004, and appeared in the *Chattahoochee Review*, Summer, 2007. "Forty Martyrs" appeared in the *New England Review* and was listed among the "100 Most Distinguished Stories of 1994" in *Best American Short Stories, 1995.*

My thanks to the editors of all these publications. To all those who gave good advice on these stories over the years, many thanks to you each. As you read this book, I'm sure you will see your influence and advice.

I want also to express my thanks to Ryan Rivas of Burrow Press, for his friendly suggestions on the manuscript, his smart and sensitive edits, and most of all for allowing this novel-in-stories, at long last, into the light of day. And to Susan Fallows, Sam Buoye, and Terry Godbey for their insightful efforts.

Finally, much love to my wife, writer and poet Susan Lilley, who patiently tolerated my going in the study and closing the door.

MORE FICTION FROM BURROW PRESS

The Call: a virtual parable, by Pat Rushin
978-1-941681-90-9

"Pat Rushin is out of his fucking mind. I like that in a writer; that and his daredevil usage of the semi-colon and asterisk make *The Call* unputdownable."

~**Terry Gilliam**,
director of *The Zero Theorem*

Pinkies, stories by Shane Hinton
978-1-941681-92-3

"If Kafka got it on with Flannery O'Connor, *Pinkies* would be their love child."

~**Lidia Yuknavitch**, author of
The Small Backs of Children

Songs for the Deaf, stories by John Henry Fleming
978-0-9849538-5-1

"*Songs for the Deaf* is a joyful, deranged, endlessly surprising book. Fleming's prose is glorious music; his rhythms will get into your bloodstream, and his images will sink into your dreams."

~**Karen Russell**, author of *Swamplandia!*

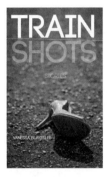

Train Shots, stories by Vanessa Blakeslee
978-0-9849538-4-4

"*Train Shots* is more than a promising first collection by a formidably talented writer; it is a haunting story collection of the first order."
   ~John Dufresne, author of *No Regrets, Coyote*

15 Views of Miami, edited by Jaquira Díaz
978-0-9849538-3-7

Named one of the 7 best books about Miami by the *Miami New Times*